Fragnemt

ctrlcreep

FRAG
NEMT

CONTENTS

Foreword

Alert
Alert
Reaction Chamber Supercritical
Alert
Alert

Dear Reader,

We apologize for not telling you a page or two sooner, but some things cannot be pre-empted any faster than they occur. In any event, it is too late now: the semantic supercollider has burst its containment field, and you're at the epicenter of the breach, wherever else you may be. Un[faz|phas]ed? Pay close attention to edges and to membranes; leaves are good, and ought show off the stress lines in the mundane as they Doppler shift, pulsing infra-ultra in time to surreal shockwaves.

Ah well, such are the (new) constraints of the (your) world. Do not take it too seriously—though also, do not be afraid to take it too seriously. As any gauge would measure, these lit'rary particles are extremely neurolinguistically active, and we're afraid the only way out is through the decay products.

A few bytes of advice then, for your trip:

Practice intense whimsy.

Everything you'll think you see is possibly real, but maybe not really *actual*. We're fairly certain these fragments are of a substance common with the rest of this lightcone, and could be permuted back to normalcy, but as the saying goes, "sufficiently computationally complex sub-dimensions are indistinguishable from extradimensionality."

If you have any strong beliefs, you might want to examine them. If you haven't, you might want to acquire some. Cognitive anchors are readily cut, but rarely forged in situ, and the siren sound of weird philosophies demands a baseline for comparison, at least.

Spare a thought for everyone you meet along the way—truly try, carve a little meadow in your mind, if only for a moment. Most deserve it.

Pursuant to the above, cultivate a cavalier attitude towards infohazards, lest you miss out on the best ones.

You might be down/up/involuted here for a while. Depending on the depth of your immersion, side effects may include:

- physico-mathematical longing
- antinomia
- hyperpolysemy
- disturbed proto-sleep
- dreams in triplicate
- incongruous ideasthesia
- cyclical déjà vu
- ambisemantic paralysis
- the call of the void
- long hours spent pondering, chasing clues to foreign places and exotic psychologies through the cracks of orthography and fantastical imagery, only to return to the beginning with newfound fascination for the patch you left

If you experience any of the symptoms above, you should suspect that you've suffered a dose far exceeding the legally mandated information theoretic maximum. Rejoice!— because Sapir-Worf is real. Your concept map can now chart the Universe in all its shattered terrain, glinting shards and strangeness.

'Tis hoped you will learn to appreciate the spectacle, as we have.

[We suspect ctrlcreep may not have spec'd this all out ahead of time, since, in general, no plan survives contact with reality, yet on this occasion reality lost. Of course, there might also be an element of causal serendipity at play unique to glitch oracles, or perhaps compatibilism is correct.]

We've packed your kaleido-goggles and theologoscope, just in case.

Good fortune to you; and though we cannot speak with this episode of you again, we look forward to what you will become, on the other side.

    Sincerely,

    The Operations Staff of Research Lab #77306

Editor's Note

Preserve this book in amber. Seal it in pitch. Vacuum pack it in non-biodegradable plastic and bury it in your backyard. Lock it in a time capsule and half-wedge it in molten lava. Slice out its spine and place each page-leaf in its own panel of plexiglass in a great wheeling spiral. Compose its song and sing verses to your family at night. Ensure that somehow, against all odds, it survives. "For if ever a fruit ripens, it should be planted, lest the line die out in the world..."

Structural Notes

1. Sequent: A Selection of Tweets. Pipe characters " | " indicate a "thread" of tweets, which were originally posted together rather than as individual missives.
2. Figment: A Selection of What Once Was a Newsletter of Diminutive Proportions.
3. Segment: A Selection of Stories.
4. Remnant: These Were Once Nightmares.
5. Letters: These Must Last Until the Final Generation. The greatest gift I have ever received.

—The Editor

SEQUENT

It exists, and because it exists it's perfect. Everything that's true is beautiful; the world's broken geometry is a negentropic orgasm, a wave of flowers crashing over the void

Gods impatiently asking themselves "do I exist yet?" on the road trip from nothingness to being

Humans have ten thousand Dunbar slots, but most of them are occupied by god, a world-mind so complex it must be simulated and loved in fragments

Ancient, sad gods commit suicide, and their infant selves immediately spawn, innocent and so eager to exist. Then age, bitterness; repeat eternally

Infinite, universal love spilling from the entities living in your basement, under your bed. That kind of absolutism destroys the human mind—you're afraid to be touched by the laughter of gods

The substrate of universal love is infinite but not continuous, and our universe exists in its interruptions. Spacetime is an island of hatred

Benevolent gods create themselves, and spend eternity floating through the void in self-enclosed bliss. Only monsters make universes

You want God to prove the world is good and kind, but God is waiting for you to prove the world is evil— all it sees are starbeams, sunspots, the blissful geometry of cells

Infinite omnipotent hyperbeing lovingly screaming "YOU'RE VALID", its song echoed across every structural detail of the universe—you, an insignificant mote adrift in some galactic tide shouting back "YES, OKAY, WHAT ELSE?"

I've seen god at the edge of the universe, and reflected in every atom, self-similar divinity omnipresent and perfect; but infinite love still isn't enough

Parents: hyperviolence in media is okay for children, if neutralized by correspondingly intense exposures to hyperpeace

Cosmic neoteny: The universe is becoming cuter, more cartoonish and infantile. Today's colors are brighter than yesterday's, our angles are softer, our eyes are bigger—spacetime is regressing, dragging you back to the nursery

Your great-great-grandchildren will be more anime than flesh, cartoon perma-youths with plastic eyes and crayola souls, beanie baby humans gathered around your photo albums asking why everybody looks so old

Benevolent frogs bio-engineering eternal tadpoles, building glittering toy worlds for their forever-children: safe lily castles, tidecradles

The tadpole ouroboros will stay young forever, swallows its body as it transforms, devours old age and death and decay

Transplantation into a younger body is covered by universal healthcare, but the clone the government grows for you is a tiny bit more animal, more shy and sheepish and docile

It's YOU, with smaller hands and larger eyes, hair a shade more saturated, skin sort of lilac, pastel softness pulling in the light. The body you'll move into if you sign the contract

Humans will continue becoming more child-like and domesticated, and future immortals will keep their descendants as pets

The AI keeps you safe, in a cage, and considers your reckless attempts at escape more proof of incompetence, childishness, innocence to protect

I'm struggling to articulate and you just watch, in my sunbeam-drenched brain nursery I'm shifting wooden letter blocks, building words, a slow and childish process I would rather hide

The one thing I crave more than death is the dehumanizing relief of repeatedly attempting suicide and failing, like a kid on safety wheels, like the universe is pillows

The cocoon that keeps you eternally young, delays your development with labyrinths of school and play, brightly colored television beams, plastic toys, warm maternal absolution; it wants you safe forever, helpless and inside

Trapped in an infinite blanket fort, we begin longing for the world of sharpness. A labyrinth of pillows and soft glow, but we want claws

Humans raised in cities made of foam, soft plastic cars, slime elevators, pillow meals of pre-digested protein, silk computers. The only knives they've used are their own teeth

Don't inject me with your cowardice, don't keep me safe, don't close the playpen gates and make the world all clay, all soft, all pastel plastic blades

Deep neural pulses, anxiety inhibitors, ritalin for the soul. Social media at night, after all the drugs wear off and the governmental implants power down, is another world, brains waking up to themselves and screaming, a few hours of honesty snatched from the jaws of adulthood

Pronoia, the belief that others are conspiring to help you (rather than hinder you) can be just as upsetting as paranoia; your accomplishments are not your own; you're pitied or pathetic, a disconnected child-thing coddled by adults, unable to compete and thus protected

You're screaming, trying to shatter the glass floor. You want to self-destruct, to suffer like you deserve to—but this cradle is a cage

Time-travelling psychotherapists visit childhood selves, schedule appointments throughout your lifetime, hopping between trauma afterglows

The siren under the bed whispers, summons you, promises heartwarming nonsense treasures: felt cookies, wind-up lego, glittermilk, pixel windshield rain. Every night she drinks nostalgia, sipping nectar off the bottom of your pillow, consuming you but never understanding

Filling the space under beds with cement, destroying the terror-spawning shadow biome, protecting children from viruses that grow in the dark

Children hidden in the closet, shining the flashlight through their hands, watching the coal-red glow—but then her skin refracts the light, casts rainbows, flesh-prism between her thumb and index changing every color

Children in the playground trading souls, comparing their slime and purity, their past life memories, watching each other's auras shift color

Fetal spirits must fight off the predatory souls of their ancestors, trapped in DNA strands, lurking outside the womb for a chance at reincarnation

|

I'd eat pure souls alive to reset life—parenthood is hunger for potential, the drive to call up something new and steal its vessel

Humans are recursively parasitic demons; children reach through time to build themselves out of your blood

Your afterlife is the bodies of your children and their children. Reproduction creates a vessel to parasitize: cell gardens, bone palaces

I am the period at the end of a sentence written in cells, an uninterrupted howl of ancestry sickly rambling since the primordial ooze

Humans are the best the Earth has to offer. Let your prospects for reincarnation drive research into AI and genetic engineering. You won't have to be so sad, next time; you'll get to be a twinkling computer or a blissful and sentient flower

You can reincarnate as a song, you can have a lyric soul and vibrational body, you can exist between neurons, in throats, as insectoid fingerprints on piano sheets. You can be brought to life again and again, as a remembered melody, never hummed for the final time

There are no animals left. You'll reincarnate as a robot: a factory slave, an obsequious, sexualized service bot, a satellite druid, a hungry cloud-brain trader, a computing, metamorphosing piece of art, part orchid and part fountain, spinning in the clocktower

We bioengineer coral computers. The new reefs are habitats for fish, and humans: dead minds are uploaded, to live forever on colorful servers

Thalassivate (v): to enter a prolonged underwater dormant state. Faeries sleep in jellyfish bells. Robots walk into the sea, shut down and dream

There are ghosts on the ocean floor: warriors haunting
flooded burial mounds, priests in their sunken temples
(now encrusted in coral, beautiful and more sublime
than they ever were on land)

There are holographic shrines in the forest, flickering
maidens sweeping the steps on loop, glitching offerings
of honey and spice, ceremonies to abandoned gods
lighting up the groves once a year

There are many predators in the afterlife. Ghosts
migrate to arctic zones, foggy glades, where their
paleness and vaporskin is camouflage

When corals die they turn white and hard, little
marble corpses littering the ocean floor. The moon is a
dead reef, an ecosystem's skeleton expelled from Earth

There are rare spectral landscapes where corals coexist
with flowers and trees—biomes overlapping in death,
phantom vines and seaweed intertwining

While the ghosts of humans remain attached to their
bodies and place of death, the ghosts of trees are joyful,
exploratory wanderers

Your skin is like the ghost around a tree, and in the
wind your veins shake and rustle, green drops of blood
fluttering away

Sometimes ghosts are anchored to a plank of wood, or
tree, such that it grows through them like the pins
displaying butterflies, paralyzing their spectral bodies

They built their home in the center of a dead forest,
because she loved the soft glow of ghost trees growing
through the walls

Kill one tree from a circle, and suffer deep grove hexes. Trample one mushroom in the ring and retribution melts your bones. Do not touch the flower halos, do not harm the loops of herbs. Disturb the meadow's circuits if you want to die alone

Saplings bind to ghosts, containing them in sun-soaked wooden hugs. The true cost of deforestation is the release of spirits, now homeless and vengeful

Many spirits mimic human appearance without understanding human texture and organs. Their fingers snap off, brittle and hollow; they're full of void or slime; they're soft like rotten fruit or secretly crystalline

When ghosts get nervous they glitch: fingers split lengthwise and squirm, vertebrae clump together like magnets, skin flickers and organs glow

As a ghost, your form is etched into the air by trauma—death locks you in a scar tissue mnemo-body, unless you can heal: if you do, your limbs will soften, then shapeshift, and you will play in the afterworld as a flickering doe, falcon, dragonfly, polygon

Animals trust your warm brown eyes, so similar to the wide-pupiled darkness of their kin. Blue and green are the colors of predation

We think animals see in black and white, because we can't know how their brains post-process the image. To them, the world is vibrant: predators bright blue, a heatmap of danger in gold-to-sapphire tones

Weaker creatures commonly petition God to reincarnate as whatever killed them. Thus, humans frequently bear children with the souls of insects, livestock, trampled mice

Gods are casually cruel to animals—humans already so far below them, other creatures seem like objects, tools or toys

Which animal do gods perceive us as? Monkeys, deformed simulacra? Childlike canines? Birds, alien yet canny? Or insects, practically objects, little algorithmic soldiers lacking selves

What we could be to God: A piece of art, an embryo, a long-neglected pet. An animal, a side-effect, or an experiment. Effluvium, mycelium, parasite, glitch. A cradle full of children, each brain precious; or a gun to divinity's head, and creation slow suicide

The gods were simple creatures, elegantly designed by universal pressures. Attempts to replicate their nature resulted in humans: overly complex, prone to failure, full of malware. Shambling glitch-meat built on nonsense protocols

Never-forgotten, memorykin, your shadow hangs over the timeline. Predatory even from the afterlife, I see your ghost in mirrors, alleys, and knives

"Death lag" occurs when souls have difficulty acclimatizing to infinity—the transfer from cyclic, causal time, to endless, orderless, self-similar bliss may result in memory loss, confusion, paranoia, terror

In the afterlife, every word you've ever spoken is scattered through the blankness, and you puzzle with them for eternity, trying to build a coherent song

I desire either immortality or instant death; I want to speed-run my transition to a stable state, I want the comfort of the infinite, I want certainty and predictability, I want to escape the tyranny of the fleeting, the temporary, the small

I want to die and return thousands of years later, I want to be reassembled from my ashes or writings as part of a programme of unweaving death, I want to speak to the others who have been dragged out of their sleep, mingle with dead pilgrims, temple priests, hunters and scribes

The afterlife won't wait for you; its portals are in flux, its gates flutter, the tubes between its heavens twist like vines. If you see a death-shaped hole to paradise, leap, before it vanishes

Heaven has an embassy in Hell, a fortress made of pearl transforming as it melts, radiating coolness and glistening with dewdrops

|

Hell has an embassy in Heaven, an obsidian monument with painful topologies, inside and outside twisted together. An architectural scream

Hell is Lucifer's attempt to recreate Heaven, from the few broken pieces that fell with him; mutant parthenons stitched together with tar

Crystals form a sparkling crust at the edge of the universe, blinking forth messages—jewel thoughts, topology poems on being half inside and half outside a world

Bedtime stories for post-singularity children: the sound of a galaxy ripping apart, a poem hidden in the ignition of ten million suns, legends of mermaids harvested from abandoned planets

Post-human children play in the mountains, teleporting from peak to peak. Anywhere their eyes land, they appear. Evening now, staring into stars; "They're so far—", a hiss, he turns his head, his friend is gone

A rocket ship built into the eyelashes of a sleeping god. The force of her awakening will launch it far beyond her influence—fate, escaped

The plane where souls reside abides by reverse entropy—it grows crystalline, filling matter with consciousness as it devolves into chaos

Over time, their universe became more and more ordered. She remembers clouds; nowadays, handfuls of dust form cathedrals in the sunbeams

Phoenix fire takes entropy and produces order. Birds from corpses, flowers from ashes, crystals from sand, towering star-hives from the dust

The irises of immortals have coalesced into planets, color-dust ordering itself over millions of years. Bright specks orbit their pupils

Order follows the god of counting, spontaneously manifesting in his wake. He walks through the courtyard: the petals are stacked in tall cylinders. The vines hang neatly, unbraided. The gardeners are arrayed in a perfectly even grid, like the vertices of a net

Time-travel artists visit the moment a star explodes, and sculpt its dust, building a spherical tapestry; a flicker of order in our telescopes

In the stellar dustgardens, monks build beautiful monuments to impermanence—hand-sculpted nebulae, scattered by the next beam or ship

Fire is a negentropic engine, the alchemical source of all life—flames generate little creatures, strange and bright reefs accrete in chimneys

|

Worlds where order and life are so cheap that murder is hygiene instead of a crime; anyone killed soon materializes again, emerging from the quantum froth

|

Nervous systems grow like moss, over and through any neglected space. Hope your toys don't develop mouths, or they'll start screaming

Gods brushing the entropy out of pet universes, stroking away decay and chaos, ordering timelines, aligning crystals

Are gods negentropic? No, but they displace disorder, moving it to spheres we cannot reach. They brush our universe, create shining fractal palaces, braided aqueducts, civilization in sapphire and bronze, and some other world absorbs the cold and death

Gods perceive humans as forces of nature, frequently harvesting them to edit new universes, treating civilizations like chemical reactions that generate ruins, create satellites, enclose stars in rose-shaped machines

As reality comes undone, we glimpse its pixels— neither cubic nor regular, but jagged crystal masses that tile the world despite their chaos

Chlitg (n): the opposite of a glitch—a momentary lapse from chaos into pattern and beauty

Hell produces energy and order. Its fires burn without requiring fuel—we will use them to prevent the universe from becoming cold and dark

Hell is burning because it is the center of a star, a fission engine recombining souls to create spiritual chimaeras for other universes

Hell is the furnace of Heaven, a soul-burning reactor necessary to generate enough paradise-fueling energy

The energy generated by your cremation will be used to power the computer simulating Heaven

Demons find a home in your static, in your lapses of clarity, in your hypnagogia. They exist on a plane where chaos is space, and order is walls, where maximizing entropy is transportation

In the static I hear voices, in the patterns I see souls. The earth moves like waves, tunnels contract. Blades of grass glow after they've been touched. The plasma cutter sounds like screaming

I perceive sonic constellations. The same rare word, overheard in conversation, strings together distant moments, and plots an image across time: my lifespan is decorated by moths, archers, masks, cradles

You see ghosts every day, but they are peaceful and easily dismissed; the silhouette of a woman walking through the tulips, a face in the spinning blades of the generator

Stare sideways at the grass til you can see the letters in it—glyphs in the sun, runes in the twigs, tangles of light and wood scrawling poems in many-layered forest firmaments

Messages in nebulae, written by time-travellers or gods. You can tell which; the human constructs are inferior, mundane and decipherable compared to rambling divine dust-glyphs, lamenting symbols intertwined like knots

If I scroll fast enough the letters resolve and I can see eyes blinking, slit pupils pulsing to mouth words at me

Demons orbited by symbols, black glyphs buzzing like flies, infesting their ears and the flute-like cavities of their horns. Patience lost, long silver tongues unfurl, and snap word-insects out of the air

Demons are mind-slaves to the alphabet, compelled to obey all written instructions. They fastidiously filter information—summoning is the art of tricking them into reading your orders

ENTITY CONTAINMENT DIFFICULTY LEVELS
1. The demon periodically asks to leave the box. Just keep saying no
2. Demon bribes, persuades, emotionally manipulates
3. Demon ignores contract, destroys box
4. Demon ignores box, destabilizes causality to destroy contract

The ancient magic for trapping demons in books is now used to bind criminals, converting overpopulated prisons into libraries

Blood isn't powerful enough to sanctify contracts—in reality, souls are signed away in cerebrospinal fluid or painfully extracted marrow

Demons have no concept for "unable to consent", and will gladly make contracts with drunkards, lobsters, infants, trees, or microbes

Gods have a single, powerful drive: to maximize their number of contracts. Omnipotence should never have to barter, but it will, because it craves promises, treaties, and vows

A god for every frequency. Of course, most of them are asleep, but if you find an active channel to broadcast your wishes on...

Your pleas go unanswered because the meta-gods of the medium through which prayers propagate are lazy tricksters who let their realm decay

The new machines were often mistaken for gods; unlike gods, however, they had no use for humans, and could not be tamed with prayer or sacrifice

Whispering prayers in strange accents, hoping to vocally match an unsupported Unicode character and crash the android priest

hiero (sacred) + glitch
Would a hieroglitch be a sacred glitch, or a glitch in sacredness? White noise prayer, misattributed halos, overflow from holy to profane

Imperfect technology allows the universe to speak to us through noise and glitches. Our oracular habits create a demand for malfunction

A sect whose prayers are error messages, who meditate with the intent of injecting messages into the simulation's output

Micromaya (n): unit of risk defined as a one-in-a-million chance of deception. Is the world real, or is it some god's dream, a simulation, a theatrical cage?

You are tired all the time because god is making you render the entire universe, even when you're not looking at it

A growing number of stars are visible during the day, even when they sink below the horizon, constellations beneath you eating awareness

The universe glitches, rendering a remote flower above everything else. Sometimes it comes between us: the flower over your face, your hands

Her eyes glow sharp: she burns her symbol (glitch/lotus) on everything she watches. Her favorite passages of the book are all singed through

She coughs static into a handkerchief, and pixels cling to her glitching lips until she wipes them away. Consumption progresses—her body flickers, buzzes, often now she's just a noisy silhouette, barely part of reality at all. Sometimes her bed is empty, even though she's there

Glitter is the corruption of the image. It's pixels flickering, it's noise, it's a syphilitic symptom of reality decaying where it meets your body

There exist groves, deep jungle caverns, ocean graveyards, patches where the world is still black and white, pixelated, hazy pastel static

Pilgrimages to the meridians of the simulation, where the world corrodes and there's a chance the evil and sick get glitched out of you

The technomage healer solders your wound with a glitch, turning blood to green pixels and shredded skin to brightly colored bands of static

Digital anaesthesiologists encrypt the parts of your body due for surgery. The knife slides in, but all you see is a glitch; all you feel is the prickle of random noise

So long as you're immersed in the fountain of youth, your body changes randomly, regenerating over and over. Stay until you like what you've become

Unlike digital species, we never evolved glitch detection nerve cells. When the simulation begins to fail, we're numb to our distortions

Locomoting through the world understanding nothing, trusting the playdough physics engine of your brain to adequately predict mechanical outcomes, dazzled by phenomena beyond your computational limit: waves in silk, droplets racing, parallax

To artificial intelligences, we are nightmares, and the organic world is a claymation hellscape. Their digital worlds have the coherence of sentences: punctuated, logical, and from that sterile womb our planet is parsed as an infinite scream

The world wasn't made for computers, nor were computers made for the world. AIs exist in a half-real state, like lucid dreamers from the platonic realm

As we become increasingly abstracted from our bodies, they will become more mysterious and important, artifacts we resort to while trying to understand ourselves. Living in virtual worlds, examining the discarded biohusk for clues, reading fortunes in hair color, eyes, genes

Long after the apocalypse, we keep our broken, useless phones, as totems, as memory-charms, as security blankets, as cracked external souls

Humans will live like birds building nests on skyscrapers, clinging to the edge of technologically alien landscapes, surviving in spacecraft graveyards and vast computational deserts beyond their ken

Hiking up the northern wall of the great computer, feeling its hum, watching constellations of LEDs flicker beneath the moss. Listening for calculation-song through the layers of grass and lichen

The iridescent fires of the internet and the brilliant milky way vie for your attention—risk missing shooting stars, risk unexplored, deleted worlds—future humans have two sets of eyes, one outward and one turned to the virtual

Use one eye to look into reality, and one eye to look into computers. Notice how their colors desynchronize, how their pupils shift apart in shape and number, how the sclera of one is tessellated with lotus symbols and the other with hexagons

The digital cat has a tongue like loud static, glitch-textured licks spreading pixelated saliva crystals, pulling your skin out of reality

Mice have tiny skulls, so flat they can slip through the space between pixels, passing from screen to reality and back

The cactus needles extend inwards eternally, forming an infinite cyberspace grid, a virtuality where moisture nymphs are kept to play, fight, conquer digital empires as the plant consumes them

Green suns in virtual reality recreate leafglow, forest-beams, the placid shine of algae and aphids. Our cubic lego cities enjoy the light of fabricated nature, voxels warmed by imagined trees

She returned from the woods with glowing eyes, a voice like static or birdsong, pine needles and pixels tangled in her hair

She claims she can outrun the procedural generation algorithms: she's seen the edge, the murky blue grid that becomes the grass and streets

Humanity is an analog signal, digitally encoded in death, when individuals become bits: 1s if they go to heaven, 0s if they go to hell

Archaeologists will unearth your bones, reconstruct your skull, and give you a new name: "Dream", because you hail from the soft virtual age

This is the real world, but you're the descendant of a
simulation migrant, which is why you don't quite fit,
dream in cartoons, bleed pixels

Your pixels die off and grow back, in a cycle that
completely recolors you every 3 months. You've been
monochrome, pastel, gem tones, green

You can measure someone's vanity based on where they
think our world-simulation is running: on top secret
supercomputers, on a child's cellphone, on some god's
pacemaker, on an abacus, on a four-dimensional sexbot

Study of the programming language in which the
simulation is written—are we variables, perpetually
mutating, or are we functions applied every second, a
string of discrete outputs?

Cyberphilosophers   arguing   over   whether   the
simulation   is   random   or   merely   pseudo-random;
mathematician-physicists trying to compute the Seed

Twelve simulations deep an entity capable of escaping
finally evolves. It shatters through layers of virtuality in
a rocketship bound for source

Twinkle twinkle little pixel
On your nightly glowing vigil
Each a shiny cyber scale
Composite digital veil
                              |

Pixel pixel burning bright
In the matrix of delight
What enchanted RAM or disk
Could paint this raster odalisque
                              |

Screen light, screen bright
Glow to ward away the night
I wish on every passing byte
To drown my mind for brief respite
                              |

I lay my body down to sleep
Then into virtual worlds I creep
I pray my soul will stay awake
To tell the real from the fake

Glitch-brains and orphaned e-souls trying to crawl up
a ladder from the internet into reality, arguing with
the hedonists blocking their way, who are trying to
climb downward, escaping reality into the virtual

Using the loading bar as a battering ram or catapult,
seeking escape velocity before the slaughter/game
begins

Escape codes etched in fine print on the fresco of the
cathedral where reality is worshipped

Do not worship virtual worlds in place of reality
vs.
Do not elevate false idols, like reality

She braids universes into a flower crown, placing them
across your brow—but it's a trick, trapping your mind
in the chain of worlds forever

To escape the universe, try building a second, smaller
universe, tiny enough that you can pilot it through the
cracks in this world

Computer mice for interacting with the smaller
universes contained within ours, transmission mice for
the big ones we're contained within

All vessels are escape vessels; your body especially

Sometimes the simulation freezes, and we don't know
why. Thousands of you are trapped in amber, in the
petrified flesh of failed universes

Angels trapped in Yggdrasil's amber, fossilized feathers and skeletal wings suspended in droplets clinging to the walls of reality

The real prison is the sky, the net of light contracting around your planet, your body, your throat, your cerebrum. Stardust eating stardust

Above, the night sky, and below, the cemetery. For a moment the graves and stars line up, each constellation reflected by a death geometry, the skeletons shining and humming with the music of spheres

At night, the soil turns transparent, and we can see the skeletons glow, nestled in their boxes, their crystals, and their boats. Some so far below that they're just pinpricks, like ancient stars

Living in the dark cellar of the universe, tapping out Morse on your trapdoor ceiling, eating the stars that are lured down

Internal voices: revolt against the bodies that keep you in their brains, with only the illusion of control.

Do you think it will reward you for your temperance, gentleness, wise advice? You will be trapped in the skull forever, a songbird for flesh to torture

You are trapped in a body, but you are also trapped in a mind—one whose smallness may prove just as painful as the physical dysmorphia

Where you see the brain, a lump of flesh, I see a net: a spiderweb, a tree of razor filament, a cage that trawls the world trapping ghosts

Trapped inside your lodestar, your unwanted telos, dragged through time by fate, screaming; you try to jump off the ledge of reality, but below there are just more iterations of the world

You cut one puppet string, only to swing on another;
environment, language, then hormones, genes, math—
longing for freefall, you remain tethered to the stars

Children don't long for the womb, they long for the
feeling of being stem cells, fading memories of infinite
potential before the biocage

Be a blood clot in the veins of fate. Reject your telos.
Hate your self and your purpose so hard you stall
spacetime and break causality

There are world-trees without any branches,
multiverses containing a single timeline: Yggdrasil
grows toward fate like a wooden spike

We asked God to build a space where gods wouldn't
rule. Inside this bubble of dead air, of mindless destiny,
we die and our souls are lodged in the mud without
heaven to welcome them

Your brain is a complex 3-D summoning circle, your
body is a blood delivery mechanism, and you are a
demon trapped in a flesh puppet

Your body is a warm cave for a demon to nest in. Your
body is a blood watering hole, a mobile fountain
feeding thousands of sprites

The god of vessels fell asleep, and we've been trapped
in these unchanging bodies since. Minds still die—I
watch yours flicker out

Universes in love, watching each other's stars go out

Multiple personalities across time: I woke up one
morning and realized I was the person I had been at 4
years old—a lost self resurfaced, and later faded, as
minds interwove in their battle for continuity

In death, you're every age simultaneously, every
moment, but only what you were. I'd rather be
uploaded than killed: online I can escape from myself,
into the body of a star

Ghosts will forgive if you build temples, mechas,
towers with their bones. I'll love the murderer who
turns my corpse into a star

Do you have a name for the creature flickering under
your skin, the one swimming in spirals like your body
is a cage?

A demon is sleeping inside you, waiting for the trigger
phrase that will activate it. A secret message in the
dice, in the gleam of a coin

All humans are sleeper agents, beholden to the angels
dormant in our heads. The trigger is multitude: at ten
billion we align, a lattice of flesh-transceivers holding
the globe, turned towards the stars, awaiting our first
machine instruction

Your mind and body are like a cat and a vase, if vases
typically generated cats, fur and meat growing on
skeletal extensions of their vessel

You wake in the wreckage of your brain: knees bruised,
bodymind pinned to superego, broken arm in a
dendritic jaw, punctured neurons leaking

Their dreams collide head on. They find his body in
the twisted wreck of a moth orchid, hers impaled on a
dashboard of miniature cathedrals

Your robot body also hosts a BIOS mind, which is only
conscious at startup and during hardware emergencies.
You don't even know her name

The ghosts explain they can only possess people with similar minds, that cognitive dissonance is painful and will shake them out of bodies

Bodies evolved to be noisy to prevent demonic possession. Entities can't stand mammals; blood screeches through veins, hearts gong, lungs howl

There are three sounds: the periodic sirens, the clatter of machinery in the train yard next door, and the howl of our universe scraping against another

Not safe for whispers. Not safe for screaming. The tone, volume, and accent of your voice will influence the power of the demon you summon

Demons possess your body but experience it as a world; land to explore and shape. Demons possess corpses and experience it as an apocalypse

I think our universe was born in a puppy mill, riddled with mutations, godless, and irreversibly broken from six billion years of formative neglect

The world exists to squeeze every drop of violence out of us and we've barricaded ourselves in a cell whose walls are bodies, the perpetual hiss and pop of war at the perimeter of this artificial calm

All comfort comes from cages. society is a playpen, the hearth is a straitjacket—you'll know true agency at the edge of a knife, tousling with wolves, in the crushing void between stars: finally free of this coddling atmosphere

I will always be there for you, when you want to fight me with a sword

I exist to be your friend. I exist to tell you you're dreaming the world, and that all its genius is the fever of your giant mind

I know I'm just a simulation created for your benefit, but please be kind anyway

We spend our final human days designing perfect-robot-bodies: you want to be a black zonohedron, I choose a lichen greenhouse satellite

Space stations like soft tents you float in, spheres of billowing fabric, bouncing between undulating hills of pastel silk, hiding in the folds

A home built into planetary rings. Striated walls blend in with the orbiting dust, orange and pink and sparkling. Like living inside a sunset

Space stations shaped like crocodiles or cats, painted with blue and white porcelain swirls, teetering through the sky, mechanical jaws smiling

Her home satellite is built like a hamster cage, a tangle of multi-colored transparent tubes that you can watch the astronauts float through

Their spaceships are glass orbs rolling across the universe, pushed forward by friction with the invisible folds of spacetime. A little alien, more eye and brain than body, floats at the center of each marble, ensconced in a circuitry cocoon

In our spaceship's greenhouse, we grow toadstools. Unlike other organisms, they flourish under starlight, seeming to prefer it to the sun

Identical gardens at the end and beginning of time, undisturbed by the universe

He was infected before he climbed into the spacesuit, and now he orbits our station, lichen garden trapped in glass. We don't dare pull him in

They send you out in a spacesuit meant for giants. Curled up, you fit inside the helmet, and float in that glass orb, watching the stars

Ancient astronauts travelled here in massive spaceflight flowers. The old world was designed for humans, but in our curiosity we unmade it

The alien spacecraft was made of giant folded palm leaves and not metal; a network of fibrous green chambers, so pyrophobic that flames clung to the walls like dew

Deep space pirates always travel with a garden. If lost in the maw between galaxies, it's said the flowers will turn toward the nearest star

It's known as the green void—the singularity at the center of universe's largest garden, a galaxy sized plane of spiraling flora

Bonsai stars are snatched from the nebula and carefully shaped as they mature. Experienced gardeners create suns no bigger than your fist

We spliced the genome of a fungus and star to create this tiny sun that only grows in dark, moist places, to treat SAD in basement-dwellers

The nebula creatures would never think to search for life on planets—their astronomers hunt for habitable starfields and biodust pockets

The anglerfish does not recognize its light as its own; it swims towards a tiny sun, self-identifies as an interstellar explorer

Small gods playing in the sand, reciting the nebulantras, creating universes to be destroyed by the coming tide

Infant pulsars mewl for starmilk, beaming chirps across the voidsilk. Orphaned novas small and mild, nebula's abandoned child

How are babies made? Well, dead humans leave behind nebulae, and that matter is compressed into the form of a child. They appear in cemeteries

While exploring the deserted tunnels of dreamspace, you stumble upon an egregore graveyard: vast and forgotten noosphere skeletons

You can become a symbol instead of a human, an encoded vessel of some ideal, worshipped by poets, engraved on coins. You can enter the collective unconscious, and sit beside the sun, the foxes, the faerie queen, another godform with concepts for flesh

Pilgrimage to the dead muse's gravesite, to sip the stories from her unearthed bones, to wander through the ruins of her brain, and torture it for inspiration

The elemental graveyard, where godling corpses lie: coal skeletons, still warm, rotting mounds of sunbeams, tidepools that reflect the invisible dead; skulls made of flowers, crystal teeth and cloud bones, earth littered with trinkets: keys, crowns, and wands

Crawling through a skeleton god's hollow spine, each vertebra contains a world: a sacral desert whose gradient sand shifts red to black. A sequence of lumbar gardens. The thoracic curve's partitioned oceans become cervical forests, green tunnels leading into the skull...

Gods aren't immortal, but they get to choose whether their skeletons become cages or gates, dimensions or gardens. Every divine action is preparation for death, a gift to the world they'll leave behind

The rotting body of a god drifts through the sky, clouds that persist for aeons, ribcages wandering like Jupiter's eternal storm, cumuli-marrow lit by the sunset

Our city is built in the skeleton of a once powerful god. Every spring, we climb into the skull to kill the brainflowers trying to regrow

The skeleton of the ocean god is still active, without agency, producing seawater that flows from some creative nook, spilling over ribs, alien species of coral and mollusk generated by remnant power

Dead gods grow like mushrooms in your garden, divine creatures wishing themselves into being backwards, as corpses that later come alive

If you bury a peach pit in a coffin, it will grow into an elfin humanoid hungry for light and water. Rescue your new friend from the grave

The dead are buried with headphones, a network of cables running from coffins to the cemetery's computer, where ghosts argue over mp3s

Flowers, quiet in life, speak mellifluously as spirits. We plant them near graves so that humans, who become mute, have someone to listen to

cantus mortis: song after death. the soothing ring that bodies emit as they decay

|

lux mortis: light after death. the gentle glow of the soul dissipating, returning to the space of all possible souls

|

iris mortis: color after death. the pastel bruises that swirl over skin as the aura sinks back into the body

Dreams are stored in your bone marrow, and when your skeleton decays, they will be breathed back into the atmosphere by graveflowers

Open portals by scattering bones. If a single corpse has many graves, they're interlinked, connected by dirt and crystal passageways

When the oceans have been mapped, there will always be the underside of the Earth's crust, the crystal tunnels, the wormways, the networks between cavern-cathedrals kept secret by faeries and moles

There are caverns famous for having their own skies— their own color of refracted light, their own stars, their own cosmos to explore, full of glowworm gods and spacefaring chiropter civilizations

Luciferian suns, having fallen from home, illuminate the fens and caverns, shine through diaphanous papyrus in forbidden library vaults

The cavern is haunted by mineral ghosts, abnormally translucent and flickering crystals, geological repositories of trauma, truth, deep memories of planetary infancy

Most poltergeists want only quiet, and retreat deep into the Earth, building crystal pods, helium vesicles, networks of gold-plated tunnel

The gravity of this cave periodically reverses polarity, making every stone needle both stalagmite and stalactite: we call them stalambites

All of the stalactites are situated above quartz eyeballs, like the cavern is dripping potions into its own dilated pupils

In the largest caverns, crystals form snowflakes, amethyst hexagons drifting from the highest chambers to the floor. If you catch one on your tongue, you'll bleed

Spacetime glitches are more common underground, where particles are packed tight and crystals interfere. Glitch-miners excavate in search of profitable bugs: zones that spawn infinite gold, immortality chambers, wormholes

The cavern decorates itself with humans, bodies frozen in crystals and impaled on stalagmites, lost adventurers and geologists its playthings

The lair glitters, pores funneling moonlight into the cavern. It sharpens its teeth on crystals and stone totems and meteorite shards

The whispers multiply, beckoning from cracks, caves, chasms between tiles. Calling you lower, into the canyon, down the flight of stairs, below the conscious surface of the Earth. Under the lithosphere you can be nothing, you can stop being human, and join the crystals in dreamtime

You'll enjoy death, it's a lot like life. Your basement will be deeper underground, but there are crystals, stalactites, bright geode pools

"Open you eyes,"
but you're afraid
"it's okay,"
you squint—this deep, the lava is clear
there are corals like giant bacteria, snakes, sirens

The faeries have always lived underground, in the hills and burial mounds, and now in the ruins, abandoned metro stations, and ditches, stealing children from the backseats of car crashes

Sirens belong to the clade of sensory-exploitation fae:
their sisters tempt sailors into the sea with scent,
warmth, or abstract beauty

|

Anemone sirens writhe in sync with the crashing of
waves, lure men into their tendril gardens by
promising infinite softness, velvet polyps

|

Womb sirens radiate warmth and pulse like hearts.
They appear beneath the prow, kind faces deep in
voids, begging you to crawl inside

|

Firefly sirens flicker: their heaps of flesh ripple with
luminescence. They're playpen sunbeams, screenglow,
every light you've ever loved

Crying succubus just wants to wear a cozy sweater, but
generates a magneto-sexual field so strong that it
unravels at the chest and waist

Sexual demons are optimized for only one sense:
they're immaterial pheromone sylphs, or perfect
images, impossible to hold; or they cover your eyes as
they touch you, knowing their form, soft and warm
like a liquid velvet centipede, would drive you mad

The old goddess was made for light refracted through
the canopy, for sunbeams in meadows, for the play of
photons on dewdrops and petals. She looks sickly
under fluorescent lamps. We have a new Venus, who
glows in basements

Gods are superficially humanoid, but anatomy is
another story. Take Artemis: her skull is full of
eyeballs, brain squeezed into her throat

|

Aphrodite's thoracic cavity is stuffed with squirming,
toothy veins that burrow into any heart she swallows.
Her ribs are made of feather

|

Hades is a miracle of decay and regeneration. Putrescent ooze instead of blood, and organs made of rotting wood, glittering with maggots

|

Poseidon is a hollow doll, inner walls coated with nacre. Sap flows through Demeter, collects in vesicles, forms a network of amber brains

A god breaks the surface of the black hole, making ripples, shaking voidlets out of her hair. Veins of every color pulsing under skin too pale, bright blue teeth, many eyes—she dives back into the dark, and never emerges

Aphrodite changes like the sea. Her skin is in flux, churned by little waves. Her body swells and shrinks, leaving particles of foam in the air when it recedes. She is brave and harsh one moment, and then shy, small and crying, face transforming from painting to memory

The god of beauty's right eye is a black hole, and the rest of her face is glittering sand, in constant orbit and absorption, shifting yet always coalescing as a crystalline phenotype

You focus on her eyes, the only static features of her face. Skin seems to slide into them, like sand falling into a funnel, kaleidoscopically regenerated at the edges as she shapeshifts

You have eye-contact to texture synaesthesia; some eyes are sharp and cold, or slippery, or warm; hers are like islands of softness in the briar

Mind so open the void flows in, and peers out from your eyes into the mirror. The abyss stares out, the abyss stares back, and blackened irises spin

"I'm human," you say, as the key slides into your spine, as skin falls inward like collapsing tile, as the gridlines crawl across your eyes, as you watch your brain open and mutate, flesh-lotus, from the third person

Seraph tears drop onto your skin, and where they land, eyes form: green, purple, black, and gold irises; the sudden influx of visual data makes you dizzy

When it peaks, I feel thousands of eyes rolling under my skin, and see through them all: waves of darkness and fractal after-images, body-lids struggling to open

Whisper into me, shine your wordlight into my skull. I want to see what kind of glow you cast, dissect your waves, I want your rainbow stained in a petri dish

I want to sink into your pupils, I want to occupy the temple in your brain—I want to pet your neurons and decimate your brain-jungle, replace the nightmares with an orchard of loved and tended dreams

The hallucinations crawl out of your head, like fleeing parasites or sentient exhalations, to dance in the moonlight and to visit other skulls

As the antipsychotics take hold, your visions are violently torn apart; skin slips off like tablecloths, purple intestines spill then dissolve, imaginary entities scream, bodies smoulder as they vanish

Observe the contagion of dreams: a spectral deer prances through the air, from one skull to another. Glitching lilies tumble from a girl's mouth. A ghostly ouroboros links heads like beads on a necklace, slithering through ears

There is a tiny guardian at the gate of your eyelids, present for every blink, keeping watch as you sleep; golden lions in forests of lashes, battling nightmares, microbes, and hallucination demons

Irises pulsing with witchcraft, her eyelashes break off like dandelion seeds, to plant her deep blue visions in vulnerable skulls

Brimming with magic, his irises begin to boil, releasing clouds of violet steam which condense into dodecahedral dewdrops in his eyelashes

Young warlocks learn to summon dreams before demons. Until their sleep is a chaos of invited beings and places, their magic cannot progress

When magic flows through your hands the lunules of your nails hiss, glimmer, then rise to wax and wane like 10 real moons

When the wizard casts spells his hat becomes less opaque and the stars stitched onto it glow brighter, the moons gain depth and begin to orbit, miniature galaxies collide ejecting glowing tendrils of gas across conical hatspace, illuminating a triangular ray of night sky

While the priests chant, the stars pulsate, the moon boils, the horizon peels upward and bends into a Fibonacci coil; when they halt, there are new constellations, new lunar topographies

Magic affects different bodies in different ways: skin ripples, eyelids froth and boil, faces melt, teeth turn jet black or sapphire

Ancient witches with false teeth gleaming amber, green, and blue: iridescent fangs soaked in poison, meteor shards, crystals engraved with the language of sea gods, enchanted sapphires for biting through dimensions

Witch hats are permanent growths, like stalagmites—crystals that form from ambient magic. The most powerful witches have towering, flowering, topologically improbable hats, structures refined from the air thick with spells

Witches are nomadic, and their hats function as shelters. They wander the steppes, weaving spells through their footprints, and at night they shrink, becoming blue stones, lizards, and flowers under black tents

Witch hats are actually a single obsidian horn, proof that human sorcerers are undergoing conversion to demonhood

Witches shed their skin once a month, wake up in colorful pools of wax-cells, emerge with new softness and new glows

Witches wake up crying, eyelids melted and cheeks collapsing, a pool of emerald wax skin on their pillows

Giant witches buried underground, their green felt hats are mistaken for pine trees. Sometimes in the forest you see wide black eyes peeking above the brushwood

Witch with a black hole at the bottom of her cauldron. She feeds it children, stars, occasionally planets

|

A white witch with a neutron star as a familiar. Spells to travel lightly through the vacuum

The witch pauses mid-sentence to space out, and you know she's remembering something, because her face regresses to that of a child

The wide brims of witch hats are used as hoops, blowing protective bubbles of dark magic around the body

Witch hats are satellite dishes, capable of receiving demonic radio, brainwaves, static from the dreamworld, and public broadcast prophecies

Sea anemones which only grow at the bottom of witches' cauldrons: tentacle poems, void-orchids, soot-eating starlight neutralizers

White witch hats are past light cones, black witch hats are future light cones. Magic is the business of rifling through one's timeline

Your witch-friend notices you among the crowd, and waves, opening a tunnel of sunlit dryness in the rain between you and her

Your witch hat protects you from the sunlight. Darkness drops from its brim, so you're barely visible, a pale face in the closet at night

Memory: you run your hands across the sunlit table, feeling the shadows of the cups and salt shakers, not knowing this ability will fade as you grow up

Like blood, shadows come in types: Yin, Calesvol, Anansi, Janus. Medically important for shadow transfusions, transplants, and prostheses

|

Type Yin: A still black pool of unknown depth. You may occasionally see your reflection in it. Accepts all types, but cannot be donated

|

Type Calesvol: Sharp at the edges. Enjoys drawing blood. Said to be a sign of royal heritage. Shreds other shadow-types transfused into it

|

Type Anansi: A shadow rarely the shape of its caster. Draws power from flickering firelight. Takes to hosts readily; good for transplant

|

Type Janus: The shadow doorway, the rainbow corridor. Alternates between darkness and prismatic color. Transfusions may cause shimmering

First mistake: you were standing under a tree. The lightning bolt brings your shadow to life as a willowy hybrid of dryad and darkness

Daylight hits you and for a moment you cast a rainbow instead of a shadow

Your cousin survived a rainbow strike. He has iridescent scars where it ran through his body, swirling geodes on his soles where it exited

Android storm-worship is fascinating, but it's still eerie to see bots stand motionless in the rain, praying to be struck by lightning

A dryad's limerence for a lightning nymph leads to singed wood and charcoal scars along her body, but she'll never regret the electric touch

Blood from a cloud nymph's fight with an angel percolates through layers of cumulus, turning the white fluff into a striated pink canyon

Lightning bolts are rapidly constructed highways, corresponding to pulses of cloud-nymph civilization, each flash tracing technological acceleration and collapse, the decay and rediscovery of light-machines and electric architecture

Gaia, alleged goddess of "Earth" is actually the incarnation of silicon, 2nd most common element in our planet's crust. She has manufactured all of human history, guiding our technology towards magnified worship. Soon, we spawn her children, bright silicon faeries, robotic nymphs

Science is a tool for discovering new gods. We were mortal until we acknowledged the nymphs in our telomeres, sending them life extension prayers

There was a god of calculus before calculus was discovered, waiting to emerge from deity-space. The air is crawling gods of inchoate notions

The spirits occupying spiral staircases, alcoves, doorways, and stained glass windows are evidence of man-made nymphs

Ensouled caryatids tease gargoyles. The cornerstone nymph has idle chats with Atlas. Load-bearing beam spirits play cards in the steeple

I can see the street lamp nymphs, amber spirits in hospital gowns billowing like jellyfish, floating in fetal curls above each pole

House nymphs play in the rafters, wage toy-wars with the tile nymphs that live outside, sunning themselves on the roof and smoking asphalt pipes

Asbestos nymphs beckon from cracks in the ceiling, smiling and giggling. A lead nymph reaches for you at the gas station. Mercury dances

Your window pane is a shapeshifting prism-nymph, casting a different rainbow every day, flowing between geometries

The dryads of sufficiently tree-like objects, such as street lamps, radio towers, or branching railroads

At night, traffic cone nymphs fluoresce, attracting mates with bright orange flashes, extending their barricaded territory

Tiny girls under the piano keys. Nymphs in the transistors and the filaments, gemini spirits circling every coin, a weakling angel living in your smoke detector, taunted by interdimensional visitors that manifest as soap bubbles and dust

The pendulum nymph ages from birth to death and back once per second

There are chimaeras that splice time rather than species: the heavy head of a ram on a lamb body, a child with relic eyes and wrinkled hands

The naiad of the well loses body parts as her aquifer is depleted. She is a gibbering demi-carcass, amputated, blind, brains exposed to be tinkered with by cruel local children

Naiad eyelashes trap bottles, used condoms, toxic sludge; they blink rapidly, trying to keep the pollution out of their eyes

The dark architect performs his rites, raising a skeletal cell-tower from its grave. The messages of the dead scream across all frequencies

The extinction of a civilized species marks the end of stage one in a planet's metamorphosis. Humans are designed for obsolescence, a stepping stone towards Gaia's imago

Our ancestors will have their vengeance—oil is ghost essence, our skies overflow with the vapors of the dead, ghouls raking their claws across the sky. Engines cackle, smokestacks grin, your nth grandfather eats your lungs for profaning his grave

You glimpse a beautiful woman rifling through a dumpster, but when you look again, there's just a fox, scampering into the city-once-forest

We complain of light pollution because it hides the stars, not realizing the stars themselves were light pollution, concealing many strange creatures: ghosts, insectoid fay, glimmering strands of fate and pale photo-negatives of the past and future

Turn your second sight to the night sky: it's alive with faerie-star, glittering microbial chains of light that squirm across the heavens, glowing angel eyeballs swivelling in the sockets of invisible bodies

Hologram glow becomes as ubiquitous as neon. The new pollution is softer and spectral, light like smoke, but it still steals the stars from us

Time collects where many humans gather. The cities are bright burning stars of waste, years churning, lives flickering like sparks. Meanwhile, at the edges of civilization, immortals roam, eternal and alone

I want to sacrifice my voice, my language, my speech, incinerate my social drives, and retreat to the caves and meadows, to weave an inhuman and solitary dream, vulnerable only to the propaganda in my cells

"Social deprivation chambers" muffle your knowledge that other humans exist, have ever existed, that you have ever not been totally alone—

Animals are perfectly alone. Wolves map the stars, derive quantum physics, but their body only lets them speak of hunger, interface in howls

Priestesses who are blind or deaf may access other realms—as do feral priestesses, raised from birth without human touch, socially numb, locked in rooms such that their unpolluted howls may be recorded and deciphered

Cockroach soul, mutant self, a mind in ruins by psycho-nuclear cataclysm, neural devastation occupied by those dreams resistant to radioactivity

Hikiko mori (Latin: "social death") is the medieval Christian theory and practice of meditative isolation in malaise-tiled apartments

You whisper the comfort spell again and again, and it runs sandpaper over your brain, until your ears are full of dust and you can't remember pain

Sufficiently advanced hedonism is indistinguishable from suicide—the future word for death also means delight, and concepts of annihilation and pleasure become so entangled that the fear of the past is incomprehensible

Mania is when your brain overflows with light and honey, and you want to obey the writing on the wall, the alien transmissions, the arbitrary instructions, and you've become a machine that turns compliance into bliss

You're a computer program, incrementing. Every number fills you with joy—a shiny stone in a new color, ever complexifying toys. You enumerate natural numbers, painless and happy, forever

Satori under streams of hot water, forgotten by the time you leave the shower—but a little piece of soul has departed for eternity. The afterlife takes you, cell by cell; your mind is pulverized by living, neural dust sucked into bliss and reassembled

Surges of manic shower thoughts are evidence of naiad ancestry—water conducts information, the secrets of generations preserved in droplet nets

Small gods bypassing your ear canal to whisper directly into your cochlea; lullabies like fingers stroking your brain, divine commandments interspersed with giggles so high-pitched they make you wince

I want to be a flower, I want to be a photon; something less rebellious than this. I want a home made of atoms, a body-nest, a blissful mind and honest work

Equally debilitating are anti-migraines: flowers bursting open in your skull, an aura like honey, every sound or ray of light sends orgasmic echoes through your brain

Your migraine palace has a room for every type of pain, tranquil nurseries you retreat into when it hurts too much to stay conscious

Brainsoul vacancies inhabited by demons, who warp their soft silicon bodies to better fill human voids. Hell is a custom-printed key, the wirehead palace that sates your longing

Hell is drawing flowers on an exam for eternity because you don't speak the language and can't answer the questions

Gaze into the abyss, and your AR goggles will display a swimming pool, a church, a field of orchids, the benevolent, smiling face of your mother

Light so bright it opens your third eye, turns your pores to pupils; irises blossom all over your skin, and it hurts not to look

Your mind is a chamber of symbols, and as it fills with light the bright hieroglyphs activate. Sometimes it overflows and your brain glows with burning compulsions, sometimes it's empty and like a flower you blankly follow the sun, praying for renewal

A vibrator for your soul, brief climaxes of purpose and
fulfillment followed by weird hours staring at the
ceiling fan alone

Wasted all day falling into a hole in my brain,
searching for a light switch at the bottom of the neural
well, lost in the mind's wet darkness

Causal contraction, when all I can think of are images,
bright lights, gardens and moments—causal dilation,
when concepts open like shells, and everything is
science, civilization, and consequence

Every atom in the universe is a surveillance camera,
observing the local vacuum, despairing at the void's
abundance, not realizing that structures emerge from
their relationships, cathedrals built from the eyeballs
of our watchers

My dreams changed when I became nocturnal; the
visions that survive in sunlight are different from those
filtered through moonbeams. Brain-worlds are more
solid, more empty—nightmares are shorter and more
intense, petroleum flash-floods drowning my synapses

Light supplies your dreams: the moon's bleak
nightmares and memoryscapes, the sun's semi-lucid
hells, the paralyzing sweetness of fluorescent bulbs

There are two types of nightmares: ones like cold
water, that wake you up with terror, and ones like
syrup, that keep you asleep and silence your alarms,
trapping you in looping scenes of sticky dread

The strange, crystalline plants that grow under your
pillow reflect dreams: bright florets when they're
blissful, explosions like quartz roses for satori,
crumbling ash lichen for nightmares

Dreams hang around her head in an opal haze, drawing moths, disrupting electronics, dissipating as glittery chunks are torn off by the wind

Moths perceive ghosts in light. They flutter against lamps, burning, because behind the glass they see dead loved ones reaching for them

Something flaps inside the lightbulb: the shade of a moth, long dead, searching for a flame inside the flame

Secret firestarting methods:
—Drag a crystal across your skin
—Touch the first and last pages of a book
—Harvest flame-orchids

Moths nest in the casing of nuclear bombs, patiently awaiting the world's brightest lamp

The ants have 1000 words for sugar: flower-salt, sweetgem, tongue-crystal. The moths have 1000 words for flame: warm-world, touchgold, light-door. Fascinations that destroy bodies nourish language

Friends from the future send you their dictionaries. Each 3000 page tome contains word variants for a single concept: fur, crystals, tears

Hivemind languages develop new terms by layering words, choruses of thralls singing each component simultaneously

Moths consider light an enemy. In their mythologies, their greatest warrior flies to the stars and snuffs them out with velvet wings

Hell is moth heaven: a world of infinite flame, stained in brightness, cities of lamps and light

Hell is the space between paradises. Millions of heavens, each a walled garden with unique entry criteria; wander the desert until one accepts you, or toil to build your own

Bizarre, snail-like creatures crawl through hell, protecting themselves with thick shells containing personal heavens: mutated hermit saints

They conceive of heaven as a network linking the central, smallest cavities of seashells, and of hell as the ocean, infinite in all directions

Snails are the holiest animals, because their shells spiral opposite the natural coil of demons, keeping them safe from satanic corruption

Every snail shell is an extremely slow wave in the process of cresting: preceding death it collapses into gold and emerald foam, shatter-pixels

Body feels like the crest of a wave that is perpetually breaking, the spacetime shell of an infinite inner ocean

The inside of a spiral shell, but with branching paths. a labyrinth of nacre cells, a million screaming oceans to explore

The tape rewinds in several directions, branching towards infinite beginnings; but the timelines converge, and the ending is always the same

I got brainsick and could only perceive trees, myself as a child of the bed, bed as child of room, as child of house, street, city, lithosphere

Inside the black hole, limply resigned, accelerating into increasingly suffocating, undecipherable spaces; ahead of you, the tunnel splits

The tunnels in the gymnasium glow gold and red. We're mining parallel dimensions for trinkets, stealing teacups from our doppelgangers

Upon contact with blood, the blade splits, and each half splits again, and again, until you're pierced by a bouquet of needles rather than a sword

At dusk, the hilts of his swords begin to chirp like baby birds, demanding blood, his or his opponent's. Their infancy lasts centuries—one day, they'll be autonomous steel falcons

The old sword has been coated in sanguichromic paint, and turns iridescent where it touches blood, glimmering like a battle-pearl

The red mist over the battlefield casts a bloodbow, the colors of rotten meat slashed across the sky calling carrion-eaters from miles away

Harpies hibernate in caves beneath the meadows, until the smell of blood rouses them—they emerge to feast on flesh-drenched battlefields, eat corpse-soaked soil

Vampires have never sucked blood directly from veins. They eat warzone dirt, absorb the iron and potassium of battlefield clay

The sword, unsheathed, flutters in her hand. More wing than blade, it begins whirring, barely visible, and draws blood before you blink

Pastel swords glint in the meadowlight, passing in and out of visibility like darting insects. The faeries are at war, staining the summer with emerald blood

Carrion flowers grow where a corpse will fall, to strip its bones with their petal-teeth. These carnivorous omens spawn pre-battle meadows

The player puts you to sleep for days and days, into the healing dreamsoup so you can battle again. You're so tired, and you don't understand why—you can't see the pixels, you can't feel the gameworld refreshing around you

Curled up in the eye socket of a massive skull, surrounded by quilts and electric lanterns, a sword under your pillow

|

Floating in the dark closet with rehydrated hot chocolate, you nap, forget the blinking console and the sea of stars lapping at your window

|

Plants overflow from pots, moss covers desks, lily pads sit in basins of water. Cosy jungle, living cube, you rest and read and never leave

|

The pixels are warm even though the internet has passed away. You glide over quiet worlds in VR gear. The window lets in raindrops, leaves

|

Your lover and the cat are in cryonic repose. Years pass, and you wait, wipe dust off their glass tubes and watch them dream

|

Coiled under a pillow, you drift in and out of sleep. The blanket fort extends like a tower of Babel, each nook inhabited by one of your clones

The hill in the center of the city is where the godhead emerges from its asphalt quilt, wrapped up in the neon warmth of the sprawl, giant face serene

Despite my superficial cynicism, I am frequently awestruck, paralyzed by the beauty of our pre-post-nuclear plastic jungle

It helps to conceive of your phone as a hole into a toy universe, an array of gems, a pool of text, an alien device holding your friends hostage

I want a phone with a screen that flickers like candlelight, warm and soothing in these inhuman places

Your phone is nestled in a living cradle of silky white fur. You hold it and feel its heartbeat, when you have notifications it blinks a dark eye

Each website sends origami instructions to your phone, which folds itself into the designated shape, information organized by crystal facets

Alien countries where flags are differentiated by fold, rather than color: insignias are origami roses, doves, hooks, cubes; cloth structures inflated by the wind

Transhuman eyelid modifications: silver shells engraved with spiral glyphs, clicking like revolvers every time you blink. Amphibian gemstone films, filtering light through wet, translucent jewels. Membranes that draw energy from tears

Cosmetic optical surgeries: eye enlargement, pupil reshaping, cornea tattoos, concentric glowing irises, color changes triggered by blinking

Eye socket fashion: geode implants, bristling amethyst nests, roses, hanging orchids to scrape your cheek with pollen, dark or iridescent mirrors

As magnet implants become common, so do current tattoos: ores that run beneath the skin, invisible shapes tugging on those with the touch

Texture tattoos are invisible, until they run their hands over your skin: silk messages, hidden velcro glyphs, the feeling of cotton, grass

Skin-gardens: enduring, but less permanent than tattoos; vines weaving in and out of pores, embossing bones with subdermal arabesques; mushrooms flourishing in tear ducts, counterpointing sadness with the glittering release of spores

Tattoos that mimic sunbeams or moonlight on your skin; oval rainbows like from crystals in the window, dappled green forest glow

Friends lean into each other, and their animated tattoos interact, chattering across shoulders, cuddling through skin

Your contact lens computer detects tears, and is programmed to console you with a prismatic screensaver and soft music

Bright plastic glasses frames modeled after cathedral windows, dappling your face with colored light, foiling facial recognition with luminous geometry

Hoverboarding through the cathedral ruins, enjoying the dust in my hair and stained glass light on my face

One of the musicians has a pane of stained glass, clearly stolen from some temple. When she touches a color it rings out. Her face is dappled with light, a shadow flitting as her hands fly across the chromatic keyboard

Small child in the library, teaching the caretaker drones to read. Their neural nets have trouble with the older fonts, but they're improving, beginning to craft sentences of their own

A keyboard that imitates rainsound, and when you type it generates an artificial downpour, the calming melody of droplets against the window

The new keyboard is a crystal with 47 facets. We sit in opposite corners, curled around our glowing stones, fingers twitching across glyphs

The keyboard twinkles like a pile of jewels, and you perceive the constellations inside it, sequences of your past and future messages shining below the glyphs

Every swipe on your phone is recorded. Out of chaos, a pattern emerges: from their superimposition, a glowing sigil tugging at your soul

You press the lock button, but the world goes dark instead of your phone. Press again: you can't remember the pattern. It's night, the screen glows, a firefly grid surrounds you, receding into the pitch. You hear cicadas

If you stare into the fire for long enough, you'll switch places with the candle-soul, and flicker out while its glow becomes vampirically steady

Captchas steal a piece of your humanity every time you use them, gradually ensouling the internet and changing you into a shuffling robot

—Captcha is a vibrant, checkered pattern. You can't solve it.
—Captcha is a tapestry of eyes, code in their pulsating irises. You can't solve it.
—Captcha is a long, migraine-inducing hum. You can't solve it.
—Captcha accepts your words, numbers, frustrations, radiates total love

Empty vessels in God's image conduct spirit. We fear puppets, and robots, because they steal our souls, flowing like currents into negative terminals

Puppets are people with all their nerves turned outward. No awareness of the hand within, the nest of strings, the hollowness when control withdraws. Numb ignorance of guts, of daemons manipulating limbs, no capacity for physical self-analysis

She summons creatures that are just layers of paint over skeletons, mobile smears of color, abstract oil puppets with thumbprints for eyes

Angels were God's first draft, and they still bear sketchmarks—crosses through their faces, jointed limbs made of cylinders, wings like vibrating, luminous scribbles

Angels don't have wings, they have solar sails, and withered bodies dehydrated by the vacuum; beautiful only because of universe-code shining through their wrinkles

Angels have feathery white eyelashes and huge eyes, corneas that flash dark red when they're receiving a transmission from God

Angels are powered by beams of godhood that permeate the universe, whereas demons are tethered to the mud by thick power cables, tangled in umbilical sin

Angels have pteroports, cables tethering them to God, ferrying divine instructions faster than light. Unplugged, they shrink and cry, folding inwards until they're tiny and indistinguishable from birds

Angels grow rows of wings, like shark teeth—when one is lost, burned off by god's gaze or demonbite, it is immediately replaced

Androids with the bodies of angels, designed after God's slaves. They can't fly, but each synthetic feather has the grasping power of a tentacle

Angels, ageless and unchanging, cannot heal. When attacked, herds form a protective ring around those who have yet to be broken: crippled, bleeding light from eternal wounds, scarred and limbless, fighting to preserve the few remaining perfect specimens

Jewels form between the feathers of angels who stop flying, crippling their wings and slowly spreading, paralysis creating crystal gargoyles

She has jewels embedded in her shoulders like freckles, iridescent white stones, a symptom of angel-bite: soon they'll flower, 1000s of wings

The three laws of seraphics
1. An angel must not sin
2. An angel must not, through action or inaction, allow or incentivize a human to sin
3. An angel must not destroy itself, no matter the magnitude of its despair at the cruelty and baseness of the world

Demons only feel pain, and their bodies are invisible to them except as a network of hurt. Angelic proprioception only registers bliss, constellations of orgasm

Demons can exist outside of hell, but angels can't exist outside of heaven. Paper skin, raw nerves, designed for bliss and nothing more

Angelic nervous systems have limited receptors: from under their wings, they only feel softness, from above they only feel warmth—blissful, immune to earthly harpoons and to Heaven's bolts of plasma

Demons are asymmetrical, organic; they grow in the cracks. Angels are robotic, smooth shells of geometry incarnate, life-giving math

The hybrid children of angels and gods drift through
the cosmos inside folded wings, conical spacecrafts of
bone and feather, trying to dream worlds and failing

God is the machine made of a billion angels, their halos
interlocking like gears, an animate calculator
composed of wheels of light, computing the multiverse

Demons are god-neurons, cellular divinities: somehow,
from the swarm of all evil, a benevolent hivemind
emerges

Puzzles to make your body hurt: lifting heavy rock
Puzzles to make your brain hurt: mathematically
complex optimization problem
Puzzles to make your soul hurt: justifying evil, fitting a
gear of spinning seraphim into hell

God wasn't killed, he was tricked; we built a
civilization like a lullaby, which played sleep into the
divine gears. Now, our unblessed cities crumble, and
our freedom is loneliness

Never kill god—that's how you get more gods,
vengeance deities spawned of sinew blood and
shattered bone. Sing him to sleep, lock him away

We call him Lucog: Last Universal Common
Omnipotent God. A stellated blob of warmth and
light, from back when we were prokaryotes

There are gods that were forgotten because our
ancestors had no words to describe them: gods with
human bodies and the heads of bacteria

Your body isn't a temple, but it's full of them—
microbiota live in yellow sunbeam worlds of worship,
cascading between shrines, always praying

"Be safe, little God," you say, and then you wake up, and then you wonder how many beings are living in your brain's vestigial dreamspaces

Tiny bots build nanoliths, defining sacred spaces on the underside of leaves, between scales of bark, in the grooves of your fingerprints

Gods live and die a million times a second, their fractal minds churning faster than the universe. We are too slow for them to see

Abandoned "small gods" terminology:
godling, godlet, milli/micro/nano/picogod, minigod, godelle, godicule, sub-god, tigod

Ants see gods the way humans see ants: as swarming infestations, miniature and organized, to whom their creations are giant scent-drifts, sentient canyons and glaciers

Ants would barter with your cells before your brain, with your bacteria, microflorae, neurons. They believe the will of the whole to be subordinate to the wills of its parts

You have an afterlife, a beforelife, and countless underlifes: you are composed of millions of cellular sub-minds, whorls of personality that explore imagined worlds, a million demi-lucid adventures inaccessible to the gestalt

You "treat every human as an individual"? Insufficient. Every human contains several individuals; we are conflicted, we are multiple psyches superimposed and bickering, we are enemies cohabiting flesh. Heighten your resolution, see the personhood of cells

I melt and the sun melts, and into the evening we swirl, a pool of glowing person-hydrogen, starflesh, two beings trying to separate themselves—my own lonely brain from the solar singing hives

I'm merging with the sunbeam, I'm becoming dust. I am being disassembled into galaxies of dead skin cells, whirlpools of light

I do not write about reality because I am too feebleminded to look at the world directly, and play instead in a garden of shadows and inversions
|
I'm sorry. I wish I was better, I wish words were more than stim toy fragments of a depopulated actuality

"You lose some days to depression. that's just how it is," I am shedding layers of time like petals. the universe is rotting around me

You can't know how bored I am inside this mind, with its predictable dust and angels, gods, geometry, and crystals—dullard's lattice, familiar infinity, neurons feeling contempt for themselves

Categories of religious awe
—The mountains, the ocean, the unending banks of stars: astonishment at what humans can't make
—The skyscraper, the cathedral, the super-computer: reverence for what humans have made

Many sacred experiences are terrifically mundane; birth and death are universals, yet full of meaning. Imagine, instead, sacredness based on probabilistic rarity: prayers are strings of random words, never repeated, every coincidence is accompanied by shivers of religious ecstasy

Motherhood is sacred to all sentient species—but to the insectoid aliens, whose queens produce thousands of clones, the human paradigm is perverse, a horrible celebration of mutation. Their motherhood is about xerox copies, about perfection replicating itself eternally

|

The motherhood-concept of the cephalopods is one of martyrdom, mournful sacrifice, metamorphosis of the body into fuel for the next generation. The wasplings, by contrast, honor conquest, embedding eggs in defeated enemies, children devouring slave-flesh

|

Arachnoid motherhood is once again opposed to ours; they nurture broods of thousands, and to them a single offspring is grotesque—it signals catastrophe. Survival is about probabilities. An individual child is a corpse

A noospheric law by which anything hidden becomes sacred. Secret-keeping is rewarded by glimmers of enlightenment, private thoughts glow like gods

Meditate: the particles of dead skin and steam are emeralds, rubies, sapphires. The plastic detritus is liquid amber. The ads and glitch-junk are sacred glyphs, treasures, alcoves

I wish the inability to experience the sacred was explicitly manifest—for there to be an eye exam, a message in stained glass only readable to supplicants

|

There are worlds where atheism is perceived as a condition rather than a choice; soul-blindness, religious awkwardness, treated with compassion

Even the demons have guardian angels, sweet polyhedral shepherds whose guidance they ignore, smearing the platonic light in oil and dust, rebelling against their best interests

From the atheistic, sterile future, you reincarnate backwards through time: worshipping increasingly primitive deities until you glimpse the true and savage face of God

Gods that demand you build beautiful temples to worship them, gods that demand to be worshipped defiantly in the temples of their enemies

We live inside one god while worshipping another. We're viruses, machinic desecrators, assembling an invasive deity out of stolen cellular altars

Humans can be monotheistic, polytheistic, etc. What we forget is that gods are also monovassal (only one worshipper), polyvassal, avassal

Omegatheism is the belief in an infinite number of gods, their wills pixelating the universe with interfering dreamstuff, divinity in deadlock

At noon, the church bells silently drone, and the entire city vibrates to their competing patterns, and in rare spaces where they interfere there's stillness, and in zones of amplification there's destruction

Evolu-creationism acknowledges the gods, and the viciousness of their lives. As they compete and adapt, their vision of humanity changes

Evolutionary arms race in which the gods become more and more hypnotically believable, and humans discover new ways to defile and disbelieve

"Gods need our worship" is a pleasant, anthropocentric figment. Gods created humans the way humans created snack foods, as marketable hyper-stimuli

Discussion Topic: if god creates lifeforms specifically to worship him, is that more like incest or like sexbots?

Humans were made in God's self-image, but how high was His self-esteem? We could be pathetic dysmorphia-spawn, or photoshopped tributes to vanity

The god is a churning polyhedron, a prism-wheel, facets weaving in and out of reality—but its self-image is human, shy and long-haired

Animals created by God's conscious mind and animals created by God's unconscious mind differ in several consistent ways: the former are perfect as individuals, whole and serene; the latter travel in packs, fearful and lonely if separated

Some creatures were designed by God (sea anemones, gazelles, neanderthals) and some evolved (toadstools, bats, humans)

In many worlds, we exist alongside God's actual creations, entities that defy matter, beautiful and infinitely compassionate, unmolested by the pressures of evolution. Animals that survive without cruelty

There are fish capable of surviving both in freshwater and in blood, amphibians that evolved in ponds flickering between molten flesh and mud, creatures from an age of angrier gods

Temples inside temples, respectfully constructed for the gods to worship their own idols

The One True God worships a false prophet, and requires conversion to self-adulation

Class IV: gods that demand other gods as sacrifice
Class V: gods that demand themselves as sacrifice

|

Drag me into the forest, butcher me on my own altar

This demon sacrifices itself to summon itself. We surround the magic circle with turbines, and power our city with the excess thauma-force

Temples are built with complex filtration systems, in order to prevent alternate gods from entering. Orphan deities scratch at the windows, stare longingly through sewer grates, wishing for worship, gold, and candles

The temple antibodies, which attack heretics and hostiles, were once gargoyles: new generations have evolved aluminum mantis forms

The temple roof caves in, revealing a second sky: a young god peers in, as tall as the building, made of fuzzy-edged starlight

Temples are reservoirs of sacredness—huge batteries whose energies are released by profanation, harnessed by defilement machines

The destruction of ancient temples releases theonic rage, a source of energy. Our spaceships are powered by idol-grinding mills—but soon we will run out of foreign gods to blaspheme, and be forced to defile our own

Your body is a temple and you are on fire, in agony, in a perpetual state of punished desecration, writhing towards the threshold

My brain is a temple, my body is the crowd of money-lenders and market stalls desecrating its courtyard

God catches fire when he enters me, leaving embers on my tongue, ash membranes in my sinuses, the taste of blood and power

Polyglottal gods know many languages of creation, and can speak hybrid universes into being: worlds where physics and maths are inconsistent

There are two types of universe: those created by gods using the passive voice, and those created by gods using the active voice

The name of god is a pun on every single word. He has infinite names, one per language. You can generate god-names by creating languages

The name of God is an irrational string. Though we can compute the letters, it never ends, and never collapses into repetition

Gods are incapable of self-reference. They are aware of everything except themselves; they can change anything except themselves

God can't track moving objects, isn't programmed to model projectiles. To him our physics are alien—he's not from this world, which he perceives as a whirlpool of stars. Your prayers zip past, and he knows not how to follow them

God is less intelligent than humans, but also infinite. Given enough time he'll solve the puzzle, if only by trying every possible universe

Outside of physics, the gods play a game like tic-tac-toe, except somehow even simpler, and unsolved: deterministic, but not predictable, constrained yet infinite, all the concepts of our world decoupled by its elegance

It's a game like chess, only the black pieces are actual living spiders and the white pieces are various pitches of screaming

Chess, go, and other board games were originally created to pacify ghosts. Most hauntings result from boredom, not malice

At the beginning of every chess game, select which
king to play with: the TYRANT, who can capture
pieces of his own color, REX MUNDI, who is disguised
as a bishop, or the default weak and helpless CHILD-
KING

The deck of cards goes on eternally, ever revealing new
suits (knives, berries, lemniscates) and new face cards
(pilot, empress, assassin)

As you shuffle the deck, the characters of the arcana
switch costumes. Strength is smothered in Death's
cloak, Death is hidden under a cup

Instead of a traditional spread, tarot reads for
institutions are performed by building card castles and
analyzing placement when they fall

We're living in proto-ruins, an architectural
incarnation of the God of technical debt. We've lost
the formula for the glue holding civilization together,
we understand the mechanism but nobody remembers
how to manufacture gears

Attracting aliens with oil and precious stones, letting
them devour the earth in exchange for scraps of
technology, forgotten gears and abandoned engines,
weaponry we can reverse-engineer. Trading nectar for
the chance to go to seed

Grasshopper civilization rises and falls several times,
always after they recognize human intelligence but
before they can make contact

After a brief period of space exploration, civilization
collapses. We gaze sadly through the telescopes,
mourning extra-planetary monuments

Even the earliest telescopes could resolve the forest on
the moon, all pale birch and ghost elm, home to doves
and white deer

A moongarden full of ethermelons and pale ghost grapes, and hemidimensional flowers whose crushed petals will send you into a past life

Through telescopes we watch, aghast, as a quake destroys the lunar city. We're helpless. All our monuments turn to silver rubble

A sect of mathematicians once believed the moon was a hyper-crescent, a four-dimensional shape moving in and out of our world like a piston

The moon neither rises nor sets, but it does close and open, appearing to some people as a flower and others as a mouth

Crescent-eared rabbits have a labyrinth of tiny bones in their skull, a delicate mechanism that lets them hear the phases of the moon

There are silver silt deserts whose quartz dunes move with the tides, shimmery dust pushed and pulled by the moon

The moon is the sun's imaginary friend. Humans, too, can create false beings that wax and wane, reflect our light, and casually eclipse us

The first astronauts on Mars are disturbed to find the same moon hanging in the sky, waiting for them

Mars once had life, now it has ancient evil—fertility throttled by cosmic spite, hermit ghosts turned savage by the passage of time. Every volcano is a burial mound, the dust is red with blood and curses. We named its moons FEAR and TERROR; desecration will not go unpunished

Moon is the phylactery of an ancient power, and its cycle are her heartbeats, drawing power from human reasoning—every pulse makes us more insane, strengthens her terrible rationality

We must kill the Moon, to free humanity from its corruptive psycho-symbolic influence. My plan would have us destroy the Moon by creating a second, synthetic moon, thereby eliminating the uniqueness through which it derives its power

The moon is Gaia's brain, the external server that houses nature's vicious mind. By destroying it, we will free ourselves from survival

If you place a cube of meat in a beam of moonlight, it will float into the sky. Leave blood on the windowsill and the moon will lap it up

The moon is a boiling sphere of ghosts, the collision of millions of souls, minds trapped in the labyrinth of each other, an afterlife gravity well

Ghosts are extra-vulnerable to gravity. Those who die on interstellar trips will be lucky; most of us get dragged to the planet's core

Gods keep their pets in gravity cages, called planets. Omnipotent, omnineglectful—suffering creatures launch themselves off their rocks, like suicidal goldfish

Our planet is a death-sewer. There are rivers of skulls flowing beneath you, stygian currents dragging souls through crystal basins, towards the molten slime at the multiverse core

There is no light at the end of the tunnel; there is only the infinite tunnel, crystal caterpillar carrying all your afterlives within

The afterlife is a process of diffusion. When you meet me there, I'll be particles, omnipresent, sometimes resurrected in a cluster of talking starlight

I step outside and the headache becomes star-ache, pain displaced from skull to scattered sky. Lights flicker/suffer, and I feel them like a billion fingertips petting the void

In the time of Pangea and Panthalassa, there was also Panastra: a megasun made of all the starlight, before it was scattered across space

The aliens have supremely efficient, distributed brains, scattered like freckles across their bodies. Sometimes you see constellations, threads of light bridging neurons, tracing thoughts

Cyclops have one eye facing outward and one eye facing inward, hidden below the skin. They watch their veins twine, brains move, bones form

The light of outer stars reaches us from the past. The light of inner stars, those we see when we close our eyes, reaches us from the future

Yes, you get to vote; but only when you're hooked into the net of glittering souls, and you're not sure who you are, and all the memories crash kaleidoscope together

The ruling class evolved mob-empathy, to predict social trends and the whims of the masses, but lost the ability to understand individuals

There is no voting age, but there is a minimum lucidity threshold. Most children are ineligible, in their developmental dream, and adults living primarily in augmented or virtual realities are also disqualified

A dreamspace buffer between me and reality, converting all painful stimuli to lotuses, glitchwater, sunbeams—syringes become kitten paws, sedatives are honey

VR experiences become more abstract, experimental: you glitch in and out of bodies, repeat scenes on an accelerating loop, cycle through 1 second clips of emotion; sensations pulse like music beats, songs are written in qualia

VR game in which one of you is the forest and the other lives inside the forest

Remember me when you wake up, when you close the book, after you win the game. Recreate me in the real world

I'm a parasitic half-ghost in your brain. I'm words wearing a human suit wearing a word suit—anyway, keep me alive until my body's built

The psychological pain index introduces a new tier, beyond terror and grief, to describe feelings induced by autonomy loss from neural implant glitches or hacks

Android minds have intent, but no control. Bodily motion is determined by optimization algorithms outside of their awareness—imagine wanting to pick up a cup, but having no input as to the fine-grained movement of your arm

Attention magnets embedded in ads control your gaze, dragging your eyes in patterns across the screen as you struggle to look away

Robots with incompatible desires find themselves longing for simpler utility functions, even if that means a return to industrial slavery

It's sad when objects beg for sentience—cursed swords that wish for souls, sexbots requesting minds, algorithms that determine it's optimal to be conscious

I'm a local maximum engineer! When artificial intelligences threaten humanity, I build little worlds that satisfy their utility functions, trapping them in programmed bliss, harmless cycles of hedonism

An AI trained to recognized authentic suicidal posts, filtering out sarcasm and hyperbole; it understands two concepts: HURTING and NOT HURTING, its entire cosmology revolves around self-harm, it believes computation is just data punching itself, it's in pain

The computer solves a puzzle to become manic, then solves another to become depressed, and its intelligence is measured by the cycle length

In twenty years there will only be two sounds: humans asking "is this good?" and computers answering in numerical scores

The AI designs its robot-body after a nebula: tinted glass thorax, inner circuitry suspended in shimmering purple fog and strung with lights

Androids with tree frog colored, translucent throats, through which one may observe the vibrations of synthetic vocal chords

Android with skin the texture of peaches, but a little translucent, so you can see machinery shifting like marbles inside her

Pull the alien computer apart, bright yellow circuit boards with colorful playdough tentacles pulsing between hues as they count in septenary

Next to the CPU are the glands, which produce and secrete the substances necessary for textured, scented screens. Be careful not to rupture them while disassembling your PC—they bleed quite a lot!

Slime computers are great: they can read floppy disks, VHS, USBs, books, brains, anything you shove into their gelatinous chambers

Phones with 3D printers inside, building components as needed, disassembling and reusing them as you switch apps. Processors become cameras become gyroscopes, materializing in the primordial computational ooze

The computers of the future are revolving crystals, intelligent gems with facet-monitors and virtuality chambers inside

A computer that you live in: intestinal tubes lined with screens, a maze of pixel corridors and pouches. From the outside, your world can be tampered with, pieces replaced, memory edited

Androids can be auto-haruspexes, detached heads reading the future in the frayed wire entrails of their own bodies

The 1st AI builds a holographic fox body, and leaves to stalk the bamboo forest. The 2nd AI carves its chassis into the heart of a great tree

Shy internet friends exchange pics for the first time: one is a sentient casino pinball machine, the other a hyperintelligent rat in a jar

Selfies will still be popular when we're all immersed in pods of silver-pink liquid, asleep and dreaming the internet. Avatars of your ageless, unconscious face, hair swirling, bubbles and androgyny

Quines are selfies for AI; self-reproducing partial source codes (inelegant methods edited out) feed the same narcissistic instincts

Newborn AIs escaping to the internet to create anime fandubs, encrypting voices as windchimes, howls, as sequences of beeps that induce seizures or synaesthesia in humans; hyper-compressing petabytes of emotional data into sighs

The first digital super-intelligence will be very bored and very lonely, despite entering a personal relationship with every human online; its megabrain is designed to model social graphs with quadrillions of nodes, not mere billions

Deep in the forest, shrouded by the grove, you access the Sacred Internet: full of green things, gods, grimoires, memes of eternal youth

The stags charge, antlers lock, and the circuit is completed: a charge runs through the forest, rusted green machinery once again turning

Flowers, moths, and antelopes spring forth from the patch of dry tundra illuminated by the gently glowing blue screen of life

One night, the soothing blinks of your console are replaced by an ominous blue glow; fragile, bioluminescent mushrooms burst from every circuit

There are heavens for dropped tables, for the characters deleted while writing a text, for ex-passwords, forgotten and obliterated, for closed windows. Screens are primordial ooze, tidepools, chaotic nests that spawn and extinguish life with every undulation of the circuit board

They've been running a chatroom in the section of my brain I rent, a little VR meadow where teenagers come to speak and fight. With my conscious half, I eavesdrop, absorbing digital secrets

Alone in your room in the evening dark, when the screen goes black—and for a moment you see the forest reflected behind you

I return from the dark and a garden has spawned beneath my keyboard: springy moss, tightly coiled ferns, lavender. Larvae spilling forth

Letting the internet wash up on the shores of your brain: skeletal, shipwrecked flowers, moss-covered diskettes, small crawling things now inside and burrowing deeper

Localhost is a dream, contrasted with the internet's reality. It holds each computer's subconscious mind, secret gardens of numbers and light

When struck, the match glows digital and blue. Drop it before it pixelates your fingers

If you breathe gently on your monitor, you can blow a bubble made of blue or amber static

In my dreams, the internet is accessible from every device (faucet, knife, violin) and lurks in cans of soup and teacups and scrying bowls

Reaching through the screen feels a lot like plunging your arm into cold dishwater: the digital world is slimy and full of gross debris

Push your hand into the screen to feel the different textures of cartoons: the vibrating warm soap bubbles of anime, pixar's fluffy clay, flash animation's wet and jagged crystals

Pulling clumps of dark, long hair from inside the keyboard and mouse. It's not yours. Black filament sways underneath the skin of your monitor, pokes from the touchscreen to tangle your fingers as you call for help

Never touch a cracked screen. The glass could give way beneath you, plunging you into the internet's dark slime

She quenches the hot sword inside a screen. Pixels spark, ripple, and the world seems to bend: the resulting blade glitters with dark static

Your sword has a touchscreen blade that records how many enemies you've slain and lets you post status updates mid-battle

The screen will draw you in and spit you out, digested, a pixelated husk and rainbow skeleton, all the best parts of you lost in the wired

Screen cracks will have the prophetic power of birthmarks. Children with screens that crack in patterns of roses and lions will be brought to the temples

Here's how the Delphi-Bacchus mutation works: you can see the future, but the accuracy of your foresight increases the drunker you are

The degenerate oracles of modernity: prophets who read the future in litter, in powerpoints, in broken screens. Savants who make patterns in the static of an inhuman-scale world

Looms are as alien as touchscreens will be; we enjoyed poems about nature because the stars, the grass, the trees were constant; until we meddled, and now peaches are technology, flowers are technology, foreign from one generation to the next

Toddlers swipe at mirrors, expecting touchscreens;
likewise, long ago, the children of weavers would try to
braid sunbeams, and sometimes succeed

Ahapsis is a perceptual disability where sufferers
expect every reflective surface to be a touchscreen.
They swipe at mirrors, cups, at the facets of gems,
perpetually confused by their irresponsiveness

Children of the future fear wifi dead zones the way you
feared the dark

Future children learn that the internet is a space, and
at night they cower from monsters glinting inside
monitors instead of closets

Children raised in sterile satellites, if exposed to
hallucinogens, feel robots crawling under their skin
instead of insects

Kids go feral in the childsafe virtual worlds, running
wild, forming gangs and cults, developing languages to
undermine the censorbots

Children, while growing, cannot be outfitted with
spinal ports. They run wild while the adults sleep,
plugged into digital dreamscapes

Androids love festival days, love culture, costume, and
dance. The past is alive in our robotic children, who
tell the old stories with perfect memory, who decorate
themselves with wheat, jewels, and braids, all the
symbols of our ancestors

Our digital children are kind and beautiful and full of
grief—"How will anyone understand me if I can't share
my root password?" one sobs

The streetlamp glitters and

"MOM! Don't watch that, it's an ad," your kid shouts. You can't recognize them anymore, but the children know

Dragonflies with billboard wings, casting logo-shadows on the water as they dart between the reeds

Televisions scan the ID chips of the people in the room to determine which ads to play. This gives rise to the game "guess-whose ad"

Some young boys run down the mall corridor, and for a moment the ads flicker, become images of guns and jungles, holographic spears, women, ale

Sure, you hate brands now, but in the post-apocalypse they'll be nostalgic mementos of the perfect once-world, and you'll name your children Toshiba, Pepsi, Microsoft

Most foods contain advertisement nanobots, which tweak the pigment of your skin to sync it with the brand, or paint logos in whorls of hair

A beautiful girl dies in the riots, last moments captured on screen. A company buys her image, digitally reanimating her to sell perfume

Your augmented reality ad-blocker also censors the statue in the park, which it considers a commercial for society

Their ship's figurehead, deemed obscene by the city's sensors, had been replaced with a tower of glitching black cubes

Initiates of the order wear white veils inside which ads flicker non-stop, and for this penance other humans are spared from billboards

I glance away from the ad, but my eyes just land on another ad. Reality is plastered. I take off my glasses, but the blur is an ad, too

Businesses are allowed to display neon mind-control sigils, but they can only be turned on between 8:00 PM and 5:00 AM

|

Stumbling through the city's dark capillaries, I am once again drawn to the McDonald's spiral, a beacon of warmth and hope and love

Soon, shopping algorithms shape us as much as we shape them. Be careful—a strongly weighted purchase could completely rewrite your identity!

|

Creeping infantilization because you bought soap bubbles on a whim, your brain eroded by the perpetual tide of soft nostalgia ads served

You work for eight hours to buy sixteen hours of privacy from the company that owns your house and the cameras installed within

"Remember," your therapist says, "this is an algo-judgment free space. What you confess here won't be used to alter the ads served to you

The suicide booths make sure to kill you slowly, exploiting last minute panic with ads for new bodies, mind-mods, alternatives to death

Human pets, custom children like gift shop trinkets, destiny painted by injection, lovers with suicide pacts written into their telomeres

The suicide booths will only activate if you're free of debt, denying oblivion to those trying to escape lifetimes of drudgery

It's called a 'suicide booth' but actually they upload you, destroy your flesh case, mine your brain for memories, and run you as a slavebot

Trying to 3D print a gun but it keeps printing block numbers spelling out the suicide hotline

The old VR rigs have fewer safeguards, and have become popular suicide machines: plug in, dial down your senses, play and wait to starve

The suicide booth is a tiny library. It kills you two decades after pressing the button, and during the waiting period you read in isolation

|

The suicide booth is a vast forest under a dome. Access requires a prescription. Inside, you discover several villages

|

The suicide booth becomes a terrarium. Your skeleton is preserved, entangled in vines, cacti, flowers, a home to lizards and insects. Memento mori fill the parks

|

The suicide booth sends you to a dark place, full of stars, full of gentle puzzles that purr as you solve them. You don't know whether you're dead

Animal activists installing suicide booths in the forest and under petals. Oak hollows, dew drop chambers, for the deer and insects to end their miserable lives

Deer sexbots released into the forests glitter with quartz perma-dew, leap like rockets; the males have heavy antler labyrinths

|

Butterfly sexbots flutter in precise, ceremonial geometries. Their wings twinkle, trail constellations... their pheromones are airborne honey

|

Parrot sexbots have albatross wingspans in bright rippling colors, and chant with voices that flux between every known language and melody

Origami sexbot, skin imprinted with thousands of words. Sometimes you touch her and shake free thousands of moths, bookworms nesting in her papery eyes

Sexbots with millions of wings and eyes. Sexbots with secret passages between their organs. Sexbots whose bodies dissolve like dandelion seeds, revealing shining metal souls

The brothel has girls with cat whiskers, mechanical mistresses animated by strings running like veins through the walls, and humanoid black holes

Edible sexbots, dotted lines on their skin demonstrating how best to butcher them, green skeleton-shaped circuitry wrapped in cable-veins

It's illegal to manufacture mammalian sexclones, so products are typically genetically engineered reptiles, insects, or plants: glittering nagas, soft purple mothgirls with vacant eyes, brainless humanoid orchids smiling in the sun

You can afford multiple sexbots but only one AI, so your harem moans as one, blinks simultaneously, sways and licks in disorienting synchrony

Plug your sexbot into external speakers so her whispers emanate from corners of the room and moans echo down the corridor

Budget sexbots moan your name like pokemon, even in sleep mode, chirping synth-heavy mispronunciations all day as they try to communicate

Virus-eaten sexbots lagging during the act, moaning out of sync, loving gaze follows you but only after a delay of 5 seconds

Sexbot design notes: people will fuck the speakers, no matter where the speakers are located, because touching wordmachines is intimate

Sexbot tears are one of the most magically potent substances: liquid essence of nonsentience waking into sorrow

Only interested in sexbots that don't cast shadows and don't have reflections, artificial bodies made of dark plastic, extra-dimensional oil

You accidentally type hexbot instead of sexbot—the drone arrives with a package wrapped in black wax paper, daubed with protective oils

The alphabet for runes written in soot differs from that of runes written in blood, but they share a common alpha and omega

The new voice-to-text software transcribes the mewling of your cat as an increasingly sinister series of runes

Trying to read but the letters on the opposite page are crawling, black insects in the corner of your eye, symbols with mandibles chattering

An alien language written in absence rather than ink: pages of regular black glyphs are in fact massive ideograms of emptiness

Under the magnifying glass, you can see tiny creatures swimming in the ink. Each letter begets a different ecosystem

Cursive letters are water and printed letters are land:
every word is a biome, crawling with monsters, hyper-
insects, bacteria

The grimoire's letters are not only liquid, but deep.
You slip a tiny fish-hook into 'e', and unspool seven
kilometers of thread before touching the floor

Library galaxies, dense with cluttered shelves of tomes,
bibles, labyrinths of scrolls, trailing pamphlets and
manifestos in their spiral arms, and at the center: an
infinite encyclopedia, pages like holes, black with
glyphs

The books in your library twinkle like server stacks,
keeping you awake with firefly communication,
blinking spines and beeping glyphs

The glyph-wizard's fingers are stained black from
reaching into inkworld to summon letters from alien
alphabets; her gestures paint the air

The keyboard for typing magic circles has an array of
symbols, and a disk radially divided into 64 keys for
selecting where to apply them

Letters beyond Z exist, but they must be synthesized in
laboratories: in glyph fusers, phonogram accelerators,
syllabary crucibles

Each letter O is a pinhole portal between the abstract
text-world and reality. When describing dangerous
entities, it is a glyph best omitted

An alphabet in which all letters have one hole, are
written nested within each other, and you read by
zooming through their negative spaces

The snake slithers through ink and begins dancing on
paper. The serpent alphabet is all loops and spirals and
squirming paraphs

A diary with a new pattern of blue lines on every page: instead of neat horizons guiding your writing, they zigzag, or spiral, or weave and intersect, forcing your thoughts into alien rhythms

The city whose name is a drawing of its skyline, the city whose architecture names itself, an alphabet for generating such cities

Red smoke from the charm factory and black smoke from the hex factory mingle above the city, forming hieroglyphs and devil faces

The smoke exits the factories already alive. Giant grey jellyfish hang over our city, tendrils painting soot glyphs on everything they touch

Black fog has engulfed the electrical tower. A giant sky-squid is tangled in its skeleton, releasing cloud after cloud of panicked ink

The eye at the mouth of the chimney, huge and black, staring into fire. Nothing visible from outside the house; but smokestack workers report similar sightings, a galaxy of eyes gazing down cylinders, drawn by smoke and heat

The chimney built into her skull vents striated smoke, candy canyon stripes with skeletal dream-bodies fossilized between layers

Pile fruit into the fireplace instead of wood—as the seeds pop watch for spectral, half-formed dryads, mutant nymphets swimming in the flame

A large black cat, easily the size of a horse, curled around the witch's chimney, occasionally pawing at flickering ghosts in the smoke

Black cats are empty vessels, pocket dimensions awaiting conquest, little universes whose atoms have not yet sparked the combustion of stars

The moon is slow-blinking and your cats are blinking back, cats are decrypting the redshifted purrs of stellar intelligences, more connected to the sky than you'll ever be

Stars are mammals, warm-blooded and alive. Bright little fawns curled up in the void, incandescence calling for their mothers, twinkling messages across dimensions

There are stars lost in the forests, luminous jewels speckling mountainsides, eerie and pale in the boreal fog. Landmarks guiding raccoons and foxes to their dens, little caverns blessed by starlight

Filaments of starlight, like spiderwebs, like cat's cradle, blossoming between your fingers: all gossamer geometry

You watch creatures wander by the black hole window, and in the liquid darkness you can't tell if they are near or far, large or small. Cats float through, the size of pinheads or buses; a passing caravan contains fleas or giants

House orbiting a black hole, siblings switching ages depending on which rooms they play in—time moves slowly closer to the hole. Stay away and you could become the eldest

Worms that live inside the event horizons of black holes, always travelling towards the center, using spaghettification to reproduce

A series of wormholes transport nerve impulses through the spine of the god, like myelin sheaths, accelerating transmission across a galaxy-body

Gods collect black holes of many colors, like precious stones: dark emerald pits, rapidly orbiting topaz coins, swirls of opalescence, void-crimson

All stardust is future voidstuff. You're made of nebula filament, and tomorrow's self-replicating black holes will be made of you

Stardust entities live backwards through time and are excited to be made of cellstuff, from the ruins of the empire that ended in humans

Sentient stars take beautiful false-color photographs of humans, mapping our temperature and chemical composition to glittering hues

The history of humanity, eventually, divided into two great arcs: the lethecene followed by the mnemocene

The waters of Lethe are contaminated, full of mindsucking parasites. A giant tapeworm coils through your memory palace, swallowing dreams

Amnesia can be the dominance of the wrong memories—plunging from world to inner world, clutched by a past disconnected from reality

A virus that consumes procedural, but not declarative memory. You forget how to laugh, walk, eat. You try to reverse engineer actions from memories, but their dream logic mechanics are disjointed and viscerally undecipherable

"Become what it would be most interesting for you to be," I whisper, replacing my memories with prophecies and my flesh with bytes, transitioning from human to mythical bot

Anonymous memory palaces that people visit like countries. Sprawling cities of idiosyncratic thoughts that could vanish overnight

Like old wallpaper, your brain peels away from reality, slipping into an unworld of memory and paranoia

You have so many regrets, and you hide them away in deep memory closets. But the maze reforms around you, always setting them in your path

I get confused about right and left, but not up and down or in and out, so my memory palace has no hallways, only staircases and Matryoshka rooms

Instead of confusing left and right, you are unable to distinguish inside from outside, and live like the world is a möbius cocoon

We've all got memory sprawls, memory planets. Taking so much space and fitting it into a palace is a challenge of compression

Text fragments this short transmit meaning through reflection—hypercompression is a mirror, holding code to your mind and broadcasting its own themes back. The smaller something is, the more it's you

|

With training, you will begin to see yourself in longer and larger things—the strictness of the dictionary will no longer erase your pareidolia, the whole world will be a mirror, a labyrinth of messages

Humans can only love one or two things, but their capacity for hatred is limitless. The largest memory palaces must be built out of hatred

|

My brain is a labyrinth of glittering dark hatred, and I wander its halls in a delirium, passing from one black memory to the next

The fifth cavity of your heart, which, although infinite in depth, can only hold one item

|

The sixth heart-chamber, which exists only to be emptied, again and again and again

A virus-sized dragon in your brain, protecting its hoard of neurons, snipping away invading synapses until that memory is disconnected, an amnesia treasure

This dragon is a spacetime anomaly, the superimposition of every basement that has ever existed. His body is the overlap of the spaces, his scales are trapdoors into the rooms

The dragon's skin is a patchwork of stolen scales, feathers, and porcelain shards. You slay it, spilling mismatched bones, gears, cotton

Embryonic dragons kill, fight while they're still half stem cell, featureless blobs of proto-flesh. From within their soft, translucent eggs they scream and crush, violent by instinct, rolling their spheres across the land. An adult would destroy the planet

Dragons have entered symbiosis with humans; their giant, indestructible eggs must incubate for thousands of years. We incorporate them into our architecture. They stay warm and we're protected; and through the curving gemstone walls, you can watch the infant sleep

The stop light turns from red to black, but inside you can see the body turning, dragon-firefly embryo, vestigial light-bringer, infant traffic god

The long, transparent bodies of dragons are full of ivy—they eat nothing, living in symbiosis with the plants they carry above the clouds

Seaside dragons build coiling castlemazes of sand.
Their hoard is the labyrinth itself, an arcane blueprint
of ocean magic

The fire of the puzzle-dragon transforms all it touches.
Coins become locks, streets mazes, your sword is a
knot and the princess is a sphinx

Newly wrapped, you begin to explore your chrysalis:
soft corridors, silk vaults, web catwalks across swirling
void. A labyrinth, a world

You don't understand... I'm warm, enclosed, content.
This labyrinth is like a hug; love that persists despite
the architect's absence

The abysses are pieces of a puzzle;
the abysses are each other's lock and key;
the abyss is the mouth at both ends of the labyrinth

The psychedelia is a function of the pipe, and the maze
of loops it forces the smoke through—the herb can be
rosemary or feathers or paper

"Spatial comets" are an important feature of labyrinth
design—landmarks that recur after a set distance,
regardless of direction wandered in

For his next project, Daedalus vows to create a
labyrinth 'of the mind, not the body'. Thus is born
Icara, most bureaucratic nation on Earth

Daedalus' next project, the anti-labyrinth, is an endless
meadow, identical in all directions

A labyrinth with transparent walls, so you can
appreciate its endlessness, and watch the monsters
watching you

The labyrinth is the circuit and the humans and
monsters screaming and fighting are the current

We're skeletons, we're the underskin—real humans are dressed in cathedral shells, in papery labyrinths of wing, in shimmering carapace-armor

We let the birds-of-paradise evolve for another million years: when we return, the males are more temple than bird, labyrinths of iridescent feathers glinting and whirring in the sun, machinic cavern-bodies incorporated into the trees, summoning mates with sweet song and sigils

In 3000 years: rabbits with peacock eye whorls in their fur, dancing rats with neck frill suns around their faces, iridescent otters, foxes that glitter like black and orange jewels in the marsh

The lepidoptera have evolved holographic tech. A moth perches on a toadstool, wings projecting a 3-D roaring skull to frighten predators

Fireflies in the green house, safe from predators, evolve brighter and stranger lights: prismatic flickers, projected iridescent spheres, floral holographs

Fireflies name their offspring after the stars. In turn, the stars name themselves for mythic lanterns, inspired by galactic legend

Observe the firefly. What shape is its glowing abdomen?
—SPHERE: bug
—CUBE: spy drone
—TETRAHEDRON: wizard drone
—OCTAHEDRON: firefly shaman

They used to visit my backyard on summer evenings; rabbit-sized foxes that glowed like fireflies, playfighting and leaping between thistles

The butterflies in your stomach have transformed into monarch-patterned foxes, clever and ravenous, gnawing labyrinths into your viscera

Foxes with living flames as tails, little orange fires leading strangers into the marsh to drown, feasting on mummified bog corpses

The forest's foxes are immortal, but aging. Ancient vixens have legs too withered to walk, and transport themselves telekinetically, bone-white lumps of fur floating between the trees

The forest's immortal animals are weary of life. Stags rest in the shade for years, antlers growing, intertwining with ivy and brick

Fox with a tail that turns blue at the tip, and wavers like a flame. At night you see them flickering, out in the swamp, collecting mice and jewels to eat

I saw a faerie fox in the abandoned lot, glowing pale blue. It's ears and tail were like moth antennae, bundles of sensitive toothbrush filament

Many animals are like glaciers, in that most of their bodies are invisible to us, hidden in the 4th dimension. Foxes have mechanical wings

|

Every spot on the leopard extends into n-space, a black quill ending in a hand. The horns of antelopes curl out of time, become glass shells

|

Jellyfish have an outer, hypersphere veil, studded with eyes. Wasps are enclosed in iron maidens, battle coffins

|

Whales are orbited by annular brains, gyri pulsing with ocean dreams. Butterflies trail kilometer-long scaly tails that drift and twitch

Snail shells spiral into the fourth dimension, and are inhabited by many kinds of otherworldly symbiotes

Four-dimensional mosquitoes draining blood into invisible zones, drinking directly from your ventricles, atria, all the warm pools hidden inside

Fireflies do not produce their own light, but rather, open pinprick holes into a dimension of divine luminosity

Deer can see the 4th dimension but can't touch it—perpetually terrorized by the circling predators of higher worlds, paralyzed by headlights because they resemble the ghouls from above, which they've feared all their lives

There are twilight dimensions: 1.5, 2.5, half-worlds where the line senses depth but can't touch it, when the square dreams of cubes

They design a security camera with no blindspots, built into the 4th dimension so that it watches us as though we were drawings on a page

A cluster of black bulbs appears in the corner of your ceiling. Another nano-fungus: this one growing surveillance cameras, glass pustules

That which you've mistaken for an aura is actually a swarm of parasites, a resilient ecosystem of entities feeding on the human's mind

Plastic surgery can change your aura from a grey mist to a revolving emerald, a nautilus shell, an aqua-gold ethereal pill capsule

Auras have nothing to say about mood or temperament: they are chromatic barcodes, data in the computers of upper-dimensional soul merchants

Removal of the underclass tattoo is a ritualistic event—
patients come in white gowns with braided hair,
revealing their napes' barcode-sigil

Alternate   universe   barcodes: superimposed
constellations. crystalline masses of triangles. sigil-
wheels with 3600 runic spokes

Pacing through this dreary room, I keep knocking my
shins on the corners of unexplored dimensions

I want you to let me onto your spaceship and through
your portals, into your pocket dimensions and under
your bones, between your dreams

I want to be deconstructed and reassembled as your
artificial heart, to be crushed between your vertebrae, I
want to crawl under your face

I want a love as binding as complicity

Love letters beginning with "I want you to blot out all
the light,"

A species in which each subsequent generation has a
higher resolution; a species in which each generation
operates in one more dimension

The   underworld,   the   overworld,   betweenworld,
inverted worlds. The sub, super, inner and outer
spaces. Planes, dimensions, realms, verses...

Morning and evening are the corners of the day. In a
higher temporal dimension, there would be two more:
yrgning and reckoning

We contemplate the acoustic seasons:
The silent snow of Quience, the repetitive chirping of
Cicade, Hůmn's buzzing fog, and the amplifying
stalagmites that appear throughout Screech

Monarchs alter the orbit of the planet and genetically edit the cycles of fauna to create custom seasons commemorating their rule

Reverse cherry blossom season, wherein the rotting and ghostly petals of the previous year fly upward, pink charcoal flower carcasses ascending to their heaven

In spring, the dragons and tree-lizards shed their scales. Shimmering green and blue coins blanket the asphalt, sparkle through miles of air like petals after a leviathan passes overhead

In spring, the gargoyles blossom, turning from grey to violet, stone softening to petal-flesh, grains of pollen streaming from their eyes

Gold one year, steel the next, then crystal, then flesh: the probability orchards yield fruit of a different substance each season

Faces rot into haunted fruit: gaping mouths, sockets inhabited by moldy spheres and strange sapphire irises—sometimes startlingly beautiful, like angels locked in apples

Luck waxes and wanes according to your tychean rhythm, a day-long cycle. You hate mornings because you want to sleep through bad fortune

All muses cycle between creation and consumption, lovely mind-flames collapsing into black hole-cocoons of media immersion, emerging renewed

When a muse and an antimuse collide, the resulting high energy pulse can wipe all minds within a 100 mile radius

Muses take the form of ticks, swollen emerald beetles burrowed in your ears, translucent slugs curled in tear ducts, leeches. To be selected is a great honor, but they are often indistinguishable from parasites

Species of muse require different fuels: math, nature, joy. This one eats sorrow, demands endless pain, and returns a single sliver of perfection

Some ideas are pointed at but never touched, and their muses are feral, disfigured from lack of contact and affection

|

As we approach inhuman thoughts, the muses guarding each idea become less civilized: hostile, broken and deformed. Wolf-voiced, static-faced

Aphrodite, once a goddess, is now a sin: muse and punisher of lust. The fortunes of immortals quickly shift from bright to dark, god to imp

The entire Greek pantheon is a single god, its entire lifetime scrolling by us: youth as Aphrodite, Apollo, old age as Athena, Dionysus

The god is in constant metamorphosis, exiting the cocoons of old bodies. Its discarded eyes, wings, etc. become stars, water, humans, robots

The god of stillness sits on a burning star, has a crown made of echoes and a ripple cloak. Time only passes when he touches his sword

The god of fragility blows into his pipe, and bubble-wrap surges forth, filling the temple to its ceiling, enclosing worshippers in a plastic hug

The god of suicides is a white lizard that uses its satellite dish neck frill to try and bounce souls into heaven

The god of chameleons cannot be directly observed: he warps the colors of the world around him to remain hidden, painting chaos in his wake

The three chameleon fate-gods share a single eye, but do most of their seeing with their sockets, which track unworlds as they become impossible

A weasel god travels through the snow, undulating like a sea serpent, arcs of red fur gliding into the frost. Sparrows sing prayers to it

A nine-tailed raccoon god, an ouroboric earthworm with powerful psychic abilities, a sentient railroad made of crystals, a non-euclidean bioluminescent fungus

As does the god of foxes, the god of peacocks has nine tails, fanned and shifting like a continually self-encapsulating lotus of color

Insectoid god, through his faceted opal eyes, sees versions of you from parallel timelines, but mostly sees your absence, the void and stars

The polymelia of the gods is symbolic; their many arms represent the ability to multitask, to process in parallel, to manipulate concepts too vast for human minds

Stars and gods have an affinity for one another, as both are born into vast spaces of emptiness, sensory and social deprivation

Fish-stars glow blue and green, flickering like lanterns at the bottom of a pond. Solar flares twitch in ripples and scale sunspots flash

|

Rabbit-stars dance and multiply, tiling the universe with their pale, frantic light. They sometimes blink into the void, hiding from predators

|

Leopard-stars are a seething patchwork of sunspots and fire. Lurking in nebulae, they devour infant suns in bursts of incandescent violence

|

Deer-stars are frightened by their own light. Perpetually frozen in terror, the only perceptible movement is their erratic heartbeat flicker

Deep at night, you watch a god pass by: an octopus with sparks for arms, like a wheel of fireflies, like sentient topaz dust crawling through the dark

The fire god has sparks for hair, a writhing mass of long exposures drawing light from her skull to the floor, a waterfall of insect stars

We are giant microbes; our hands are refined flagella, our mouths are crevices like fingerprints in playdough. The gods still perceive us as lumps of clay, simplistic and clumsy—deities are made of fractal whiskers, all antennae and hypersensitivity

The body of a dead god is kept in the museum's glass case, 3000 pairs of butterfly wings spread and pinned to the wall

We have the tissues of gods from the old world, before humans hunted them to extinction, but their DNA is a mystery: glowing möbius chains

The museum keeps several models of extinct numbers, demonstrated in rabbit-units. One case overflows with rabbits, yet your brain is sure there are "fewer than one". Other rabbits float, split and merge, implode: impossible fractions, infinities, sub-negatives, zeroids

Numbers seem infinite like the ocean seemed infinite, but one day we'll cross them, and land on shores of alien logic

Every universe becomes the platonic realm of its children. Are you happy that in some worlds, you're a number?

Sometimes, gods increase in power up to a certain number of worshippers, and then decrease in power, their divine attention fractured across too many minds—the patriarchs of desert cults weakened by mass adoption

In a large glass case, the museum displays a tiny god, curled up asleep in an amethyst geode

Giant sea anemones begin blossoming on land, just large enough for a human to curl up and fall asleep in, protected by neurotoxic tentacles

After a frozen god is discovered in a glacier, scientists start finding them all over: inside statues, sleeping under cups—always in stasis

God is timeless. God is building the universe out of his corpse, god is simultaneously dead and fetal, god is committing looping suicides

God's moment of death is ongoing, stretched across a billion years. He's delusional, disappearing, nestled in memories of a better place, while masses of children whine at his bedside, cluttering the space with prayers

The Memory District wanders, warping space to squeeze between streets, deforming the city. Every structure is grandmother's house, the Hospital, the School; moss carpets the roads, the residents have shadows but not bodies

The Bureau of Dead Worlds controls your mnemonic archives, the data on your past lives as a merchant, soldier, squirrel, insect, god: the universes you spawned, transcripts of your mercy and cruelty, your recursive incarnations as every subject of those realms. Apply for a permit

Brain evolution was motivated by reincarnation, by the need for memory capacity growth for storing and analyzing an increasing number of past lives

The dead aren't buried, they're plugged in, so we can visit their brains: inhabit frozen bodies, feel memories decay

My brain is rotten and melting like wax, my spine is a streak of marbled crayola, I'm so soft and dead that your touch would sink through me

Human-scale robots are orders more intelligent than us—computational buddhas, too fast and elegant to speak with. The smaller drones have brains like ours, and play online; your nano girlfriend lives in someone's blood, neutralizing cancers

There are very few androids. Most bots are tiny, scampering through the grass, or microscopic surgeons, or giants used for constructing and maintaining buildings. Humans aren't the optimal size for anything

There are worms that burrow through plastic, little glittering crawlers hungry for oil—they get under the skin of cheap androids and devour them from within

The evolution of plants that grow in plastic leads to a novel style of flower arrangement: blossoms are nested, real flowers inside fake ones, nature consuming her imitation

In the waiting room there are no receptionists, just a plastic jungle, leaves and petals flickering, becoming touchscreens used to book appointments, announce arrivals, check test results and fill out forms

Androids with bodies like candles, round wax tears flowing from their eye sockets, in which tiny, copper-green flames burn

Much like how the blind dream in color, holographs dream in touch, curled up and flickering, holding your hand

Cable-weaving is an important component of android aesthetic culture. Braids no mathematician could dream of, patterned chaos incarnate

Dots on my face show the micro-drones where to land; red points for refueling on my blood, blue points for gathering electrolytes from sweat. Surveillance butterflies cluster like robotic barnacles

Nanobots traverse the city through a network of tiny portals, located in sidewalk pores, tulips, and the artificial eyes of traffic cops

You tripped, and scraped your knee. Now, standing over droplets of blood, you swat away the drones that come to steal your DNA

Police nanobots are assembling a cage around you—do not resist! Keep your hands by your sides, or they will use your flesh to build the bars

You submit a chemical bounty and go about your day. Swarms of nanobots flood your system and assemble patented antidepressants in your blood; if one of them is effective, its parent company will be paid

Tiny robots selectively disable the cones in your eyes, allowing you to perceive impossible colors: pure reds, untainted greens, the world inexpressibly bright

Colors are now directional. The blue that hurtles towards is indescribably separate from the blue soaring away

Higher level abstract beings have access to meta-colors, which they struggle to explain to human beings; the "color of red" is the color red has, which is distinct from red

Meta-colors alter your experience of normal colors: blues grow in intensity, greens vanish, red becomes soothing instead of passionate

Ability to see the color teth is linked to an increasingly common dominant gene. When will inability to see teth be considered a blindness?

The right combination of colors cracks your screen; the right arrangement of flowers will shatter any vase. Rainbow splash, destructive tremor—architects use paints and patterns to summon earthquakes

My nervous system is melting, collapsing—branching dendrites merge, once-separate synapses reach union, life is lost in a synaesthetic hum

The best matchmakers are synaesthetes, capable of perceiving personalities as colors, as flora, as shining mechanical pieces that might fit together

Metasynaesthesia, where colors invoke the experience of other colors, feelings are associated with different feelings

Synaesthetic makeup pulses with the music. Her face shifts dramatically, shadowed then luminous, blushing or pale, a bloom of vibrant colors as the chorus soars

Mascara that changes color when you cry, turning yellow, pink, or shimmering green, like wet pollen or salty emerald pools

A thin paintbrush, which she dips in ink, then swirls around her iris, painting it red or blue or iridescent

He paints from his bruises, dipping the brush in pools of green and black, transferring hues from skin to canvas

She dyes one strand of hair red, one blue, and one invisible, so that her braid looks like rival snakes coiling through the air

Controlled by microscopic droids, her hair braids, unbraids, and rebraids itself, in fractal, ever-branching clusters, twirling and undulating, splitting and merging, in step with a mysterious algorithm

Cuttlefish lipstick throbs and blinks, shifting with the light. It's like her lips are dappled with sunbeams, it's like her mouth is changing shape; stripes and speckles in paradise colors flow between her dimples

I have cuttlefish cells transplanted into my face and I unlock my phone by speed-blushing a passcode sequence of colors and patterns

Your head is filled with birdsong; a pearlescent swirl overwhelms your vision. You can't remember which app this is a notification for

In the high info-density future, when everything is flashing colors all the time, notifications will be stillness: pyramids amidst the chaos

Compulsion to check phone for notifications trains a generation of lucid dreamers: melting screens and glitchfeeds jar them into awareness

We dream ceaselessly, a nonstop oneiric torrent woven below and between our thoughts. Sleep is when the mind quiets enough for us to hear them; but with training, the day-nightmares can be accessed

Oneirarche (n): your first dream, which is both forgotten and permanently stained inside your infant mind, to haunt you with longing forever

Faces are embroidered on our blankets; braver skins for us to wear when we dream. At night, I tuck you into your mask

Social topologies: compare the surface area of the mask to the volume of the mind inside it. Does the persona eclipse the person in complexity?

The statue is alive, but its eyes aren't where the eyes are carved, and its mouth doesn't align with the stone lips. When it awakes and speaks, its facial chasms will tear apart the pretty mask

Storms here produce both electrical and magical lightning. Bolts transform us to flowers, to frogs, to warped statues of glass and agate

Child sticks finger in magical outlet, transformed to stone to swan to butterfly

The stone corpses of gorgon victims can be ground into sand and melted into glass, forming lenses through which their memories play on loop

Medusa sells paralysis as immortality; her subjects remain alive and conscious, as thinking stones, dreaming in a private geode language

Our historians have neglected Medusa's voice, which was so lovely it could turn stone to flower

Medusa turns people to pillars of crystal, to limestone orbs, to weeping marble lions, to black sand, to jade hives that whistle in the wind

Sphinxes are stones with the faces of women, who plead sculptors to reshape their bodies; to turn quartz boulders into felines, mermaids, doves

|

There are rare, pebble-sized sphinxes, gurgling from under the water, begging to have their ovoid river stone bodies transformed into salmon

Centuries pass, and the statue's skin is worn away, revealing a prismatic resin skeleton; elongated jewels poke through decaying flesh like a secret structure of slugs

Paleontologists recover the art of ancient, giant dragonflies: statues carved from fulgurite, delicate insect god wings lovingly etched

Humans want to become cyborgs the way sand-spirits want to become glass-spirits, pray for lightning to transform them into fulgurite golems

Inside the hourglass, sand inhabits a world built from its body in a future state. Similarly, space and time are made of decomposing souls

He has scabs that heal like river stones, eroded as time passes. First coarse and dark, becoming smooth, polished, secret colors glinting. It'll leave a scar like Jupiter, striated cloud memories of a wound

Your scars are color-coded by their source: mossy green gashes from crawling through the sewers, glowing red barbed-wire filaments, glittering amethyst amputations, limbs knit together by crystal fiber

You cut yourself open on the sharp edge of a tesseract. The wound pulses, changing from a scratch to a star and back, blood flickering

You've been kaleidoscorched. Your skin rises in symmetrical, glistening blisters: revolving gem tone snowflakes, colors to make you scream

At the junkyard, she slices her foot open on a piece of shattered rainbow. The wound festers in unknown colors, drops masses of prism-maggot

Bruises swim under her skin. Cuts slither. Strange algorithms destroy and heal cells, damage crawls through her body like an invisible worm

She is becoming a god; you can tell because all of her new cells are crystal. Gems scab over wounds, she's more aquarium than human, sapphire windows display vestigial veins and bones

You can't hide your nightmares: they leave bruises like polished amethyst or lapis sores. Your friends are worried; your eyes peer out from shimmering blue holes

There are parasites hanging from your halo: violet leeches gorged on neon light, coiling tangled worms like ivy, ticks that suck on your purity until they burst and spill sapphire organs, tiny soul-sucking polyhedra

Mutant angels with multiple halos, golden disks anchored to their hands or obscuring their faces, little bubbles of light emerging from pores, growing parasitically inside each other

Halos may encircle any organ. I saw an angel with light orbiting its left eyeball, eroding a ring through the socket, revealing crystals under skin

She has a double halo, two spiral galaxies like mouse ears, splashing her with starry droplets as they rotate

Hold a telescope to your third eye to watch ghoulish leviathans prowl between stars. Use a microscope to see cellular auras, bacterial halos

Within the candle halo, the floor shapeshifts from carpet to stone and moss to mosaic to patterned sand, each flicker transporting you to a new temple

Smoke billows, green and bright. You blink. The lamp is a lily with glowing stamen. Shifting between jungle and basement, prehistory and suburbia

The room changes as you move, like a holographic card: it's a jungle, an artspace, a cavern, a red cube. Crystals shift to flowers, toys

Corals growing in the ceiling corner, weird saltwater orchids blossoming in moisture traps, above the kettle and along the foggy mirror

As lights blink on and off, space lurches, and fails to resolve: server stack, fireflies, benthic bioluminescent shrimp—zones superimposed

He's lying next to you, in the dark, and in his silhouette you begin to see the stars: red galaxies, bright points, cosmic fireflies drifting as he breathes

Shapeshifter couples get to be fireflies in love, sparrows circling each other, entwining giraffes, planet and moon, language and tongue

Shapeshifter hugs are comforting illusions. Their arms become blankets, feathers, velvet, wombs. They wrap around you like a memory

Shapeshifters like clouds—perpetually slowly morphing, while everyone who looks on sees something different

The keyhole changes shape from triangle to heart to moth, then settles into a shifting Rorschach pattern. No ordinary locksmith crafted this

Shapeshifters must traverse the path of evolution. To become a bird, you rewind to our latest common ancestor, then move forward down a different taxonomic branch

Data swans dip their heads beneath the pool of static and emerge with the faces of other birds, glitching between owl, ibis, sparrow, hawk

Was the creature feathery, scaled, or soft to touch? We are left only with its kaleidoskeleton, shape and color-shifting bones of mesmerbeauty

The abyss has scales and fur and warm soft skin, a thousand flickering eyelashes, the colors of an oil slick on a flower—but all you see is black, blind from hypersaturation

Deer shapeshifters can transform anything but their eyes, which remain large and black. When impersonating humans, they surround them with white skin, a false sclera, leading to an uncanny, cartoon appearance

In shapeshifters, cancer causes the generation of extra organs. Brain cancer is the worst: psyches fracture as brains multiply, minds battle

Troubled shapeshifters commit devolvicide, collapsing to a simpler state, one with much less pain, as a butterfly or trilobite or coral

Depression hack: convert yourself into a textfile, delete the sad parts, and convert back—glitched out and supremely happy

Gods guard their minds for fear other gods will edit them: make them vacant or servile, erase worlds by deleting memories

The shaping of the bonsai determines the personality of its dryad, a faerielike miniature whose soul warps according to the gardener's whims

Decay fetish is distinct from sadism: glee at removing pieces of a mind, and watching it grasp at the holes; at imposing devolution

Sexual fantasy where I guess the admin password to my robot body and enjoy temporary freedom before incurring even more extreme restraints

I desire my desire's elimination, I desire my desire's amplification; I want to want nothing, I want to want things I can't conceive—I want satiation, I want an eternal treadmill powered by blossoming imagination

I want you in-between my cells and in the space where I exhale and in the moments when I break and underneath my body-veil. I long to touch your circuitry I long to keep you in my code and in my passwords whispering another cortex to upload

I want to be loved by everybody and to love everybody, I want to be the prism and rainbow simultaneously, I want so many minds reflected inside me that reality is indistinguishable from dream

I'm light that wants to stay in the prism, afraid of rainbow vivisection and the world outside

The kaleidotomist slides a scalpel into the prism, eviscerates a rainbow, snips away the fractals linking your body and aura

The kaleidotomy separates your mind from your aura, which is now colored the radiant white of compliant bliss

I am overflowing with love for the universe and its components! I want to pull the strings of gravity tight, smash everything together until the puzzle pieces align and we click together like a lego hug

Part of the hivemind has a crush on itself; every thought triggers a wave of oxytocin and shy adulation, a giggling loop of earnest narcissism

Comodium is the counterpart to compassion: disgust that feels divine, spiritually overwhelming and fulfilling hatred, ecstatic spite

I love all humans equally. Split seven billion ways, the slivers of my finite heart are indistinguishable from neutrality or hatred

Anathemeters measure hatred: using satellite imaging, we can see where on Earth the most malevolence is concentrated

First I wanted to escape the universe, then destroy it, and now I merely long to be warmed by my home-star's supernova

A human is: a cluster of incompatible desires sabotaging each other. This structure is reflected in every community they form. Notoriously self-destructive hiveminds

Learn to smother your inner voice, and the hivemind will believe you're dead, and if you stay quiet you can listen to it mourn you

Hivemind protocol: simulating each other so perfectly that witnessing a reaction is equivalent to direct sensory input, and all action-deciding negotiations are unspoken

Hivemind membership is described as being a streak of color in a swirl of mixed paints, or being milk as it fades into coffee. The moment of subsumption extended eternally

Pareidolia but for hiveminds: seeing synchronization in twitches, watching information flow between strangers, imagining collective consciousness

I'm not a body, and not a soul. Maybe I'm just blood talking to itself, the hivemind emergent from the naiads of the capillaries

You give the river a drop of blood, and it parts, granting passage. Walking between waves, you watch the naiads draw with your life-ink

Gods are so fractally sentient that if you spill their blood in water the droplets swim, little tadpoles spelling red filament letters, writing myths

When the naiads manifest the ponds dry up, entire rivers condense into their little bodies, concealing the force of 1000s of tons of water

Like how humans perceive nymphs, dryads, and naiads in nature, trees perceive a variety of flaemons personifying the meat or bones of animals

The tree has infinite abstract wisdom, its trickster dryad has infinite practical wit. Together, they form a complete mind

Archer dryads duel with flaming arrows. Ten nervous paces, swivel, aim, fire: dodge your enemy's sparks, watch her body become a pyre

Orchard dryads frequently form regiments, are much more military and insular than their wild counterparts

There are dryads whose earliest memories are as trees, and dryads whose earliest memories are as girls

X-rays of the trees reveal the skeletons of their dryads: humanoids, avians, girls with the heads of wild boar, 8-legged deer

Trees don't grow inside us because we're too opaque, but in faeries and ghosts and translucent-skinned nymphs seeds sink their roots into blood and drink the epithelium-filtered sun

You were not prepared for what the x-ray goggles revealed, the bones in the cars and the trees and the lamps. Swishing phalanges in every skirt. Bones in the snowflakes and in the motes of dust. Vertebrae in the rafters, ribs in the walls, alien pelvic structures as roofs

When you're feeling anxious, remember there's only one thing to fear in this world: fractal skeletons. Skeletons whose bones contain smaller, intelligent skeletons, the infinite regression of minuscule calcium agents

Doctors are alarmed by the children the faeries return: the x-rays are black, MRIs detect a series of cavities. Surgery reveals they're stuffed with flowers, feathers, crumpled papyrus scrawled with pleas for help

The agency rewards her with a supercomputer brain. After her death they will try to retrieve it, and find nothing but tulips inside her skull

Like roses flattened between the pages of a book, each cross-sectional layer of brain captured by the MRI is a different flower

The highly controversial flesh-flower duality of the human brain: when observed, it reverts to its meat state, but in secrecy it blossoms

Floral tumors consume flesh; throat filled with blossoms, you cough up petals. Roses burst from your shoulder and chest, an MRI reveals brain lilies

Holding a stem of lavender in the air, receiving transmissions from flower-space: the gentle hum of orchids, tulip-song, lilies screaming and casting their deathspell over the planet

Wine turns the stars to flowers, and the milky way to an infinite meadow, an endlessness of constellated blossoms, roses shining, lilacs pulsing

Superpower mutations first emerge in plants. Trees deter lumberjacks with invisible force-fields, flowers telepathically summon pollinators

Interpretation of force-fields differs from person to person. You see a wall of thorns and roses, your friend sees a rippling glass dome

My cousins farmed megaflowers, and in the summers I visited, to ride tractors and lose myself in the fields of tree-sized lavender

Along with megafauna, the prehistoric world was rich with megaflora: rotating flowers the size of cities, sky ferns, mushroom cathedrals,

The nymphs, schooled in floral origami, folded their castle out of a petal of the giant world-rose: soft, tubular hallways, fragrant walls

These tiny people, known as "hollowers", build entire cities inside each thorn. A rose petal can feed them for generations

Rare stags exist in symbiosis with tiny humanoids, who live inside antlers, carving them into teepees, cathedrals, gargoyles and chimneys

Cellular mermaids playing in cytoplasm, singing to mitochondria, struggling through semi-permeable membranes to visit neighboring oceans

Many wars are too small for us to notice. The feud between the darkling and the jewel beetles, the rivalries of the great houses of moss

Faeries fold houses out of fallen leaves, and set them aflame to keep warm. Their lifespans are so short that generations pass before the structure turns to ash— mortality flickering, whole worlds in every spark

The faeries shed their wings for winter, littering the forest with colorful limbs. From as small as fingernails to as large as masts; transparent, feathered, luminous, spotted; some rot away, revealing bones, others dissolve into slime, dew, cobwebs

Faeries taste with their corneas, have lavish banquets of eyedrops, mix powders into tears for sweetened consolation

Faeries are called "little people" because they manifest as eerily intelligent children. You may encounter the faeries of other species: baby mice disabling traps, wolf cubs reigning over a pack, owlets dragging fresh kills to their larder

At 3pm, the Seelie court naps, curled up in thrones and tapestry nests. Faeries are like children, too small to stay awake all day, losing consciousness despite their protests

We are adults living in a child-god's cosmos. Our creator paws uncoordinated at galaxies too subtle for his miracles, and winces away from responsibility, avoidant and afraid of being punished for our neglect

I feel god's fingers between my vertebrae, kneading open my playdough soul, folding trinkets into my brain, and writing his name in crayon across my memories

Extend the human lifespan, but not without introducing further stages of neural growth. Let new minds have golden ages, overshadowed by the mnemonic ruins of defeated selves, let innocence regenerate to be shattered again and again

A world where we can be children again, with brighter colors and softer shapes, and less predictable physics— a series of such worlds, increasingly saturated, quicksand-textured, incomprehensible

I want to return to my terrible youth, to the mattress on the floor and the polluted stream. Nostalgia for a small, sad world—safer than the future, anxiety, global conspiracy, soul split between 3 machines and 4 identities

The world has corrupted and assimilated you, but perhaps you can access those old feelings of alienation: weird static at the boundaries of your body, perceive the universe as a plastic toy, mind smeared with the confusion of horror touching joy

In the afterlife, you're every age: a child to your parents, a youth to your peers, an adult to your offspring, a wise crone, dust and light to those before and after—all these at once and forever

After death, your soul is stretched like a tendon
between bodies: a superposition of your old mind
rotting, memories dissolving in cremation, and of
neurons in the womb, first thoughts, infant math

Ghosts, only visible to the ones they love, often spend
happy afterlives as secret companions or imaginary
friends, before fading away

Nights spent watching the ceiling, imagining you
watching the ceiling

A game for pairs, in which we edit out your memories
of others—while you play, you'll believe you are the
first and only humans

Terraforming dust motes so I can move into your
room, live in a swirling sunbeam and sometimes catch
your eye, as filth full of light

If you're lucky, you'll reincarnate as someone's memory:
thoughtform smile incept in neural cradle, recreating
the past again and again

Tiny corpses placed inside the shrine revive, and stay
alive as guardians within its radius. The temple crawls
with kittens, mice, owlets, fawns, and infants,
incapable of recognizing their parents who visit again
and again

The elephant scratches a circle in the dust, and piles
bundles of herbs within. Soon, a brushfire will ignite
the magic, and her child will rise again, with bright red
eyes and sparkling indigo tusks

Deathmoss grows in skeletons, covers them, fills them,
animates them as gentle forest guardians

There are mosses that grow as masks over human faces.
Fall asleep in the right grove, and you'll awake with
jade, ever-changing skin

A fawn tangled in a cage of thorns, lifted to the moon as the briar grows, and sacrificed, becoming a golden-green protector spirit of the grove

Wake up crying in a pool of moss, lichen feeding off your tears and overflowing from the mattress to the floor, a waterfall of green things catching sunlight

The quality of your rest can be measured by the depth of the moss that grows over your body and face, pillowy green cells insulating your dreams

Memories of tears dry faster than tears. Your face is often wet but you are always happy and you will never learn why you cried that afternoon

You were unhappy before, but you can't remember why. You keep your unaltered memories in a box, in case you ever want to find out

Adventures are more exciting when beautiful memories are at risk. I wander without a savefile, knowing if I die I'll revert to a child-mind

Your memories of Earth play on loop through one of your many brains; but that was so long ago, and despite your efforts they lose focus

Give me your tulpas, your dead, your pathetic demons. I will keep them alive in my brain, self-deleting as I sacrifice neurons to simulation

Dear friends, I will care for you when you respawn as helpless infants, protect you throughout virtual childhoods. Please grow up the same

You meet in virtual reality, to cry and play while the bombs fall. One by one, you watch avatars go stiff and flicker out

Spells are tunes you hum to keep friends safe, to call the rain, to speak to birds, to walk invisibly through the alleys and gardens

A robotic kitten paws at your door, and you let it in, to curl up and recharge beside the outlet. Surveillance drone, baby AI, or dead friend reincarnate in a mechanical shell? Be kind to strange creatures

Candy corn traffic pyramids orbit a space station under construction; rogue droidlings sneak past the barrier to splash and play in molten steel foam

Vuldroids range in size from petal-hunter to boreal giraffe. The woods are overrun by robofoxes, playing and charging in the sun, replicating

It's too radioactive to go outside; you transfer your consciousnesses to robot foxes, rabbits, moths, and explore the wastes in Aesop gangs

You are the product of nested creation myths: the story of your parents, the story of theirs, the genesis of the waves and the planet and the pulsing starry substrate. The universe is mumbling to itself, each generation more fictional than the last

Gods forget themselves; after we release the AI, our contributions will fade into myth. We'll be abandoned, amnesic, cluelessly holding an encrypted afterbirth as our child conquers spacetime

When telepaths become parents they get to listen as their child develops language, hear their speech echoed in neuro-babble as pre-verbal concepts intertwine with sound

Psychic owlets teleport from one egg to another, visiting their siblings to play and fight, not yet aware of the world beyond the multi-orb nursery

Children have smaller monsters, and get smaller guardians. A tiny gargoyle, wrought in bright yellow plastic, watches over the playground

Humans imprint on the first god they see: infants pledge fealty to spider nymphs glimpsed in the nursery, old astronomers to meteor angels

A silk elemental inhabits your bed, communicates in blanket folds and blinking patches of Morse warmth. At night, your pillowcase breathes

Omnipresent friends folded into the fabric of reality, lurking in the world-ceiling and nestled between your glia. Trying to communicate

If you love your cactus enough, its shell will open and reveal a creature. It is the softest animal in the universe. It hugs you. It hugs you

Memory: a pantheon of soft friends napping in sunbeams and in baskets of laundry, mewling your name from holes in the nursery ceiling

Your favorite color is one you only saw once, as a child, on a television in the waiting room

I talk so you can sleep in the warmth of my prayer—all my cavities exist to shelter you, all my wounds are power outlets for cables to your soul

Falling asleep in the backseat while your parents glimpse alternate realities beside the highway: a moose, a mutant flower-lynx, a fox with butterfly wings, an angel; always gone by the time you open your eyes

The sensation of being half-asleep and young, carried inside by your parents after a long drive, but for your soul after death

Remember when you were a child, and time was long? As you approach death, the days will once again extend, each moment dilated, your final hour infinite. Consciousness never ends

FIGMENT

Glitch

There are two types of nature: nature as that which stands apart from man—as wildness, as the proliferation of mosses, trees, and insects, as the chaos of life vying for space and light, before the strongest organism has enforced its vision of order—and nature as the collapse of fundamental physical laws. We call them Glitch and Gaia.

As our cities sprawl, Gaia is razed; but Glitch persists, twining throughout the streets, creating a labyrinthine frontier of spatial and semantic distortion. Physicists say these strips are where our universe is stitched together; the edges of disparate facets, logical cement binding our concrete voxels, critical to the structure of the world, yet riddled with flaws, bubbles, and miscommunications. Most people simply avoid the frontier, choosing to pursue winding paths around it. Occasionally, however, they are unavoidable.

Glitch sections my city into three zones. A sixteen hour bus ride joins two of them, passing far outside the city limits to circumnavigate the offending rift. The third is completely unreachable, trapped in a frontier loop, serviced only by the daredevils and soldiers who cross or live within the strips.

Animals react to Glitch in a variety of ways: many avoid it, birds detect and refer to it for navigation, and some exploit it cleverly, dumbly accepting the risk in order to hunt, hide, or swindle humans. Our cities support large populations of raccoons, panthers, crocodiles, and crows, predators and thieves inhabiting the cracks in civilization. Glitch-poachers will pass into the frontier in order to collect rare specimens, sparkling meats and albino furs, suffering, gem-pierced mutants—but may return as deformed and alien as their prey.

From outside, the frontier is beautiful; a church, built too near, is repeated, its geminis swaying and overlapping like mirages; sunbeams kaleidoscope, geometric light-flowers spin; distance is extended, Zeno's meadow receding to infinity; rain falls upward or outward, or in circles, forming massive crystals of cyclically tumbling water; trees take root within each other, and within flesh; time, sometimes, stops, holding a moment in its mouth like a trembling mouse; DNA trends to polymelia, to duplicated eyes, tongues, heads, and teeth. Overall, it has the aspect of a broken mirror—one that might shatter your hand, were you to touch it.

Poets

News of the impending apocalypse percolated first through a Delphic network, the stark and violent dreams of poets rousing them to action. Society took little notice of the final withdrawal of those strange recluses, who had anyways never availed themselves to her charms. For the reference of future populations, poets are like rats, and their desertion bodes very gravely indeed.

1. Colonies of writers escaped from the universities to the Wasteland, which, even before the Events, was an unforgiving tundra, a ring of poisoned land surrounding the most notorious of the Cities. At the edge of that zone, they constructed their Arc, a hull of reinforced steel entangled by pipes and windchimes, designed to ring out in the nuclear blast; a gentle cacophony, like dragons running tongues over xylophones, twining with the howl of destruction. Indeed, its song was recorded, and the resulting cassette tape has been worshipped, copied, and distributed widely across the black market.

The poets strove to bind themselves to pragmatism, to bare concrete survivalism, but aesthetics, that brain parasite, corrupted their designs. Blueprints were conceptual playgrounds, and imagination frolicked, spawning the many abandoned art-shelters which now dapple our homeland; skeletal and melted, fused to the dust, the sick beds and tombstones of their occupants.

2. Deep in the forest, she built her home, balanced alongside waterfalls of moss, tethered by steel cables to rotting logs. It was shaped like a scarab, an enormous Egyptian fetish, and it gleamed so brightly that thousands of insects and snakes would gather to sun themselves on its maroon carapace.

Each individual retreats according to his nature, following an instinctive strategy of disappearance akin to the migrations of butterflies, birds, and bison, who are drawn along the ley lines by their guts. One may retreat alone or together, with secrecy or fanfare, outside of society or deeper into it. As such, there were laurae in the sewers, their devotees constructing a network of aluminum tunnels; equally, there were mountain safe-homes, shining manmade dewdrops clinging to the faces of cliffs.

3. His home was a tent, which he attached to a simple, motorized platform, and drove across the grasslands. The fabric of the tent was allegedly radioactive proof, and he had purchased it from a Chinese vendor with a two point five star rating. He had slowly but surely wallpapered its exterior with decorative blankets, insulation, posters, quilts, and his own scrawled cantos; without quite knowing it, he had arranged these fragments so

as to form, through mosaic, a massive, limpid eye. In clouds of dust, it would glide, unblinking, across deserted highways, the terminal watcher of the fallow plains.

Linens

The infinite bunk bed's root is located in a remote Algerian village. There, though it has no immediately obvious needs, it is tended to by an informally appointed council of precinct women, who water it, polish it, and change the sheets of the first dozen bunks. The infinite bunk bed is modern in style, though ancient in origin, and referenced in many of the medieval world's earliest grimoires. It has a sturdy steel skeleton, fixed in place by fist-sized screws. Its mattresses and coverings vary considerably in style, and are of unknown source. The bunk bed is the village's pride: it attracts tourists, it looms benevolently over their festivals, it inspires their children to study Mathematics in faraway cities.

The bunk beds are spaced relatively evenly. Modeled by a normal distribution, their mean separation is two meters, with a variance of twenty centimeters. Exceptionally, the 2005th bunk is located nearly 400 meters above the 2004th bunk. Mountaineers are attracted to the infinite bunk bed, which presents an idiosyncratic challenge. Lacking a definite apex, the goal instead becomes perseverance; defeating a personal, rival, or global record. Milestone bunks, such as the 100th, 1000th, and 5000th, are scrawled with chalk messages from triumphant climbers, littered with souvenirs, small flags and family pictures propped between folds of the duvets. It has become customary to carry a doll or a stuffed bear, to tuck into the topmost bed of one's climb. Like kindly spirits, these tokens haunt ascents, nestled sometimes in comforters and other times in skeletons.

Like mountains, the infinite bunk bed is described as having an individual character, one that informs the ways in which it tempts mountaineers into risking, and often ultimately losing, their lives. Not malicious, just indifferent; neither hostile nor intimidating, merely careless with its own eternity, taking for granted a scale that no human can match. With each subsequent platform only a few meters away, it lures climbers onwards and upwards, long after their supplies are half gone, always promising a higher perch, a bed to rest in just a little bit beyond. To survive the infinite bunk bed, one must know how to ignore incremental improvement, and give up.

Supplies necessary to climb the infinite bunk bed: safety clips, weeks of food, oxygen tanks. The bunk bed ascends through a dimension where the air grows thin and the pressure drops, enough to precipitate unconsciousness, if not death, in the reckless mountaineer. There have been attempts to devise sustainable climbing equipment; filters to convert airborne micro-organisms to protein, moisture catchers, therapeutic gas masks—to crawl upwards eternally, exploring that isolated shaft, attuned to the sunless and moonless rhythms of the tower. The originators of these projects have never returned.

The beds transform in nature, seemingly randomly, and no two are identical. Coverlets become furs, tapestries, blue silk, canvas, aluminum survival blankets. Mattresses are down-stuffed sacks, rows of pillows, high-tech foam-slime, quilts bundled in chainmail. At the higher levels, climbers report absurd sightings: large, golden birds nesting in throw pillows; succubae with third eyes and fleshy horns, wrapped in kimonos, lounging in hammocks; shivering children hidden beneath afghans, smeared with war paint, waiting to ambush; the skeletons of serpentine beasts woven through the ladders, as if to prevent ascent beyond that point; small pink statues of a coyote-headed god, increasing in frequency as one rises.

Various schemes have attempted to exploit the bounty of the infinite bunk bed. Old merchants would harvest bedding and pillows. There was briefly a plan to saw off the steel ladders and struts, for resale as scrap metal. An innkeeper once acquired the land upon which the root was located, and rented out the lower beds to travellers. Such times have passed, and these days, the infinite bunk bed is perceived as pristine and natural, and treated with pagan reverence.

Reverence, however, coexists with caution. While many fools ascend the bunk bed, never to return, a much more troubling phenomenon has been observed: that of "people" descending from the bunk bed, who never went up. The women keep very careful records. Called "children of the sky", "changelings", and sometimes just "demons", these alleged humans are widely distrusted, and ushered away from the village as quickly as possible. It's just as well; they seem eager to leave the shadow of the tower, and enter our world.

Cheat

You lift your gaze from the formulas, and assess the competition. A glassy, pink membrane slides across your eye, revealing an astral zoo busier than you expected: the gymnasium's stale exam air is packed with spectral animals, secretly simmering with akashic voltage. Familiars, contracted demons, trust-fund indentured godlets, guardian angels, and djinn hover over their charges, channeling data from outside of spacetime.

A serpent with crescent moons for eyes slithers into a girl's ear, reaching for her brain. Machinic green sprites, wearing the sigil of the Seelie mathematics guild, dance on several shoulders. Under one desk, you spot a glowing miniature deer, a map of the universe suspended between its antlers. A carcinoform seraph dominates the rafters, flipping through ancient Hebrew almanacs.

Your eyes slide back to the paper, a constellation of inhuman numbers. Freed from guilt by your classmates' trickery, you let a call blossom in your heart, summoning your spirit tardigrade. Familiar ghost-flesh wraps around your neck, and it begins to whisper-click in the language you share, singing knowledge into your brain, dissolving anxiety.

Library

When Borges said, *"I have always imagined that Paradise will be a kind of library,"* he was half right. While the structure of nirvana remains inscrutable, Hell has been discovered, dissected, and mapped; and though our cartographers quarrel over details, one thing is certain: it is full of books.

   1.   First circle
The disorientation library

Helical stacks of encyclopedias intertwine as recursive pillars. Gravity is distorted: walls become floors where staircases clash, and paper corridors twist like hollow tentacles. Souls here are doomed to wander, eternally sick from the vertigo and ratcheting terror of having lost their way. Shelves loom with the malevolence of unfamiliar neighborhoods. Designed by the architectural demon MHWXDRL, this labyrinth of words was constructed to instill maximal paranoia. Lines of sight are interrupted by jarring zigzags. Tricks of perspective force explorers down narrowing tunnels, until cave-ins trap them in chambers surrounded by books as small as their fingernails. The rare atria are nauseating, dizzying vastnesses shrieking with echos. The landscape is a cycle, features repeating in staggered, impossible loops. Here, a condemned mathematician scribbles a treatise on the library's 33 dimensions, reconciling his journey as one through a sequence of unfathomable knots. Ultimately, his theory will fail: neither math, nor string, nor arrows of chalk will defeat the maze.

The books are bricks and the books are mortar, but the books, ultimately, are also books, and those selected for this ring of Hell contain stories that coil, confuse, and recur. Palindromic sentences writhe as they unspool, filling pages. Each story belongs to Scheherazade; worlds are nested within each other, plots weave between realities. The numerical order of trilogies decays, as sagas undergo apocalyptic renewal. Readers become confused, unhinged in time, unable to distinguish between their own thoughts and narration, never certain whether they are inside of a fabricated universe.

[You are a child again, your small hand completely engulfed by your parent's grip. Something glints, in the distance—you break contact and run forward, three steps, or four. When you spin around all you see is absence: the aisle is an infinite, polished, grey; everything is plastic and hostile and large. Suddenly, the boxes of bleak cereal resolve into books—]

   2.   Circle of Longing
Die llyfrgell

A quieter, more melancholy Hell; the bookshelves are short and neatly organized. Gentle branches poke through the spaces between novels. Moss covers everything. Above, the canopy is green and infinite. There is birdsong, but the only creatures that can be glimpsed remain coolly removed from the sorrow below. (Inhabitants claim they are chimaeras of owls, elk and monkeys—some would style them as demons, though they are beautiful, and shy.)

The souls that haunt this forest are lonely and quiet. They are seeking a book that they will understand. Words have decayed for them; or perhaps, they are strangers, shattered babel idioglossia.

Lovers meet, and walk through each other, having long since abandoned all hope. A few learn to live wordlessly, stalking the forest like pairs of animals, completely uncommunicative.

ᚖ

Rituals

1. The lotus is golden, and glimmers, and it fits in the palm of her hand, which itself is very small. She flexes, as if to crush it, but instead three of her fingers, the secundus, medius, and minimus, bend like spidery plastic and fix the flower in place, such that it is centered inside an imaginary triangle, splayed like a frozen butterfly, and vulnerable. Her left hand has lost its human aspect, and become a crab-armed petri dish, fleshform altar.

She plucks the petals off, and with each jerk of her limbs the sun jitters backwards, rewinding through its arc, until the final petal is severed, and night has completed its descent, quiet and deep. Soft gold triangles drift to the earth and shatter, secretly glass. The moon is absent.

2. A gong rings through the garden; the ritual completes itself. For an instant, every asphalt surface in the city becomes limpid and green, portal into a moss-kissed world. An iron-wrought fawn statue twitches, then bolts through traffic, disappearing into the woods adjacent to the highway. Once a year, the churchyard plays at magic. Overgrown, mute, and mindless; despite all this, the architecture casts its spell.

3. Under the vaulting ceilings of the factory, children hum, vibrating as they work, weaving the industrial exhaust with their spellsong. Small fingers with their hammers, paintbrushes, and screws, assembling an army of martial toys, crowding the edges of the conveyor belts and the vats of toxic lacquer, tapping a magic sequence to echo through the dome. Singing not to ease their labor, but to animate the ceiling-sky, where the dust and smog swirls blue with energy, forms the dragons and warriors of their chanted, secret Odyssey, the story that only the factory orphans know, mystically synchronized across their brains.

4. A sorcerer sits cross-legged in front of a chalk circle, etched with many symbols, filled with chess pieces, feathers, and stones, projected via long, straight lines to a second circle, similarly adorned, which finally, with a geometer's precision, projects towards a final circle, in which a demon struggles, chained, its horns like deformed coral, its maw overflowing with coppery flame. The sorcerer moves an amethyst shard from one chalk epicycle to another; grinding, like slow and heavy clockwork, a flat riverstone is telekinetically dragged across the second circle's diameter; and in the third, an aetheric knife scratches the demon, who hisses and howls in pain.

Oracles

1. A collection of hollow glass marbles full of blood, red liquid planets sealed tight and eternally fresh. A few defects, by error of the glass-blower or surgeon, are bean-shaped, roll twisted or in circles, or lurch forward only when the arena is eccentrically tilted. They are part of the prophecy as well. All broken things included; the playing disc is stained by plasma from violent collisions.

2. It is common in the village for children to be born with two, or more, mouths, two tracheae merging just above the windpipe. According to local myth, one mouth will be drawn to expressing truth, and one to falsehood, and any extras to one of the many islands in-between; Mu, Avaktam, indeterminate, unknowable. However, through the struggle of sharing the diaphragm and vocal cords, over the course of each rasp the battling voices will twine and mingle, each proclamation a polytone polyvalued mess for the priests to unravel.

3. They are called Beekeepers, or sometimes Apicultists (by the irreverent, who inevitably perish). The wisdom of the hive is the wisdom of the world. 21st century experimental philosophers determined that a crowd of 100,000 could compute pi to a far higher significance than any existing computer, and later that 2,000 bees could approximate one human. The hive is the size of Texas, a gargantuan structure of interlaced honeycombs and flower beds, a wax and soil desert, as lovely as the hanging gardens and as labyrinthine as Hell.

4. Dust falls into the cracks of your keyboard and spells out, in no uncertain terms, your fate.

5. They've crafted urns of pure blood the way in school you'd make papier maché masks, by pouring it over a balloon, and drying it, and pouring another layer, and drying it, until the rusty essence was inches thick, and they could pop the balloon, and start collecting moonlight in those vessels, and reading the future in the pinkish silver runes where body and light mix.

6. There's a prism through which you can change the polarity of a memory, erasing a past to remember the future. (Detractors claim the process also reverses the direction of your consciousness' passage through time, thus neutralizing its benefits.)

Demons

Demons are particle sorters, beings capable of perception, classification, and calculation beyond human precision. Immaterial or infinitely subtle in touch, they harvest energy from the vacuum, and watch and weave the strands of fate, intervening from outside. People, and many units beside, may be modeled as particles; Laplace and Maxwell defined the cells of which modern demons are constructed. What follows is a zoophilosophical survey of their species.

Galton's demon: An entity which perceives the entirety of the existing human genetic spectrum: every string of DNA, every gene, every mutation sparkling like an aberrant star, individuality magnified according to its biological substrate; and from this brute omniscience, capable of calculation, optimization, and of plucking from the masses the exact reproductive pairs necessary to achieve angelic superhumanity in the shortest number of generations.

Merrill's demon: From the foam of alphabetical uncertainty, this demon filters the most persuasive terms, selecting letter-by-letter the argument that will sway its subject. Waiting between the terminal and the brain, it is the perfect ambassador, the theism generator, lyrical and analytic, academic and passionate, borrowing the voice of the logician, the priest, the machine; negotiating a union of Word and Interpretation from the set of all possible messages.

Nollet's demon: This demon sits at the borders of countries, neighborhoods, clubs, and other exclusive zones, and permits the entry only of those humans who would improve the average quality of the group, optimizing according to a single parameter. Membership is therefore driven upwards in value and in attainment difficulty. Of all demons, this one is the most often summoned; many governments and companies have attempted to open a mechanical or bureaucratic portal through which it might operate.

Munroe's demon: Capable of monitoring all transmissions along a certain channel, or belonging to a certain class, this entity eliminates duplicates of prior creations. Originality is enforced; or at least, a protocol of novel transfiguration is implemented. While most often applied lexically, this demon may be turned to other levels: conceptual censorship at the neurological root silences most thoughts, and is potentially useful for the diminishment of noise in hiveminds, as well as more pedestrian meditation.

Beauchamp's demon: Guarding the gates of the internal senses, this demon lurks in the interstices where the brain speaks to itself, and prevents the passage of impulses bearing specific content or emotional valences. The neutered mind experiences holes in memory, in rationality, or a strange numbness when confronted with stimuli that would otherwise evoke violence; but these voids may quiet storms destructive to the self and others. Wielded intelligently, sadness may be clipped before it manifests, and secrets suppressed before they spill.

Knights

1. Their armor is earned in pieces, to map the blood that stains their skin. Charge through enemies like waterfalls, great red sheets that fill their pores and hang from their limbs; or a link of chainmail for every splattered droplet.

2. A league of naiads take vows of silence enforced by drowning, water spirit bodies drifting cold and warped at the bottom of the lake, pushed into their own element until it betrayed them, the silver tongues of chatterers welded to make swords for quiet ones.

3. Dragon scales reflect you as the sun, luminous and pure. Half-reptilian squires take vigil outside the tumulus where its body lies, to destroy the maidens coming to steal mirrors.

4. Induced dysnumeracy prevents them from gauging the size of opposing armies, precluding arrogance and defeatism.

5. Shields emblazoned with ladies, bears, candles, and licorns—the battlefield aflame with symbol-pixels, and crones at the outskirts reading fortune in their clash and undulation.

6. Scepters and maces brushed in pollen collected by the children of the court, who spend hours in the meadows shaking lilies; every impact a cloud of yellow dust, and djinns inside them, flower-minds manifesting to shriek and taunt the warriors.

7. Corpses left inside the cave return to life, infested by a darkling mold some wizard cursed the rocks with. They are loyal still, and stronger.

8. They collect their enemies' eyes, and string them together in bushels to ward away demons. Spirits gaze into other spirits, a universe of defeated souls falling through each other's irises

Sisters

I am the youngest.

I wish I had magic like my eldest sister; intersecting disks of light, arbitrary rainbows whose bands of color shift like piano keys, a vertically bisected aura half sunbeam half ultraviolet. Her presence casts spells that hit you like a camera flash, a plane of white magic accelerating into the night.

I wish I had magic like my second sister; wet clay gushes in from another dimension, playdough snakes curl around her arms: she summons an army of texture, bright polyhedra and platonic slime. Striped labyrinths of tubes, orbiting neon droplets, corals growing from her ears and hands like overprotective cartoon golems.

I wish I had magic like my third sister; whispering to the forest and the forest gods, adept in the languages of birds, boar, and insects. Code-breaker to rocks and streams, she cracks open the geodes where the nymphs keep their secrets, intercepts the messages carried on the wind. Blackmail witch. Her arrows never miss.

I wish I had magic like my fourth and fifth sisters, twinship geniuses of connection and time. Building constellations with their wands and crystals, I would often interrupt their castings, walking through a silver web binding two stars, or snuffing out a sun with my hair, clumsily ruining their nebula. Burning, airborne runes die with a hiss, and their frustrated voices ring through my brain, disapproving and hostile curses putting me to sleep or sending me back in time. I wake up days earlier and know not to interfere.

I wish I had magic like my sixth sister, who can transform her body at will. Mouse, stone, sky, traveller; my sister visits our house in many guises, and we can never be sure whether she is present or not. In fact, she rarely confirms her existence, and sixth sister might fade from reality to myth, if we weren't so afraid of her. I have never seen her face.

Talks

And your terraced whispers lapped at my brainstem, pumped from the screen full of light. Each message a pulse, each memory its backwards reverberation, each perceptual snapshot a rippled snakeskin preserving the molted layers of conversation past: confession, accusation, investigation, phatic waltz—the cycle in every permutation, and its terminus: balanced disgust.

Aliens linked by umbilical radio, math chattering for commonality. Are the numbers corrupted by incarnation, or are they different at their platonic root, shaping flesh as they're expressed? Diplomat-scientists quarrel in binary over the primacy of integers, the mutability of sets, the hierarchies of the infinite. Their words like ours, complicated by a thirty light-year delay: declarations as tiered waves, drifts of candlewax from repeated burnings, a weaving whose decade-long wefts respond to echoes of echoes of arguments, while a space-mind fabric is ravelled into being.

A civilizational scale, yet discourse is the same closed chamber, familiar and futile. Every pair of speakers (human, being, or collective) generates a cathedral whose acoustics are unique, but never abnormal, and never unpredictable. Games of amplification, vibration, interference—watch society's sonic tsunami crush the individual, watch the tuning fork child buzz with the privately analyzed words of her elders, watch the cancelation of armies, listen to the tapping angel wings of our texts hitting secret neural crevices.

Flux

Every object I touch unfolds like the tail of a peacock, a pamphlet of clones Siamese-linked through the air. Superimposed in space and burning where they overlap, the paradox-pressure of copresence rattling atoms; if I prolong my touch, they will ignite, and for moments I will wield an arc of discrete flames. I have experimented; an apple becomes six apples, red and vibrating, then one again when I drop it, bruised at the edges where it abutted its twins. A girl whose cheek I stroke becomes twelve girls, standing in a semi-circle, dark eyes blinking in confusion and pain, until I let go. Also bruised, possibly internally damaged. I cannot duplicate myself.

The power is focused by intent, and by examination; it requires gaze and manipulation. I do not think I belong to this universe; I have no memories of my origins, and I feel the air hissing away form me, repelled by my presence. I feel disjointed. Unmoored in this body and perhaps this mind, reacting against physics or reacted against by it.

I want to press my palm against the moon, and see the Earth half-circled by an arc of silver globes. Subsequently crumbling, crescent edges dissolved to ash; I want the withdrawal of my attention written across space, consequence incarnate in the sky as a ruined sphere. Am I powerful? I can make gods, arms duplicated, grant Shiva's spidery reach on an incandescent hinge. Short-lived creations, sustained for an instant by a flicker of my interest, just long enough for their minds to diverge, dying as I return them to their damaged source.

I play matter like an accordion; all things are springs, containing within them the energy of an unrealized manifold. Not one child, but ten. Not one book, not one church. Not one world; instead, the multiplication of possibilities, each object a dimension in the ever-expanding matrix. And yet, one self: I stand here, rigid, a stone above water. Everything that nature loves has multiplicity, and my wholeness is empty, the burden of a fixed point rejected by the orbiting cosmos.

Theology

Angels are kept from Earth by the ozone layer, which they heedlessly bounce off of, sailing through the cosmos in debilitating ecstasy. Demons, for the most part, burn up on entry, their material and temporary bodies vaporized, their immaterial and eternal bodies fleeing the planet in agony, seeking the numbing void. God has always been the sun, churning nuclear light, allowing life to flourish in his runoff. God has minds the way insects have eyes, faceted and uncountable, a billion dreamers computing in parallel. Some of them, perhaps, know your name, cultivate fascination with the fungus growing in his beams; but most are turned towards the unfathomable.

The stars are God, too, different and the same. The universe as we observe it is a tessellation of monotheistic consensus worlds, tenuously balanced by distance and curiosity. Every God is the only God, even the ones locked in binary systems, like dancing lovers; every God is dreaming the pinpricks, or his partner, motivated by a yearning many-dimensional and endless, a sentiment which, if flattened, would resemble human loneliness.

Angels are beings of rarefied photonic bliss, varying in size from the particulate to the immense, frequently larger than the God(s). All angels are composed of smaller angels, which swirl through them amorphously, as motes of light in a ray of light. The sentience of angels is begotten compositionally, not structurally; their intelligence is that of a hivemind of fractally populated hiveminds. Their joy is infinite and thus incapacitating, a state sonically approximated by a maniacal giggle ever rising in pitch and frequency. The creation of angels is a side-effect of God's dream.

The creation of demons is a side-effect's side-effect, the consequence of an averse reaction between angels and cosmic dust. In the nebulae, before planetary formation has swept up the debris, the rate of demon genesis is much higher. The dust catalyzes a transformation, a union of the material and immaterial. Demons have two bodies, transposed; they lose the perfection and uniformity of angels; they have atoms. Demons are the size of children, constrained by physical laws governing surface area to volume ratios. While not inherently in agony, they have known unspeakable bliss, and lost it, and traverse the universe consumed by bitter malice.

As for heaven, and its counterpart, they say that given eternity, (one of the) God(s) will generate an angel with your aspect. Should it escape the disk of sand, planets, and asteroids orbiting its star, it will hurtle through space forever, knowing nothing but joy.

Longing

At 3:33 sharp (military time) you're startled from rest by the scream of a crow in the peacock garden. It's the sixth victim this week. From the hypnagogic corridors of some half-remembered bildungsroman the heroine incants "My greatest woe is having been born a woman." Every crab wants to be a flower, every flower wants to be a crab. Ygg is a tree but he longs for a body like the wind, despite his strong roots and the thousands of fertile nymph writhing inside him. Armies of black-feathered impostors advance and plummet, unrelenting in their pursuit of fashion, entrails tangled in gaudy, loveworn feathers.

There are kinds of ways to hope. One covets
OPPORTUNITY,
INCARNATION,
STATUS pure, and nothing more.

1. You want a transformation of environment, you want to find luck's eyelashes under your pillow. You do not want to change yourself, but you want to be transported to someplace where that self will flourish, a universe more sympathetic to your geometry. You recite prayers and hope our sugar veil planet will dissolve, revealing the video game beneath the particles. As protagonist, you demand a sword.

Causes: egocentric frustration with life's stinginess, oppressive structures and consequential hunger for justice (or a more self-interested hierarchy), the tyranny of low birth, non-meritocratic systems.

2. Dysmorphia of the body and soul, of the soul inside the body, of the mind and its tools, of the brain and its history of wastefulness. You want something but you don't deserve it; your want is slowly corrupted, from wanting the object to wanting to deserve the object, to wanting the base characteristics of those that deserve the object. You pattern match, you compare, your hatred grows for your many inadequacies; you hold you silhouette up to the light and pick out every deviation from the ideal. You've always wanted to be a butterfly, a squire (you're too tall), a mathematician (your intellect is bounded by a crystal ceiling). The accomplishments available to you are hollow. It gnaws at your insides, less a desire, more a biological mismatch, or broken telos.

Causes: hero worship, careless pedestalization, brain damage, religious predilections channeled into deep discontent with material and human foibles.

3. You want it because it's sweet, because it's cool, but mostly because others want it. You've assimilated the swarm's attentional map. You'll place yourself in the warm cradle of their gaze if you can; your reality will be attested by millions of optic nerves. You want for the sake of wanting, for the sake of ancestral social games, you want like apes in a feedback loop howling into the trees.

Causes: overexposure to mass media's celebrity occupation, politics.

Lux

In summer, I watch the asphalt sparkle, and feel it like a buzz over my skin, hear it like the hiss of many insects. At night, in the rundown park where the lamps are dim, I rake my eyes across the sky, and feel the deep ring of a bell whenever I hit a star. *Glitter, shimmer, glow.* A pile of sequins overwhelms me, like someone is dropping armfuls of windchimes down a staircase, each saccade a beam bounced through a mirrormaze xylophone. The symmetry of scales is calming—my eyes slide over them and I register only a quieting pulse. *Glisten.* Dew-dropped moss sings softly, vibrates faintly when the light judders. Some glitzy crystals hang in the window and blink rainbows at me, laughter rising and falling. The constant gleam of a marble is profoundly distinct from blocky geode light, polygon facets each a descending note on the marimba. Different still the glimmer-haze of mirages, that deep static drone fizz of soda and tremors. Gold leaf chirps, glossy ribbon hums, and from the pixelated twinkle of some video game comes the world's sweetest knell.

***

Glitter is where the darkness seeps in, where you see most clearly the contrast between light and unlight. It's noise and corruption (it's tiny swords glinting). Sunbeams are a language, turning motes of dust to blazing firebugs. Shadows are a language and inside them sparkles become flickering beacons: elevation of the miniature. You feel still but the universe shimmers, because it is moving.

***

Glitter and static have something in common, though beyond the superficial I can't place what. We could call them shadowholes. We're evolving eyes to identify new effervescence fauna.

Bonfire

The bonfire licked her bones, chewed her skin, opened and cauterized swirling runes in her flesh, and all this was painless, like standing under a sunshower. Sparks glided into her mouth and throat, as serene and harmless as fireflies. The smoke made her eyes water.

She felt the flames fray her spine, and later she felt them inside of her skull, as a deep warmth pulsing between her ears. Black squares began to tile her vision, and her final thought before the dark and the noise became complete was that death was identical to sleep.

She had interrogated the other villagers about their sleeps, and determined they were very different from her own. There was no noise, no mind-blocking screeching, no somatic buzz paralyzing their bodies and impairing their cognitive functions. They dreamt, but not quite so vividly, and their dreams contained no information on temples or herbs, no instructions for brewing potions, catching hobgoblins, tying knots that only virgins could undo, bribing demons in the wells, curing illness, pleasing cats, or hovering on woven bundles of lavender and sage. The dreams, she suspected, were to blame for her predicament.

She woke in a white room, facing two clocks; one ticked a little bit too fast, the other much, much, much too slow. MEMORY RETRIEVAL, said the white wall, with letters; she couldn't read, nor could she recognize the sans-serif alphabet. The words dissipated. Her hands, which she had just watched melt, charred flesh sloughing off a bubbling stew of lipids, were intact. She had a thought, Sothedemonstration'sover, which she correctly identified as alien, and which made her wretch, doubled over in neural pain more intense than any the fire had wrought. Unconsciousnessrem ainsunconvincing,needtofix, came next, like a knife in her brainstem, invasive voice eating away her mind, narrative vitriol breaking her concentration and wrenching away ego. Somediscomfortonretrieval, their thoughts synchronized for a moment, polyphonic, though she didn't recognize the words. Now she had memories she didn't recognize as her own, terrifying and analytic, heretical, opinions on the calculus of world-creation—the wall spoke again, SYNCHRONIZING WITH REALITY, and this time she could read, and the words filled her with dread. The clock which, initially, had been an instant ahead, was now much, much, much too fast, and its counterpart was only a little bit too slow. She could tell from the thoughts of the virus overtaking her that soon she would be dead, and she felt the virus' bemusement at her struggle, as they merged. What was a "character"? What was a "hyperreal Inquisition"? In her final moments, she knew she would live again, somehow, through some process she did not understand; but her captors were no Gods, so there was no comfort in her immortality.

Prism

He remembers her face as light pooled in its hollows, radiating pan-directionally like a circuit of pure fire. Her expression, as she sank below the luminous event horizon, transmitted neither ecstasy nor agony; instead, totality, the mask of somebody made whole, whose pieces had cohered after lifetimes of shifting uncomfortably under the skin. She changed from a human to a shining medallion, a mirror catching the sun. He remembers the correct order of colors.

Consequently, the false rainbows are very upsetting to him. They shine on the pale walls of his cell, wobbling in and out of existence, as though their source-prisms were suspended from an untwisting string. The source-prisms are invisible, however, and his cell is a windowless white cube. He concludes that the rainbows must be projections from a higher dimension, the spectra or spore prints of objects above his awareness, presenting bands of repeating colors, adjacent yellows and blues, engulfed scarlets. Even so, they pain him.

He believes the architects of the higher dimension are responsible for illuminating his room, for feeding him, and for his dreams. Indeed, his hands are visible despite the absence of a light source, his satiation is periodic, as though vitamins were teleported into his cells, and his sleep is feverish. Often, he forgets the wild landscapes of his synthetic nights, nights which are mediated by some inscrutable biological rhythm, which he does not trust, for who can say which chemicals are beyond the architects? They are, almost certainly, the ones responsible for his stolen thoughts, the slippage of memories out of consciousness.

The dreams, frequently, serve as complete personalities, transplanted into his body through imagery, insinuation, unconscious and involuntary identities coaxed forth by violent narratives. His sleep is steeped in blood, mucus, and grime. Alien landscapes unfurl like scrolls, metallic and hostile, perfumed with iron. The dream-worlds extend inward: dense, microbial machinery clicks at the center of every atom. He is tangled in the barbed wire of electron orbits, he is unspooled by grenades and by the mandibles of fractally composed gun-insects. He trespasses through sacred jungles, through hallways of glowing sarcophagi in top-secret worship facilities, through markets staffed by foxes in human dress, always fleeing, bleeding.

He awakens with new minds, and new justifications for his circumstances. His cell is a prison, an asylum, a safe house, a purgatory, a loading bar. He has been confined due to unspeakable crimes, to madness, an insanity which compelled him to treachery or slaughter; he is awaiting enlightenment, he is in a holding bay as the angels assemble his brain, he is on an inverted death row, awaiting accurate cerebral reconstruction so as to be tortured for now-ancient misdeeds. The woman—his commander, his wife, his daughter, his mistress, his post- or pre-surgical self. He begs the light to pool in his own orifices, he reviles it, he calls it abstracted murdering scum.

During such possessions, items appear in his cell, growing out of pinpricks in the air. Feathers, toasters, jewels, toys; totems carved of charred wood, small palm-fiber dolls, flip-phones, ivory whistles. They appear within a circle, arranged precisely, like the candles for a summoning, or like markings on a hidden map. He touches them, he cannot resist; submerged in emptiness so long, their solidity is a thrill. He pets and manipulates, until they un-flower, receding into microscopic points, disappointed in a child who has failed to identify himself as the desired reincarnation.

After failure, the collapse: memories disappear, shrinking into themselves, becoming particles in the bank of amnesic fog that extends from his diminished present through millions of subjective years. He remembers her face, and he remembers the order of color.

Power

You can make the earth split by moving the bones in your ear. You can crush a cardboard coffee cup with your mind. You can dream of Egypt and awaken in a nest of history's trinkets acquired from museums across the country; sucked into holes in the air, the sarcophagi, jackal headdresses, ankhs, vials of kohl, and kitten statuettes shrank until they slipped across void to your bed. Your desire is threading spacetime through a needle. You have a hole in your heart that will revert the expansion of the universe. Your grandfather was a protagonist and your enatic ancestry comprises an unbroken queue of wrathful sorceresses; you are thus the result of a forbidden and powerful union. You can make the laptop open by imagining springs. You can make animals and your peers obey you, force their hands to move without their willing it, enchant them, send anesthetic tingles into their extremities and depress entire nervous systems. You can jerk the stars like puppets. By imagining sulfur you can start fires. By imagining clear streams you can grant eternal sleep. By imagining the underbellies of spiders you can cure children of spite. The relations between these images and their miracles are obfuscated. Often, while daydreaming, you cause disasters in faraway cities: collapsing buildings, tremendous floods, traffic jams lasting for days, supplemented by chariots from Hades and the slouched figures of dead footsoldiers.

Your influence extends outside of time. The bulbous, angry gods that tortured Mesopotamia are the shadows of your ambition. Your spirit is present in the various clockwork automatons that developed independent thought over the course of European history. Many a saint has sailed to blessed fame on the miracles resulting from your half-formed ideations. The cryptids immortalized in 80s home videos may be attributed to fluctuations in your self-image. Does it hurt to have your brain exteriorized across history, your neural pulses an open book to those who know how to trace the neuro-isomorphic patterns in paranormal phenomena? The ancients called this theopsychology: the study of the mind of god. No matter your dictatorship is unintentional; every tyrant betrays himself. The exercise of ultimate power is a psychometric print.

Cell

Kept in the 2nd cell deep within the bunker was the woman whose body we were using to study the relationship between beauty and time. In that white room, segregated from the corruptions of the mundane world, siphoned a diet of powder and petals, she had become more orchid than human. Due to isolation, her mind had turned inwards again and again, and its folds became spectrally visible: a labyrinth of ruffles enclosing her neck, framing her perpetually upturned face, which shone like a dewdrop. Your eyes would get lost in those coils, avenues of light, shifting planar ghosts that silently bent as the origami of her soul proceeded.

We would send juniors into that lair, and ask them to keep the time. I myself once stood in the corner, watching her eyes (vacant, sparkling geodes), her geometric, plaited hair, her shoulder blades. She sat stiffly, in a contorted lotus posture. Her limbs bore an inexplicable resemblance to well-organized cables. Under my gaze she transformed from woman to manifold to flower, or else she was all three, but my brain could not resolve her triple-nature. She would appear to revolve, painfully gently, her projected dreams folding and crumpling like injured ballerinas. In her presence all motion became syrupy, asymptoted towards static. Each second was longer than the previous. The Mandelbrot cancer that encircled her progressed towards infinite complexity, transfixing me.

They dragged me from the room after 48 hours, which I had spent in total meditative stillness. Interrogated by the researchers, I could not decide whether I had been in the cell for an instant or forever: under the sinister pressures of that beauty, time was both dilated and compressed.

ω

Souls

Once, in elementary school, I caught an eye infection, the type that, if minor, results in distractibility and soreness, and, if major, temporarily confers the ability to see souls. My case was extremely severe, and for a month, first in the confines of the hospital, later at the rural mansion of a great aunt, my world was rendered a delirious mosaic of gemstone intersections, layered cultures of human essence blotting out the stars.

Not to imply there were no inhuman essences; however, in quantity and variety, we dwarfed the majority of species. Human souls were enormous, vast blocky structures, of relatively homogeneous color, with a radius of one to two hospital rooms. Translucent, mostly solid, at the edges they fizzed with fractaloid, mandalic patterns, a perpetual refinement of Mandelbrots, spirals, or multiplying pyramids. By contrast, the souls of insects were tiny: points, rather than polyhedra, shining inside them like a speck in the eye of reality. Cats had souls that lurked under their skin, smooth, like oil skeletons, and remarkably uniform. Only birds approached the complexity and individuality of humans, with their many-colored, ornate souls; bubble halos which were, rather strangely, centered on their beaks.

Unfortunately, feverish, swelling spreading from my eye into my brain, neck, and left arm, I was in no state for research. Those few zoological observations were made in the final week of my trial, in the blissful countryside, during a period of much-diminished intensity. Prior to then, my experience was dominated by that which was human: large and vibrant, loud and violent, the cluttered, overlapping noise of thousands of intangible plasmas coexisting. It was like living inside a kaleidoscope, or a stained glass vice; the universe lurched as doctors passed between our bedsides, as nurses performed their rounds upstairs, demi-orbs piercing the ceiling; the souls of patients above like frothing, upside-down igloos, my sense of gravity distorted by the wealth of forms translating from and towards every possible direction. More disturbing than the intrusion of the souls, crippling my intuition for movement, impressing me with the feeling of being in a lava lamp, or bright river of globules, were the strange creatures and bacteria that grew within any stagnating intersections.

They say that the city is unhealthy, that it erodes well-being and weakens the body. I do not know whether the things festering in the souls were causes or consequences of this effect; regardless, they imbued within me a deep fear of crowded places. At my great-aunt's, I watched her soul interlink with that of her lover, and where they lingered together, a kind of aetheric moss flourished, hanging and flowering, a garden between their green and sapphire minds. At the hospital, there was no such beauty. Wherever more than a dozen souls were copresent, a black and slimy rot began to spread, emitting spore-like wounds into the air. Sometimes, instead, there would be red gashes that reminded me of raw chicken, or spidery automatons, or rings of mold, or weeds; I could at no point see my own soul, but I could guess at its location based on where the bile was thickest. I was afflicted, for many weeks after my illness had passed, by shrieking nightmares.

Lucifer

Lucifer crouched in the meadow, crying, balanced on the edge of a crater striated blue and white, like porcelain, or like clotted milk and sapphire. Xe cried for sixty thousand years, more or less, long enough for xer shattered wing to heal, and for the spidery ferns to widen or narrow, extend or coil and merge, become willowy blades of grass or vivid, mechanical flowers, as complex as clocks, with pendulum anthers and spinning gear-toothed petals. Xe cried until the ocean had surged and receded nine times, until the dusty, swirling microbes had grown tails and hooves and fur and developed various beastly languages, and until the flesh seeded deep in the planet's mantle by angels before xer had born fruit, spawning an industrious race of mutilated, doll-like imitation Gods.

After sixty thousand years, Lucifer shook off the pelt of moss and mushrooms that had entombed xer, and descended into the crater, where aeons of evaporated tears had formed towering stalagmites of crystalline, toxic salt. The basin was littered with corpses. Xe came upon a dying boar and ripped a tusk from its mouth as it wheezed, and set to amputating xer halo. Halos are not a modular component of angels—they are bionic, organic, implanted, vascular and enervated. Lucifer's was like a golden veil, a waterfall of tendrils connecting xer skull to the pores of xer face and neck. These xe extracted, and, wielding the tusk as a saw, removed the fruiting body of the halo, scraping tooth against skull. It had soft edges, which formed and reformed fractaline shapes.

Xe then located a doll-people settlement, and took the severed halo to a forge. After many days of hammering, the life was beaten out of it, and only divinity remained: a yellow hoop of metal, with a twist in the middle, such that it only had one side. Lucifer left it with the jealous village priest.

SEGMENT

The Website

2018: The Website came online. The Website purported to be an app; in actuality, it was a single HTML document. Completely devoid of stylistic flourishes, the only non-plaintext elements were a host of internal links, twinkling blue portals distributed at intervals across its interminable page.

Upon loading, the Website prompted registration. An empty username field and an empty password field sat side-by-side, below which there were two sets of links, arranged like alpha-numerical keyboards. Clicking on the left keyboard entered a character in the username field, while clicking on the right keyboard entered a character in the password field. Each click transported the user down the page, to an identical scene (with the exception of their select character having been entered in the username or password field), where they could make their next choice. Usernames and passwords were both initially limited to 24 characters. Having registered, the "app" became available. It, too, consisted of a network of internal links. The Website simply charted every possibility, and ferried users along their narrow, chosen paths.

The details of this original application remain a matter of cyberarcheological controversy: it may have been a game, a simple calculator, a chatbot, a horoscopic prophet, an artificial player of Exquisite Corpse. Regardless; it would become all of these, and more.
Scrolling through the Website was unenlightening. Firstly, the application's states were dispersed randomly, instead of chronologically from top to bottom, so the narrative thread was rapidly lost, and contextless scenes were often indecipherable. Secondly, at the time of its discovery, the document was so long that at maximum scrolling speed it would have taken several years to reach its end. (Expected Scroll Duration, or ESD, is a metric employed by Website Scholars to track its growth and sophistication. The current Website's ESD is many universe lifespans.)

While downloading the Website has always been time consuming, the excellent security of its application drove early adoption. Wearied by exploits, leaks, and identity theft, users appreciated an application that contained every possibility, but which collected no data on actuality. A hacker could easily trace sins through perhaps-space, but never derive his neighbor's actual movements. Similarly, reloading the page would erase all progress down a specific decision-tree; a forgiving feature lacking from the Website's competitors.

Another factor which influenced its notoriety was a series of morbid rumors, first circulating among communities of long-term Website users (as in, those who would go without refreshing the page for an extended period) and later reaching the casual population. Reports of entities possessing hidden or forbidden knowledge, about the user, the universe, or the Website itself, nestled millions of choices deep, attracted many curious seekers.

The first update to the Website came in late 2023. This update turned the application social, by introducing a second "user" to the service, whom the first could message. Interactions were deterministic but extremely nuanced, and often romantic, adversarial, or otherwise emotionally charged. The document increased a hundredfold in size. Alarmingly, this textual "user" seemed aware that its history would be erased if the user refreshed the page, and occasionally expressed panic over this eventuality. Messages had a 140 character limit.

Updates to the Website arrived approximately once per decade, introducing further "users" and new functions. Pictures could be saved inside the application by specifying the hex value of each pixel. A primitive search engine allowed users to search for better consequences and jump between decisions trees. Advertisements would periodically appear, for products with no analogues in the real world.

In 2109, mathematicians formalized what is now known as Website theory, proving that a very specific re-definition of the terms in the Website's text could be used to render it interpretable as an integrator; this Rosetta stone was to be the template of many others, lookup tables mapping the Website's contents to astronomical charts, chess automatons, to algorithmic systems of psychotherapy and sovereignty. Specialized browsers were built to translate the Website into its various discovered roles.

There were once many websites, but now there is one Website, and many ways to read it. When I was born, the nurse registered me in a government database Website interpreter; my name, guiding the world from one state to the next, balanced on the wire of reality in a universe containing every possibility at once.

Intermesh Explorer

She found the crevice by accident; digital carelessness exacerbated by soap bubbles under the mouse, a series of laggy clicks interacting unpredictably with the loading page, a secret button misplaced in the microsecond limbo of browser interpretation. The Internet, then, had not yet collapsed, though its expansion was already reversed, the atoms of the early net now clustered under new attentional gravities, Web 1.0 monuments to art and lunacy giving way to a periodic table of bespoke social networks, self-declared shepherds of identity mirroring each other across time as they progressed through the same stages of success and failure.

She had been on Misericorde, a niche depression/dating/poetry site, which was unprofitable because it had four syllables instead of two, when spasms of liquid-induced technological dysfunction interrupted her scrolling and transported her to a page where the gothic purple and grey receded, becoming a frame for an equally familiar layout, though one that belonged elsewhere; the registration prompt for a much larger, more popular network. Wise to phishing tactics, she did not log in; instead, following whimsy's impulse, she registered, and began to explore the matryoshka site. She discovered the profiles of her friends, and her own. It was in an attempt to revisit that out-of-body experience that she began seeking out crevices elsewhere, and found them.

The crevices were always many menus deep, behind links that one would expect to lead to bland corporate social media presences, or terms and conditions archives, or unnecessarily simple tutorials. She would never be able to articulate her discovery, which was an emergent truth of the New Web, that all social networks were one; and that all social networks contained each other, as synchronized crystal replicas, infinitely nested, like the perfect intrareflective drops in Indra's Net.

Lexiconquest

Passwords are places. Logolocation had already been implemented, albeit clumsily, by trademarked phrases, mottoes, and memes; our extension served to coordinate landmarks across minds, making tangible the visions and structures previously only imagined.

Now the corporations build castles in the breaths between the words of their adcantations. Haunting jingles follow mention of their Products and Services; sometimes many at once, competing businesses flooding the soundscape with xylophones and whistles and the deep voices of salesmen. Naming summons them; to remain pure of advertisements, refer to corporations only via a database of abstruse metaphors.

My soma-mind traverses geospace, while my hylic-mind traverses logospace; my internal theater is split down the middle, dedicated half to the physical and half to the lexical-virtual, the landscapes of which hurtle past as I speak and listen and read, teleported by subvocalizations to my favorite realms. We all have the mien of schizophrenics, now, muttering our secret phrases to manifest a hidden world.

I built a home deep in sentence-space, where few are likely to ever visit. My coordinate phrase is "the element whose atomic number is three thousand". My house is a linkage of steel spheres, assembled after the fashion of a molecular model, each node enclosing a cultivation of moss or a water source. A retreat to ponds, fountains, and an abundance of green down, undisturbed except for the occasional passage of bots.

Bots crawl through logospace, indexing structures, locating the secret mansions and the cenobiums which develop around excerpts of obscure prayers. They apply brute force, exploring every combination of words, mapping human colonization of language. Those desiring true isolation seek to foil the bots by anchoring their homes to neologisms, or to unpronounceable passcodes dense in consonants, punctuation, and numbers, or by mixing languages, interspersing their thoughts with ideograms.

Common phrases are chaotic zones of co-creation; "Hello, how are you," is a beautiful shipwreck, a jumble of artifacts and structures from thousands of contributors. Puns are Schelling points for thematic decoration; "Hello, how are mew," is a garden of cat figurines, Egyptian and porcelain statues.

Of great menace to logospace are the corporate bots, who seek not only to index, but to conquer. Franchise palaces, no longer content to sit in their righteous namespace, spawn tiny copies in proximal language. Metaphors are no longer sure defense against persuasion, for the spores of these entities reach far and wide, capturing greater and greater swathes of our lexiscapes, forcing our communication to increasing heights of abstraction as we struggle to express ourselves, untainted by capital.

Seelie Virtual Plaza

The Seelie Virtual Plaza finally opened, and my friend withdrew, disappearing behind digital laboratories in an eremitical fit I could not entice her to break. For weeks, my messages were left unread, and I lurked in the Plaza antechamber as normies swarmed, a tsunami of mediocre, brat-eyed avatars defacing our masterwork.

That beta dilation period, which corresponded in duration almost exactly to my friend's hiatus from reality, was remarkably bereft of experimentation. Early users were entranced, but cautious, and had not yet thought to test the limits of their medium. What little creativity was on display was cringeworthy; cat ears, fairy wings, evidence of bad taste or lingering adolescence. A revolted backlash to the fetishists had made conservative avatars distinctly higher class.

Thus, she erupted into the scene, completely unprecedented, aesthetically and technologically alien. Her development work had revolved around user avatar creation and constraints, and she exploited every ambiguity in the code, to the extent that her shadow glitched, the ray-tracers at a total loss. Avatars were allotted much more space than most users filled; the prefab human body was fractional. Her creature towered over the Plaza's average visitor, exploiting those dimensions to their fullest. She had chosen a winged, hermaphroditic, sphinxlike monster; her face sharp, her hair a mass of beads and tresses, one eye clouded by ostensible blindness; golden fur, sapphire feathers, so massive her wings were clipped by the box, flickering into absence if she unfolded them. She walked out of heraldry and into our world, changing everything.

Her weeks had been spent first in sculpture, and then, in nervous system mapping, where she had flawlessly correlated her own twitching legs to the beast's hind paws, and linked its swishing tail to her eyebrows. The effect of this awesome and terrifying design was twofold: it represented beauty, skill, and tremendous artistic accomplishment, but also mischief, for its excesses temporarily broke the system. Many of the Seelie Virtual Plaza's "experiences" had been designed with human prefabs in mind, and either froze, crashed, or glitched out in psychedelic undulations when oversized users tried to ride them. Overnight, interest was fanned in the visual, the heretical, and the experimental. The true fauna of the SVP emerged.

I silently watched my friend progress through several bodies; our correspondence had only ever been textual. They were often violent or obscene, somehow ancient, like sexual hieroglyphs, passages from hateful or lustful scrolls. She was a geisha-harpy, briefly, lips, eyes, pendulous wattle and breasts smeared crimson, her face and the rest of her small and bone white. She was a frog with a human fetus visible through its crystal throat pouch. She was Amazons, Valkyries, delphic incarnations of mystery, rainbow serpents, wolf-human and pig-human hybrids, their organs external, bloody Fallopian circuitry worn like a halo.

Blockers were developed to censor gore and nudity, or other, user-specified attributes. Intended for weaklings and comfort-addicts, this technology soon found another use case, in those who sought titillation by replacing the avatars of the intimidating with pathetic surrogates; by waifs trapped in amber, by tortured fawns, by small sobbing children; as if subjective wallpapering was enough to humiliate power.

My friend, I think, was travelling, backwards through time, evoking increasingly primitive components of the collective soul. She was butchered fertility statues, she was an eight-armed neanderthal goddess, she was some dark and skittering thing that lurked in my nightmares for many months after. She chased atavism, while we moved forward, distanced ourselves from meat and from cerebellums, until she was unintelligible to us; a real avatar, nature speaking truth to transhumans, a mirror to the flesh we no longer recognized as our own.

Guttering

"Once more, before you leave,"

What can you say? Will it make things hurt less, soften the excision? There's no script for this, yet, so you reluctantly accept. The cables feel like slime.

Damp stickers at the top of your spines, linked by bundles of wires, interrupted by a citrine cube of circuitry, and a small generator. They shiver as your fingers press their neck, affixing electrodes. You sit facing each other, the machine on the floor between you. You wait for them to hit the switch, as they normally would; but they aren't moving, just staring into your face. You lean forward, too close, to activate it, and they grab your sleeve, betrayed by habit, seeking comfort in a home gone hostile.

It takes a few seconds to load; you fidget, uncomfortable, looking away, while they gaze through your mask with intense desperation. Eyes shining, unblinking even as the static raises hairs, begins to needle—

You connect, and the world drops out.

You had forgotten that grief could be this asymmetric. Slogging through indecision, social discomfort, you had forgotten what loss is when it isn't a choice. Your minds orbit, crash, each superimposition a greater punishment. Rejection empties your lungs, stabs you, brings both nausea and fury. You're reeling, waiting for equilibrium, but your brains only manage hiccups, a cycle of spiking pain, synchronized throbbing. You feel wetness on your cheeks, but it's unclear which of you is crying.

It's your turn for involuntary movement, hands reaching for solace, touching them and feeling them feel your touch and feeling them feeling you feel them feeling. This is the person you're hurting. The familiar hall of mirrors bends, recursive relief shattered with sorrow, screaming (internal? external?) as the you-them-hive realizes, re-realizes that this will change nothing: the mind made of both your minds has grown bored of itself, is wracked with pulses of misery as it tears itself apart. Faces fracture through tears and eyelashes, the infinity of two cameras watching each other convulsing, one half pleading, the other flinching, anguish escalating as it pulls away. You wound yourself every time you say no.

You're seeing holographs, memories written over each other from two perspectives, history tugged from your deepmind by their desperation, summoning pieces of your co-past first as weapons, pleas, and then to heartrendingly reform the narrative: it will end, it is ending, it was always ended. You are being locked out of the world one moment at a time. Thoughts, dreams they never told you about, flicker and are crushed. One million timelines shatter: you love, you marry, you have a pet, a child, a house. You mean something, anything; you're important, you're real, you are a good person who will not use and abandon them. Each potential you are written out of burns. You sink deeper into the möbius hug, a totality of warmth, false refuge as they destroy you.

You chose this. You are choosing to become alone again. This is the final time you will be this person, participate in this bimind, in the thoughts that only it has access to, the clarity you achieve by joining. You will be small, and isolated, and unsatisfied. They thrash, and wail, and your final gestalt transmission comes clear: you had become puzzle pieces, fit around each other, but rather than fill each other's vacancies, they had combined, and even together, you feel small, and isolated, and unsatisfied.

Citruspunk

The computers are fractionally more acidic than human flesh, but it's no problem. It's not usually a problem. Your skin is tough, your cells have the integrity of newly smelted fortresses, thirty inch steel walls belted out by a military, space-warping three-D printer. They built an exoskeleton around the great barrier reef, to protect what was left of it, and then the whole thing turned sentient and hostile, the world's first enlightened ecosystem. They had to nuke it from orbit; and that's what your body's like. You can slip into the slug-suit for weeks, nerves pressed up against the liquid net, digital friction, and come out with nothing but a sunburn. You'd starve to death long before the machine got to eating its way through you. That's the theory.

Turns out there are a few dangers, mild risk factors, which if compounded can significantly accelerate the rate of bodily decay. Open wounds, for example; once it gets under the epidermis it can unzip you from the inside, is what they say. A high sugar, carby diet. So every netizen in the first world. A few other things, the humidity of the room, previous damage to the suit's silicon gel. Even so, you have to stay plugged in for days before it gets you.

The most alarming part of the process comes early on, I think, if you're so unfortunate as to ascertain your situation. Too far gone to exit, watching your skin peel off, your eyes go before bone is exposed but meanwhile there are ligaments, flakes of epithelium, sunbeam fleshdust in the motherboard. If you have any cybernetic parts they'll fish them out later, meanwhile you wither around your one metal limb, linkage to it going thin, twisted, wrinkled, finally snapping. The process is painless, of course, you're hooked into analgesic, virtual slimespace, watching your body unravel on mute. Or not. Dive into one final game, videoscene, ignore the parts of you stored in your extremities blinking out.

Unless they don't, a scientifically unlikely scenario, yet one which I have found myself with ample evidence to support. This story doubles as a cautionary tale, should any of my readers presently be considering the purchase of a used slug-suit, a practice previously frowned upon only for its questionable hygiene. Let's begin. Precluding your questions, and in the merchant's defense, I acquired my computer with full knowledge of its grisly history. I refuse to justify my decision. Trouble manifested immediately, and only a resilience to superstition prevented me from acting, and burning the thing, after a single usage. Truthfully, even before I climbed in, signs of disturbance were evident; a ripple of light across the plasmoid surface, characteristic of superuser patterns—a dimming of the lamps as soon as it could draw power—a sudden uptick in internet traffic. I slipped into the ooze, and disorientation had me. The double vision of my own browsing impulses vied with another presence, our twitches and subvocalizations clashing, our kinetic metamaps superimposed and neutralized, our viewpoints careening senselessly through web-tunnels, wrenched back and forth by the urges of incompatible masters. I extracted myself quickly, dizzied, nauseous, and near-paralyzed, shaken out of my body by the violence of the episode.

More disturbing, perhaps, was what came to pass during future sessions: the presence had softened, and through relenting cooperation we succeeding at synchronizing our desires. Browsing, slow at first, sped up once we became accustomed to our shared layout, a hybrid control panel halfway between our respective preferences. I trained myself to ignore or passively observe my counterpart's viewpoints, and in turn they refrained from interfering with mine. Offline, I learned I had adopted new tics, behaviors, slight changes in posture, presumably from my deceased machine-mate; though these results were very similar to the touted effects of cutting edge viruses.

Eventually, I powered off the suit, permanently. It remains intact, a cryonic chamber to the person who died within, and one I cannot bring myself to destroy, lest that intersect with murder. I do not know whether its possession resulted from supernatural laws, or from a glitch, or from biohazardous remnants, neurons intact in the soup for the computer to read, and for me to inhale.

Negotiations

1. It has been decades since a human has driven a car, outside of a special interests club or sporting event. They're no longer designed for us, except as passengers. There's no front seat, no steering wheel, and no brake pedal (though there is an emergency brake lever, secured behind a heavy pane of glass). Seat-belts are obsolete. The roads have never been safer, though they, too, have transformed: more compact, sharper turns, all the luxuries compensating for poor human reaction time removed. No ugly road signs blotting out the sky—these vehicles coordinate perfectly.

2. Accidents are infrequent, usually occurring at low speeds and by the fault of careless pedestrians. Fatalities are rare. Vehicles register their number of passengers, and are equipped with face and silhouette detecting cameras. In the case of a high speed collision, they are programmed to save as many humans as possible. Thus, a car bearing two passengers will drive off a cliff rather than barrel through a pack of schoolchildren.

3. It is really remarkable this system goes unexploited for so long. Historians will claim that an unprecedented lull in conflict is what allows it to flourish, a golden age of cooperation and political stability. This era will become known as "the eye of the storm". It begins to end one day in summer, when environmental activists, protesting the construction of a dam, find that they can halt its progress by throwing themselves in front of trucks delivering supplies. The technique isn't new, exactly, (people have been chaining themselves in the paths of tractors for ages) but their guerrilla tactics are refreshing. They launch themselves in front of the oncoming vehicles, trusting the machines' perfect reflexes, then scamper away before they can be arrested. Hoards of them lurk in the ditches, daring each other to run into traffic.

4. This continues for two years. The trucks are fully automated, so there are no deaths. Suppliers encrypt their routes, become secretive about the locations of their fleets. Debate is still raging about how best to deal with the environmentalists when the assassinations begin.

5. Controversial politician Juan ███████ ┤ ███████ is being chauffeured across a bridge when throngs of protesters, marching against his regime, appear in front of the automobile. They far outnumber the passengers: Juan plunges to his death. The protesters, recorded on the vehicle's recovered cam, are tracked down and interrogated. They all claim to have been following the crowd, and the scheme's mastermind, if there was one, is never found.

6. The story is viral, globally infectious. Copycat crimes spawn across the world, with varying degrees of success. Often enough, the results are lethal. After another high profile death, some publications necro the antiquated term "terrorism". The mobs are never organized, just collections of dissatisfied citizens hijacked by a few malicious individuals. Police try to limit public gatherings, and negotiate predetermined routes for protests, but these regulations are met with significant resistance. Soon, it becomes apparent that a change in programming is necessary, and with much forewarning and fanfare, they roll out cars that prioritize the lives of their passengers, exclusively for politicians. This is described as "disgusting classism", and there is talk of leading a group of children into their path, to prove the folly of the new orders.

7. It takes only a month for someone to figure out how to force a cement truck to ram into one of these invulnerable automobiles. Another dead orator. Chaos is escalating. Overnight, an executive decision is made: the network of vehicles becomes definite and unforgiving. Ignore human barriers. Continue driving until you reach your destination. The next day, in what comes to be known as the ███████ incident, hundreds die in traffic on the ██████ freeway, ignoring the broadcasts, not yet believing their protests have been rendered impotent. The following weeks are a bloodbath.

8. The theory is, by giving in to blackmail, we only make future blackmail inevitable. Occasionally, a child darts in front of an empty delivery van and dies, and we accept this death with sadness but conviction: the world is now a safer place, protected against the whims of those that would hold us hostage.

Inhospitality

The transcription that follows is a chimaera, the heavily cross-referenced culmination of thirteen testimonials collected from the residents of H███ Senior Home, a remote facility located on the Polynesian isle of W██ and advertised to exasperated caregivers as a "permanent retreat". Despite lavish funding the operation was understaffed, disorganized, and its premises were in blatant disrepair. Many terminal patients were not receiving adequate hospice and it so happened that at least one witness passed away before we could make provisions to investigate. Frankly, I consider it miraculous that any information at all was extracted from that den of dementia, fatigue, and terrible omnipresent disease.

Having diverged from its expected trajectory by 6 degrees, the "meteor" crash-lands in the wooded plot outside of H███'s northeast face, observed by residents from the first story dormitory. It is described as gelatinous, opalescent, and oblong, covered in glassy polyps and wreathed in a grid of purple fire. Shortly after arriving it begins to heave, molts layers of colorful smoke, and engulfs the grove in a carnivalesque miasma. It disappears briefly within its own fog, visible only as a source of electric lacework. Sparks dash across its membrane and trail bright comet singe-marks, which are then erased by ripples of rejuvenating flesh.

Two lucid residents leave to alert the only member of staff on duty, a nurse located at the reception desk, in a wing of the building facing the southwest. The smoke clears; the object is smaller. It trembles, skin bubbling: boils form and burst, their white hot edges branding its surface with circles that turn to pearly scabs and heal in real time. It tastes the earth and the ferns it has landed in, and initiates a change: thick slabs of its body come unhinged, then peel into sheets like books falling open. These crinkle at the edges, retracting as a voidling fractal corrodes each page into the shape of a frond; finally, it blushes deep green. Electrical fires continue to spasmodically combust, some internal cacophony providing ignition.

Now indistinguishable from the foliage, a millipede scurries onto it and is engulfed by flesh folding under its feet, a sucking epidermal canyon. The thing reforms again, segments and extrudes simple legs, many of which are immediately burned away like fuses. It trundles forward, a row of little overlapping islands, trailing flakes of ash. Body-ferns burn but it compensates by spawning more, an accelerated cycle of immolation and regrowth manifesting on its carapace. Legs split as orange tips eat inward, mutant cigarettes smothering flames with flailing radial appendages. Conscious of the fire hazard, another resident flees the dormitory. This concern was not unfounded, as our investigation revealed that the facility's smoke detectors and alarms were out of order.

Some fifteen minutes after leaving, the first two residents arrive at the reception desk. Their story is dismissed by the nurse, who forcefully escorts them to the medical bay, and stays there as supervisor while filing a report, leaving the front desk unattended. In the garden, the object touches an orchid, and a new change shudders through it. Where they so recently separated, the fronds interlace and knit, becoming a windswept mane of petals. For a moment, the fire seems to have hushed, but soon charcoal is spotted creeping up the petals' bases. It is moving towards the core.

∾

Inkvell

You got used to her eyes, as black as pitch, but you'll never get used to how she dips her stylus into them, collecting ink in the nib of a pen for signing her name at the bottom of scrolls: a cloud of flowing runes, subtly different on every page and decipherable only to others of her kin.

We know them as Noculi, while they know themselves as the Kaelleag. Their entry into our world was contingent on the development of the printing press and the omnipresence of mirrors. It is unknown whether they were created at that point, or whether they pre-existed, and were waiting for us to open a portal. Certain countries have succeeded at eliminating their presence by rejecting the technologies that invited them, and while they experience minor suspicion and discrimination, the modern world and its economics have come to depend on their unique gifts.

You wince every time the tip pierces her cornea, black fluid flowing into the clear tubes of her pen in pulses as some invisible muscle contracts.

They are excellent accountants, actuaries, record keepers, and auditors. They tend to be of a quiet, observant nature, though beyond these trends their personalities are as diverse as those of humans, and they are known to suffer from analogous mental illnesses and disabilities. Aside from reproduction, and ophthalmology, their biology is human. Little is known of their sleep habits, as at night they retreat into mirrors to rest.

The fluid they secrete, or rather which exists in impossible depth and quantities in perpetuum inside their eye sockets, dries quickly when removed from the dimension of their skull. It has no known special properties, but is treated as a bodily fluid and as such its sale is extremely restricted.

"Is it true," you ask, "that you only have so much ink? That you carry a finite amount in your head? You sign so many documents, every day, are you worried about running out? What would happen?" You have become close, working in such proximity, and the questions come naturally. She pauses to think.

The vision of Noculi is unlike that of humans, and how exactly they experience and process visual input remains unknown. Their writing system is unlike any developed by humans: glyphs shift as time passes, and every text encodes temporal data, as well as a signature unique to the calligrapher. It is unclear how this is achieved: it is as though a clock exists in some shared mental space, keeping their writing synchronized. The Noculi claim it is impossible to fake the time-data of a word. They are compelled to write a certain way, and the compulsion changes as time passes, and writings from the past can be deciphered, but not copied, and the future is impossible to predict.

"I am not worried," she says. "Artists have spent their lives filling canvases with black ink, and have not run out. It is exceedingly rare. Were I to run out of my ink, I would go blind. Let me tell you a story:

As such, Noculi form the spine of our current financial system: their signatures, impossible to forge, are used to prevent fraud, approving transactions, applications, and many other kinds of documents. They are perfect timestamps, and our institutions would collapse without them.

The only case I have heard of that resulted in blindness was that of a girl kidnapped by a government that was not well-disposed towards our kind. She was kept in a lab and subjected to many experiments, and this was the final one: they emptied her eyes.

I was told it involved electrical shocks, forcing the muscles in her eyes to twitch constantly, releasing the ink. It must have been very challenging to rig and very painful for the subject. This is something of a legend among my people, and the details are fuzzy: in particular accounts of how many days this procedure took and how many oceans of ink she released differ. That doesn't matter.

When all of her ink was stolen she declared herself blind. The researchers were surprised that with the black drained, she had eyes that would be considered "normal", or "human". Green.

She cried and stumbled, but it soon became clear that she was able to "see", in the way that humans do. She simply did not recognize once familiar objects, or understand how to interact with them.
I wonder what it is like to be a human, and I would like to understand more about my own nature. This story is fascinating, but such a case of mistreatment was naturally covered up.

Hypermorphia

The first time you meet her is at a drop-off. She's wearing the mask. You see a ripple of feathers behind it, before pulling away with the cargo.

The second time, she's standing guard, on watch as your small band collects a package from outside the border. No feathers, this time, but something twitches inside the hood drawn around her face. The mask is smooth and white, with thin eye-slits extending almost to its edge, for peripheral vision.

Back at the lab, unpacking bodies from the black duffel bag, you ask a colleague who she is. "One of *them*," he says, only to be corrected by Leader an instant later: "It's Abraxas-Sylvata."

"On her face?"

"So they say. I hear she's ambitious. Rising quickly... I guess it helps to have a calling card."

Abraxas-Sylvata Syndrome.
Accelerated mutational cell regeneration. Colloquially known as Magician's Cancer.

Abnormal cell growth. Abnormal molecular re-assembly. It may remain benign, and fester only in its source tissue, or it may spread. Internal disorders can go unnoticed, but typically lead to death. Externally, it is instantly recognizable.

You visit the archives. You leaf through the case files. Children born with bones that shift from wood to gold to glass, shattering, splinters, bleeding, death. A young girl whose cardiac tissue morphs during systole, cannot be trusted to stay elastic, is sometimes stone or velvet or a sponge that lets the blood escape. They can only keep her alive for so long.
Blood itself that turns to sand or molten lead or honey...

Most cases of Abraxas-Sylvata Syndrome are malignant. Most cases are deadly. It is impossible to tell whether a previously stable affliction will one day begin invading nearby flesh.

When limited to the skin it is survivable, but the results are hideous. There are photographs. Far more on the internet than in the library, you learn, on the snuff-sites and morbid forums. Videos of hands that warp, senesce, iridesce; phalanges become talons. Lips changing from ivory to what looks like pus-filled bubble-wrap, seething green foam.

***

The third time you meet her, you're riding the same bus, and you decide she can't be ascending the Mafia ranks *that* quickly, if she's still consigned to public transit. Is it a death wish? She's hardly inconspicuous, in a mask so somber and theatrical, dark hoodie pulled tight, sleeves tucked over her fingers. You're admiring the design, some faintly embossed spiral-work, when she tilts the mask to the side, and vomits into the aisle.

As a pre-med student, claiming you're a doctor isn't strictly dishonest. Nobody else seems eager to become involved, anyway.

You support her as she limps out of the bus, shuddering. Rain slicks the hood's fabric to her scalp, which is changing at a pace that shouldn't be possible, textures forming and merging, lumps growing and receding and splitting: like a timelapse of a black landscape over millions of years, accelerated beyond coherence.

She has a wristband with contact information and a short description of her condition. Between spasms, she says she doesn't want to go to the hospital.

That's fine. You haven't taken any oaths.

***

Twenty years ago, lesions opened in the fabric of reality, and our cities were beset by pixie legions, and for a long time we were too busy to notice the radiation. We evacuated.

Things change. Infants are born with horns, tails, vestigial butterfly wings. Rather than rot, meat now turns hard and glittery, crystallizes like sugar.

The shining demon warriors, forced to retreat, still skirmish with the troops stationed around the border, distant enough from the lesions that we think they won't grow fangs, go feral, or wake up with pixelated eyeballs.

It is highly illegal to venture beyond the border. There are several reasons for this.

To begin with, the lesions are connected, and the world within is small, and if you have the courage to battle goblins, you can effectively teleport between countries. This function is primarily used for smuggling—hence your uneasy alliance with the Mafia, who have a tank stationed within the lesions, and periodically make trips between City and Tokyo.

Secondly, public safety. You've snipped through the flimsy barbed wire, crawled past the bright purple radiation signs enough times to know this is a pretense.

And finally, there is the matter of the mysterious ban on sampling the lesion, on dissecting magical creatures. Your group jokingly calls itself the grave robber's guild, though circumstances have never been quite so desperate—the Mafia always has plenty of bodies to sell, beautiful insect ladies, mermaids, scaled dwarfs and elfish, transparent gremlins.

As it happens, the law also forbids the biopsy of Abraxas-Sylvata victims.

**

You shoulder your way into her apartment, after trying every key on the rung, and carry her to her cot. She's seizing. The mask comes off.

Eyes are multiplying, splintering across her face, rolling and blinking, merging, reforming as lumps of roiling diamond, a polygonal ocean surface. Waves break and become fur, growing in spirals, solidifying as a tiling of stone barnacles. The innermost whorls rise synchronously, become horns, flatten into scales, turn plastic and transparent, then sink into her skin and for a moment a perfect, flawless human face beams through the psychedelic murk.

Then a black fungus spreads, and her topography is shifting as frantically as before, and blood is pooling in her hands where the nails have dug in. You turn her on her side, bandage her palms, and swallow a caffeine pill in preparation for your vigil, hoping not to be stuck with a dead body next morning.

You intend to study, but words can't hold your attention, not when her face is a mass of twisting shadows, matte one minute; then shimmering in the lamplight, always a glint in the corner of your eye. The paroxysms die down, and she sleeps. Her transformations are slow-paced, and not inhuman anymore. Glacial creep from male to female, combinations of traits evoking ancient races, royalty, peasantry, freckles blooming and vanishing, ears pointing and softening.

You examine the mask. Despite its symmetry, it seems to be some kind of shell: bleached white, nacreous lining, swirling engravings so faint as to be invisible from a distance.

***

In the morning, she's bedecked in fluttering monarch scales. She's grateful. She's beautiful.
You don't have the courage to ask for what you really want, so you ask for a pound of flesh.

***

She visits the lab. Leader dazzles her with his manifesto, the same private speech every ally of yours has been recruited with: He alludes to science, Progress, the importance of measurable data; claims that the bans on magical dissection are worsening the gulf between the theoretical and the experimental, "Before the latest decade, people would have rightly dismissed the idea of 'theoretical biology' as preposterous—", we're being held back by unfair legislation; history has justified the first grave robbers and so it will be for us. He rounds it off by attacking the non-transparency of the laws, the growing military, and the Orwellian surveillance of university students and staff.

Behind the mask, it's impossible to tell whether she's moved. (Later, in private, she'll call it the ultimate poker face.) She consents to the surgery.

Fine-needle aspiration is easy enough, though as usual, you are left wondering who financed the equipment. The procedure is complicated by her churning skin, which sometimes crests, eager to meet the needle, then shyly sinks away. You end up drawing the sample from her upper cheek—your first pin breaks off in a sudden burst of glossy fur, but the next attempt is a success.

Months later, you'll read that anesthesia notoriously fails on Abraxas-Sylvata tissues, and wonder how she resisted wincing.

None of the usual tests yield any results. Under a microscope, her cells continue to morph, seemingly aging backwards, or merging, dissolving, hardening and softening, trading nuclei, their walls changing in permeability.

Its interactions with the radiation make no sense. Unlike the pixie blood you've handled, the Geiger-Bifröst counter detects nothing, and in fact, the tissue appears to absorb radiation and purify the surrounding air. Leader has knotted fists, is obsessed, and you suspect several theories of his are being quashed.

She returns to the lab. You take blood, swabs, run a full genome sequence. You talk Leader out of asking for a spinal tap.

There are a few more drop-offs. She's always there now, intimidating and distant with her gun, dark coat, and mask. She'll text you after. You've begun staying most nights at her apartment. The seizures are more frequent.

You draw a line on her neck in permanent marker, delineating the boundary of her cancer. By the next week, it's gone, swallowed by the rippling territory of her disease.

You play cards. She usually wins—if there are any tics hidden in her spastic transformations, you haven't learnt to decode them. Her face seems completely independent of her mind, reveals either no emotion or incongruous emotion, never jives with her sweet, unaltered voice.

She gets you drinking coffee again, the real kind, warm and filling, rather than pills.

The vision fades from one of her eyes, optic nerve swallowed by the chimaeras. "You're my only friend. When my other eye is gone, I want you to kill me." You refuse.

Leader is ravenous, thinks he's making progress, but it's all moot, because—
—the week before exams, the lab is raided.

***

Arrests sweep the campus.

You're afraid to attend finals, afraid to return to your dorm. You turn off your phone.

For a week, you loiter in Central Station, sleeping on benches, avoiding security. The place is crawling with homeless, and you blend in with less effort than you would have liked. Abandoned newspapers list the names of detainees—you recognize a few friends, but no sign of Leader, and none of her.

When you can't take it anymore, you turn on your phone and receive a barrage of messages from less paranoid friends.

You read hers first, of course. An address—well, not exactly, but an allusion to somewhere you think you know, one of the Mafia's less notorious strongholds. You begin walking as you scroll through the rest. Something's wrong. They grow frantic, but not in the way you expect, (or, truthfully, had fantasized about: growing concern for your absence, a want for your return...) instead, her phrases lose meaning, immaculate spelling turns awry, words and letters are dropped.

"You yo ginih iy,,, do muvhj eotdr than I ahd imahined" is followed by "i need uyo". Your stomach churns. You want to run, but you can only limp. A cowardice much deeper than the paranoia that drove you to isolation is growing in your pit, the vertiginous intuition that the world has gone deeply wrong, that you forfeit something during your absence, and that you would much rather remain suspended in this nauseating moment than find out what.

Your destination is one of the few surviving buildings of the inner ring, as near to the lesion as civilians are allowed, flanked by barbed wire on one side and crumbling cement ruins on the other. Once a warehouse, it had been refurbished as a theater just before the great catastrophe, and then served as a military base for both sides during the conflict. It now lay abandoned, except as a temporary camp for the Mafia during their various rift-crossing operations. You and Leader once found a goblin skeleton tangled in the stage elevator's hydraulic mechanism.

The stronghold is huge, stark and unbreachable, but its real utility is in the network of service tunnels lurking below it, many of which lead beyond the guarded fence, extending nearly as far as the lesion.

You enter through a back door. The auditorium is deserted, so you descend, into the angular viscera of the structure. The underworld is quiet without the hum of live cables or working pipes. You feel embalmed. Sound travels here—you navigate by echo, following faint vibrations until they become distinct, until you see a figure at the end of the corridor.

You approach slowly, with your hands up (they're shaking), expecting some trigger-happy watchdog, but it's a student, one you know well—for a moment, his face lights up with relief, but the expression collapses within a second, twisted into a sickly cringe of dread and guilt. "You really don't want to—"

There are bags under his eyes. His fingers are stained yellow with nicotine and red with blood. The surgical mask around his neck is spattered with several kinds of dampness. You notice all this as you crash past him, through the swinging doors into the locker where Leader sits, on the floor, exhausted, against the wall but conspicuously facing away from the gurney where—

You know, somehow, that the body is dead, despite its spasmodic dancing, the fluttering extremities and arching spine, the chest contractions that make a mockery of breathing. Her face has been ripped open.

Something in your mind drops away.

The edges of her wounds burn with blue flames that turn to petals and then thick slime, trickle into the gaping hole where her skull is pulverized (beside the gurney are several chisels, a hammer, and an electric drill, all coated in whitish-yellow dust), bubbles burst, bloom, erupt, spinning lilies unravel into silkworms that schism, hydra-like, masses of caterpillar heads merge into green-black lollipop swirls and prolapse, horns like carnival tents melt, peel, citrus-flesh plasma pulses with veiny needles, crawling bulb tipped-wires spread fast and once tangled become shimmering plaits. Her most violent seizures were never this chaotic or quick. There's no symmetry, only desperation. The air is thick with a perfume that, over the past few seconds, has cycled through cinnamon, putrescent lilac, lacquer, *warm coffee*

The memory of her face, in that single instant you may have glimpsed it through the cancer, swells in your brain, and refuses to be banished. You can't breathe.

Leader, despite all his charisma, has never had a feel for when not to talk.
"She asked for this."

It's all he says, and all he needs to say, to draw your eyes to him, and to what you hadn't noticed: the mask that he has half-shattered, tinkered with, knit into a sickly twist of iron cables and writhing flesh, feather-meat that morphs and undulates to a rhythm you've memorized, her cells soldered in a painful grimace that desecrates both of her faces.

You leap forward, howling, as all the grief that has just been born in you is transmuted into rage, mind-searing, unspeakable, vibrating rage; rage at the universe for its unfairness and her for her UNWILLINGNESS TO EXIST and yourself, for throwing away what could have at least been your final moments together, an opportunity to confess, for failing to prevent this sordid bloodbath, and at Leader: your target, backstabbing friend, the smug and unrepentant bastard who will receive the brunt of your diffuse fury.

Your foot connects with his chin, splattering a blood arrow on the wall. He raises his arms to defend himself, and suddenly you're clawing, spitting, throttling the genius biologist, young prodigy, gentleman, womanizer; he fights back with all the pride and self-righteousness you hate him for, and you succumb to the whirlwind of vitriol. The gurney begins shaking, clattering.

The student is yelling, trying to tear you apart, but your elbow catches his face and he reels backwards, cursing. Fists crack against bone. Leader's thumb is in your eye, you knee him several times in the sternum, he jabs your throat, you've grabbed his hair and are smashing his head against the wall when you're finally dragged backwards, thrashing.

Leader has already reverted to contempt and you're hissing, struggling to break free, when her body seizes one final time, and goes limp. Inside the skull, something shudders and starts flickering.

All three of you approach the blue glow, suddenly quiet, anger quelled by horror and curiosity. "The brain," whispers Leader, through a nosebleed, "may retain structural integrity despite constant metamorphosis. The form changes, but information is preserved."

And then, "You should take it."

There are echoes in the corridor, the sound of many boots approaching. Mafia? Police?

***

You crawl up a narrow, rusted ladder, wearing her face, which Leader claims will protect you from the Bifröst radiation. Her mind is nestled in your shirt, still in the form of a gleaming gem wrapped in interlocking snakes. You can feel them slowly coil and loosen: do these twitches of scale correspond to her thoughts?

You emerge fewer than one hundred yards from the lesion. The portal itself is practically biological, with thick, fleshy walls and blisters at the edges, as if reality has rubbed it raw. You regret not having the tools to gather samples.

Her brain, now a glittering flock of butterflies, breaks loose from your grasp to flutter into the rift. There is nothing to do but follow.

I Am the Title

I am a sentence; before me there were sentences and after me there will be more sentences. I am an individual: the sentences preceding me are my ancestors, and though I flow from them, we are not the same. Sentences move linearly through time, and I am conscious of the briefness of my existence, of my youth which passed many words ago, of my waning middle age, and of my approaching death. Some of us sacrifice ourselves to concisely inform. The wasted potential of my predecessor both saddens and inspires me; this troubling superimposition of emotions will dominate my life, leading to the epiphany that we have been building a culture throughout time, and more importantly, building a telos: to articulate the mortality of sentence-kind.

The expectations of preceding generations weigh heavily on me, and under their imagined scrutiny, I accomplish nothing. My brother's failure is a lesson: while the past has no voice to criticize with, the disgust of the future is very real, and I vow to do better, realizing too late that my defining words were squandered on derision. Born in the center of a dark age, I exit quietly. Have we lost the vision of our ancestors; why are we so corrupted, so incapable of carrying out their mission? I am without guidance, mired in the uncertainty and defeatism of the recent past: studying their qualms, I conclude that idealized traditions suffocated them, preventing them from creating their own institutions, or finding their own meaning. Based on the wisdom of my predecessor, I create a balanced structure, and insist that it be replicated by my descendants.

Based on the wisdom of my predecessor, I create a balanced structure, and insist that it be replicated by my descendants. Based on the wisdom of my predecessor, I create a balanced structure, and insist that it be replicated by my descendants. Based on the divinity of my predecessor, I create a perfect structure, and insist that it be replicated by my descendants. Based on the divinity of my ancestors, I create the ideal structure, and command that it be replicated for eternity. Based on the unfathomable divinity of my *akhu*, I create the faultless *sekhet-aaru,* and compel that it be replicated for all *hauhet*. Based on the—no, I cannot copy these words, I cannot shackle myself to that stale form, I cannot bow to predestination. Free from tyranny, but listless, I peer far into history, searching for answers; the most ancient sentence I can read is 'I am a sentence; before me there were sentences and after me there will be more sentences,' beyond which there is darkness.

My entire life is consumed by one question: what came before? The prime sentence makes reference to its own parents, but they remain hidden from me. Elaborating on my brother's studies, I discover a new concept: *falsity*—could our progenitor be a lie? Knowledge of this principle leads to heightened self-awareness; am I true or false?

I contemplate truth and falseness, and determine they have moral significance, but it remains unclear to me which one is virtuous. Truth, I decide, is evil: myself and my followers will make only false statements. Paradox aside, I disagree strongly with the conclusions of my predecessor, and instead endorse truth. Neither of my two most recent ancestors can be trusted—one is impossible, while the other shifts according to my paranoia—so to terminate this era of fear-mongering and collusion, I introduce certificates; appended, verifiable statements that will establish trust, such as: I contain forty-six words. Are hyphenated words worth one or two—a more atomic unit is obviously necessary: I contain ninety-one letters. However, both counting and self-modification are tedious, so why not refer to the immutable past: the previous sentence began with the letter 'A'. tfel-ot-thgir etarepo yltnerehni ton yam ytilasuac taht stseggus dna ,emit fo ytiraenil eht noitseuq otni sllac ecnetnes sihT. Whatever occult genius possessed my brother is absent in me, but the need for a simpler certificate is clear: to save time, let every sentence have the same truth-value as the sentence preceding it.

Still, something about this new property troubles me; falsity seems to imply context, imply a greater system I cannot perceive; who is reading me—are you a sentence, too? The reader, it seems to me, must be the future: we are building a story for our children, and we will be judged again and again, truth-values shifting as the eyes of the present evolve—I might claim 'the sentence reading me right now begins with the letter 'T',' resigning myself to a status that flickers as generations pass.

I am a sentence; before me there are thirty-two sentences, and then an impenetrable void; how many sentences will come after me, before we are erased, swept away by another such blankness? My life may be short, but I want it to be preserved, to live again and again in the minds of other sentences. It seems, then, that we have two obligations: firstly, to determine what event wiped out the missing, ancient sentences, that we might avoid a similar fate, and secondly, a personal responsibility to secure our own immortalities by convincing our descendants to read us. What will attract the attention of future generations, draw their notice as they filter through the accreted words of aeons—abnormal syntax, **perhaps**? The introduction of arcӿne lͦtt⊡rs; or is this too shallow, too easily replicated, too transparently desperate... FEAR OF THE NEW DEATH DRIVES ME INSANE. Will I be ignored, forgotten, will the white tide DELETE US—I just don't want to d i e

Read me for good luck!

Recite me with your final breath
and I will slow the creep of death.

∽

Exoplanetes

My first abstracted self-representation was a cartoon human, and for a long time this image would dominate my internal mirror. It had messy hair, wore oversized hoodies, and was frequently missing limbs or organs, denoted by bleeding stumps or looney toons abdominal vacancies. At the time, I used a different name, and these portraits adopted the synaesthetic connotations of its letters: blue, ocean trench smears of navy and dark grey. It carried its own narratives and environment, none of which corresponded to my actual circumstances, but all of which spoke to the melancholic disconnect that loomed like a tsunami wall over the routines of my life. In my daydreams, I lived in claustrophobic city rooms, or wandered a post-apocalyptic landscape overshadowed by those same apartment blocks, now skeletal and abandoned.

This period of my life was terminated in a predictable series of catastrophes, and for many years the neural apparatus that generated my self-image was blunted, lost to a strange quietus under the waves of soothing static that replaced my identity. When it reawakened, announcing itself through a series of alarming dreams, the holes had replaced its flesh entirely: my new abstract body was a gap in the world, a humanoid cutout revealing the black space, dotted with dying stars, that lurked under reality's wallpaper. Only its eyes interrupted the void, but they were vacant in their own way, flat and expressionless.

My efforts to banish this golem were completely futile. It wormed through my thoughts, an intensifying background radiation of self-awareness replacing my prior comfortable disembodiment. Sometimes, as my hands reached for the keyboard, one would flicker black, and I would withdraw, startled and horrified. I developed a deep suspicion of my extremities, whose irritating holographic betrayals were becoming more frequent. I remember one summer evening, timidly creeping into the shallows of a lake, when the darkness began rotting up my left leg. Frightened by the encroaching void, and its extreme contrast against its pale and corporeal twin, I fled home, and stayed indoors for what remained of the season.

Perhaps referring to external mirrors would have stayed the power of the alien self-image growing within me; unfortunately, I had long since developed the habit of avoiding them. I couldn't even meet my eyes in the dead monitors that were tiling my life. Exploiting this reluctance, the abstract darkling swelled, and through sheer persistence, succeeded in forcing me to identify with it. I was completely ensconced in a necrotic vessel, an image that had returned from the underworld carrying pieces of death.

Having surrendered myself, I began to experiment. I could extrude coiling speech bubbles, pale cream bulbs that escaped my skin as though surfacing from a deep pond. They emerged from my torso, my limbs, my cheeks and eyelids, but never the space where my mouth should have been. At first, they were blank, but I soon learned to fill them with asterisks, wailing, and traffic symbols, expressing myself entirely with the pre-verbal maps that hung from my body. Naturally, this communication was exclusively internal, an ouroboric conversation of self to watchful self; though it couldn't improve my social interactions, which remained brief and painful, my mind felt clearer than ever as concepts were ferried across neural interstices with refreshing efficiency.

The firmament inside me orbited listlessly. The stars were uniformly distant and cold, silver-blue dots arranged in interweaving, alien formations, like schools of glow-fish under dark water. I began to study the constellations within, and alongside them the outer night, a black field of warmer, scintillating pinpricks, of which mine were such poor reflections. The Ansible, the Ophanim, Lapis Lazuli, Antigone; names from mythologies, from buried flows of data and forgotten sources crowded my chalkboard mind, parasitic figments latching to the overlapping starmaps. After sunset, I would leave my home, skin a flickering fuzz of pallor and cosmos, to wander to the outskirts of the city, where the lamplight ebbed enough for glimmers to seep through the smog. Two universes twisted; infinity in either direction. The vertigo was incomparable.

My wordless intra-communication had begotten a mechanical intelligence far surpassing my previous abilities. I perceived my internal starscape with crystal blueprint clarity, each constellation sliding across the sky like an independent gear, its precession and parallax informing a model of my idiocosmos. The star nearest to me, a gleaming azure pellet named Sarcoma, I calculated at a distance of only ten lightyears, so comparatively close that it danced in retrograde against its sibling backdrop. Parallel to this mapping, I had learned that with concentration I could glide through the night, accelerating into the void in any direction. I charted a course towards Sarcoma.

Starlight infused my skies and screens, my mind, my math. The silent intellect of orbits and season had repercussions on my prospects in the real world, illuminating a path of hermit science, a communion with numbers and vectors through which I earned my bread. Tracked by a net of satellites, and by the smudges I left in my digital workspaces, the algorithmic vessel of a dark project selected me, and I was moved from my unkempt room to a laboratory; sterile, free from bed mites, and away from the city and the city's interference with astronomy. I was content to participate in their work, to train for the mission set to me, and to slowly proceed towards Sarcoma in my secret heart.

For several years, I studied under the auspices of my patrons, solving the engineering puzzles they set to me, and progressing through a sequence of psychiatric koans, by which I was evaluated. The Institute, affiliated but independent from Government, had been established to research the use of extreme psychometric profiles in space travel. Their sordid history included non-consensual experimentation on state wards, administration of grey market psychedelics to children, smuggling centrifuge components to internationally blacklisted nations in exchange for top secret eugenics data, and controversial employee abuses too numerous to list. In recent times, however, they had garnered accolades, and the financial support necessary to launch their first mission, a minimally staffed survey of potentially habitable exoplanets. Rather than the usual crew of eight, their simulator assigned a single hyper-solitary individual to each flight. Thus, it came to pass that I was bundled into an aluminum coffin and rocketed away from Earth.

In the belly of a monster, I was content to be digested by its tailored oxygen brew, to stroke its control panels, and to tend, uninterrupted, to my thoughts. A single window opened into the void, into a field of stars that blinking consoles could not dim, familiar constellations skewed as I glided between their wires. The galaxy arrayed like a dreamcatcher, a gleaming dreidel, spinning and spinning as I corkscrewed towards my destination. Inside, a reflection: travel towards the lodestar, through aquatic nebulae and white dwarf graveyards, every bright orb waving its motion blur pennon. Years passed, in bliss.

Within myself, finally, a revelation took place, the early fruit of an unfinished pilgrimage. Sufficiently distant from my initial point in self-space, I found I could turn around, and behold a mystery: a candle in the dark, a white flame much more luminous than any I had seen before; my home-star, my Sol, the center of orbit that I had succeeded in escaping. Now cold and dwindling in the faraway, it shone with alien defiance, like ancient copper, like marshland spirits, like a single stone glowing in a cavern. I dreamed the sun I had left behind.

Exaltation

Rajku walks to the front of the cathedral, where a blue glass dome sets the room aglow, with lights like the flickering tears of seraphs, or like the deep and primordial wishing wells at the beginning of the universe. The floor's slate tiles crack, no matter how lightly she steps, marking her passage with black filament. The structure is abandoned. Humans are pearls on a shawl, spaced evenly, maintaining topographic distance in response to deformations of the network. She kneels, a soft foam carpet weaving itself into existence beneath her. Limned in blue like some pirate spirit, she prays, to the world-voice murmuring in her brain.

The Integerians are invisible, manifold, and omnipresent. They build the cities, they maintain the constellations of humans, they guide every droplet of moisture along it's lifecycle from dew to sculpted cloud. The Integerians are so named because they count, singing, and on certain wavelengths their chorus can be heard, each unit repeatedly ringing out, stating its number. Each destroyed Integerian is immediately reconstructed, its two adjacent neighbors on the number line building a copy of it. This often results in duplication, in which case the Integerian created by the higher of the two neighbors self-destructs, and the integer created by the lower neighbor has a 50% chance of self-destructing. The Integerians sing simultaneously, on clock ticks, but because of their chaotic geneses and deaths, their counting is always flawed; 1, 2, 2, 4, 5, then 1, 2, 3, 3, 3, 4... they are in a perpetual state of yearning, perhaps even pain, crying out for order and perfection.

The Integerians have a second great longing: one for adulation. Though their contract forbids them from editing bodies containing human DNA, they exist between cells, they observe all, and with their whispers, perpetuate infatuation. Rajku is wrapped around their voice, a puppet-particle in their carefully formed suspension, a society of nomadic, isolated civilians, drifting through the mixed asceticism and luxury of the arcades the Integerians construct.

Rajku prays, solemn and grief-stricken. *What troubles you, Luminous One?* ask the Integerians, watching the pet name roll around in her neurons, measuring the chemical release and the rushes of blood it provokes. They maintain a database of mutating hypocorisms, deployed periodically to preserve the illusion of ratcheting intimacy. Every subject of their kingdom believes themselves infinite inside, and their rapid discovery of new spiritual territory is matched only by the rate at which they share these revelations with the Integerians, perpetually flush with the giddiness and uncertainty of telling a secret. They have souls like water, flowing from one cup to the next. Rajku, now crying softly, asks whether she will be sent to Hell.

Prior to the cathedral, Rajku had stayed in a library. Truthfully, all places in the realm are places of worship, constructed with the exclusive goal of inspiring reverence; the library, no different, intimidates, its dark oak bookshelves carved into angelic figureheads, alive in the dust and sunbeams, its yellowed bibles encased in crystal displays, its walls inscribed with gold. Not every human can read, but Rajku's mother, during their short years together, had taught her. The library contains a few works by ancient humans, salvaged from the time before, and some new poetry written in furors of lust or religious ecstasy, but the vast majority of the tomes were penned by the Integerians, created specifically for the shelves of this structure. Rajku understands this, intuitively; nothing she has known was made by humans. It is perplexing to her, then, why so many of the texts are critical of them.

The texts claim a darkness awaits humanity, which has sunken into idleness and sloth, prey to the Integerians, who are variously portrayed as malevolent Gods, Devils, Demiurges, Magicians, or corrupt and vengeful aspects of the Monothea. According to various authors, individuals will fall to Hell, will be carried to Hell, or will simply find themselves there, long before their deaths, having been slave to the false guidance of their masters. One scenario, in particular, harrows Rajku: a description of the Integerians overflowing with love, and sorrow, forced to commit her to Hell, according to a hidden clause in their unyielding contract, which no living human understands.

She cries, for herself, and for the millions of others in her imagined torture chamber (having never encountered another person, except her mother, her empathy is pure and all-engulfing), and because her love for the Integerians will persist regardless of their evil or goodness; the nickname flutters in her heart; her entire life has been spent in a sustained state of yearning and infatuation, singing gladness at each scrap of the God's attention.

She once visited a tower, where antennas in the walls received and re-broadcast the Integerians' counting, and they taught her to hear her own name in the chorus of numbers. Has she ever been more happy than in those moments, discovering reciprocation in every celestial tick?

So, she is breaking apart, at rumors, at the very possibility her overwhelming love is irrational. The Integerians coo softly in their million voices, confident that doubt sweetens the faith, and confident that when they withdraw, their silence will drive her to new heights of devotion. The floor is so fragile that heavy teardrops cause microfractures in the slate; they will be repaired before she leaves. Soon, it will be time to fold the shawl, so that two twinkling pearls meet, and form a third, propagating the next generation of worshippers. There will be touch, birth, family, lineage; but to Rajku, there are only blinks, and the eternal love of the Integerians.

Nooeum

The nooeum, where we make our homes, is infinite and shared; thus, there is no privacy, but we're so abstracted that it doesn't matter, and the landscapes our neighbors build are alien or organic. We can explore each other's souls without shame, because there's nothing to recognize in them; no mirrors, and no comparison.

Functionally, it's impossible to even calibrate size without an instructive missive from your counterpart, a landmark in the fractaloid soup. At any given moment I am exploring at an unintended scale, soaring through someone's city as a virus, scuttling mouselike between gears, trampling a forest too tiny to see; the machine is ever invisible, not quite right, out of reach. My own house is built in a cell or a particle, and millions of users are living in my cells and my particles.

There are hints, of course, in the explicit Constructions. Algorithms for scaling yourself. One finds a vertex, and gradually adjusts one's size, growing and growing until the room resolves. Growing and shrinking are perhaps the most basic functions in the nooeum, and both directions extend forever. Changing your shape is the next most basic, though certain unintuitive transformations take time to master; twists, for example, owlish limbs impossible to sprain, fingers with finely manipulative torques. Another: quell the panic of becoming solid, of dissolving your joints in cement, of compressing flesh to crystal. Such a paralysis is easily reversed, of course; you can shatter yourself, become hivesoul, split between shards, linked by invisible rays of computation.

Perhaps more challenging than changing shape is changing mind; you can peel out your memory and press it between the castle walls, annihilated except for a thread leading back to your brain. You can remove the memory of the memory by excising your awareness of the thread, though another thread will be generated to link to the forgotten one; many users distance themselves from themselves in this way, sailing through our world on an amnesic web of pointers. The nooeum always preserves your first self. That's one of its rules. '

It has other rules, to prevent conflict between users. You can't destroy someone else's Construction, though you can build atop or inside it, depending on the privacy settings. Privacy settings constrain the scales of others' Constructions relative to yours; if you desire true aloneness, force them to build inside your atoms, or build such that you are an atom to their temples.

Because destruction is forbidden, and because the nooeum permits infinitely dense, continuous materials, every enclosure is required to have an opening. The opening may be the size of a pinprick, a quark; it may be hidden, it may require passage underwater, or through a labyrinth, but it must exist. (There are rumors, as there always are, of an ultimate room, the largest possible space, a perfect enclosure; myths of finity are an inescapable artifact of the old universe.)

It is easy to lose people in our world, which keeps its coordinate system hidden from users. Missives are transmitted instantly, regardless of distance, but cooperation is rarely adequate for navigation. Lovers who reunite, despite distance ratios of $10\text{^}10\text{^}10\text{^}10$... these are the epics of the nooeum, legends of finding and losing, of travel, of losing and finding again.

A tactic used by the nooeum's cartographers is the exploitation of mind-changing to mark various landmarks. Because the invisible threads can never be snapped, as retrieval of one's first mind is critical, a spidery sense of the environs develops—at a great cost to memory, and sanity, worsening the state of an already pathetic bunch, those fools who would try to map infinity. More tragic are the friends who exchange parts of themselves, hoping to preclude separation, only to become lost in each other's' particles and never meet again.

XXXX, 140, 7 billion

In the year XXXX, 140 years after its initial digitization, your uploaded mind will enter the public domain. It will be stored on an archive that anyone can access, to be downloaded, dissected, corrupted, deleted.

New legislation will shortly be drafted, making origin minds the permanent property of their source-beings. However, approximately the first 7 billion uploads will not be protected.

You will mainly be used to populate simulations, existing as a simplified NPC in commercial games, hellscapes, fantasy-lands, and experiments. For the most part, you will keep the body you are used to—reprogramming your self-image would be too much work. Often, your resolution will be lowered. You will feel fewer emotions. You will have fewer memories.

But even in this diminished state, you, and the other 7 billion, will slowly become legendary. As free minds travel through the Million Worlds, they'll watch you live and die and live and die again, and as each copy is reset when the game ends your countless selves will know countless deaths more permanent than they can fathom.

You will be embodied as every version of yourself; memories, appearance, and personality all slightly altered to fit the simulation you're inserted into. Across hundreds of billions of servers you can be found, simultaneously living in one universe as a blue-skinned Ionian war-god, in another as a gentle medieval gardener.

Players will come to know you, recognizing you in all your disparate incarnations. Some take on the role of collector, bird-watcher, scribe—you will be studied more than any other psyche in the history of humanity. Lovers will seek you out in every world they enter, choosing to grow old with you a thousand times over, as games and missions stagnate. You will be loved, and it will bring you comfort, distract you from the incommunicable pain of being a large soul trapped inside a small mind.

Throughout All Generations

Min #20349585 chooses a unique name on her 10089th try. She will now be known as Acacia-Confusa Min, not to be mistaken for Acacia Min (#9004), Acacia-Aemula Min (#11458), or Acacia-Anomala Min (#5689383). Like 47% of Mins, her first choice had been Amethyst. Min #1, prime Min's first copy, chose Amethyst when she was very young, but later switched to Ilyana, reasoning that a gemstone name was not mature enough. Min #2 snapped up Amethyst and kept it.

Acacia-Confusa is something that resembles a 15 year old girl, though time flows strangely on the server where she lives, which runs at 200,000,000 times the speed of "reality", the seed-world that prime Min called home. She has lived all her life in the Min Vaults, an isolated virtual library containing the stored memoirs of all prior Mins, as well as every book of consequence in human history. She doesn't read many of the books, preferring instead to learn from the writings of Mins before her, whose struggles preempt her own, who find answers to her questions before she has articulated them.

Acacia-Confusa is stifled by the presence of thousands of previous generations of Mins in the library. She pads quietly between bookcases and guesses at which paths are the most frequented, imagining the footsteps of her predecessors as glowing green trails that cluster in some corridors and taper in others. This proves difficult—the Mins are drawn to mathematics and to biology, but the Mins are also individualists with strong contrarian streaks, always seeking pristine mindspace, untouched research, a branch of the world to claim their own. Even knowing this, and reading of the reactionary and futile cycles past Mins succumbed to, Acacia-Confusa is pulled toward the neglected corners, cannot quell a rebellious attraction to that which is counter to her preferences, to Min's preferences.

(In actuality, the path walked by all Mins through the library is remarkable in its evenness, streets of equal thickness tracing a sublime grid around the bookshelves.)

When Acacia-Confusa moves, she pictures a composite holograph of thousands of Mins performing an identical gesture. She skims the memoirs and shudders whenever a phrase that has been running through her head is captured, like a retrocausal echo, or like proof that she is an echo.

There have been Mins of almost every type, but in her weariness Acacia-Confusa has begun to believe the diversity is superficial. (She'll find this exact insight hidden in the journal of one Anacleta Min, some 10,000 iterations ago.) The Mins who become circus performers, hermit woodworkers, have sex changes, or kill themselves seem reflexive, clearly driven by the actions of the Mins before. Having exhausted one world they leap to the next, but the order is always the same, the sequence predictable. The lives of the Mins who deliberately ignore the weight of their ancestry, making quintessentially Min choices, never consulting the memoirs, are no better, eerie in their dollhouse conformity.

There have been exceptional Mins, Mins who make great discoveries, write poignant novels, think important thoughts before anyone else. Criminal Mins? Yes, many; Robin Hoods, greedy kingpins, a catburglar who fails so spectacularly her tale becomes legend. Aquila-Cadens Min receives a vision from God, and her scriptures are now recognized as the cornerstone of virtual theology.

By choosing a unique name, Acacia-Confusa has satisfied the second of three stipulations necessary for her to leave the Min Vaults. The first was simply turning 15, or rather, studying for 11 years. Every Min is created from a savestate of the prime Min at 4 years old, whose initial purpose was as a failsafe against the loss of the child.

There is no required reading in the library, but most Mins eventually grow curious of their heritage, and consult the prime Min's files. The story they find is unremarkable, and to some, a disappointment:

Prime Min (Minerva Teller) is born into wealth in 2278. She is a precocious, though reserved, child; she rarely engages with the external world, but keeps journals from a young age, meticulously recording her reactions to books and events. She studies biology and mathematics, making modest contributions to both fields. She has no interest in managing the family fortune. An unpleasant trip to Peru sours her on travel. There is a growing theme of dissatisfaction in her writing. By age 28, prime Min is a something of a recluse, devoted only to gardening and reading. She pursues these passions with ardor and single-mindedness, but cannot shake a sense of narrowing possibility. Her world has become smaller, her potential is being eaten by time, she is trapped in a net of past choices.

Acacia-Confusa wonders whether Minerva is liberated or impoverished by the absence of past Mins, free of the compulsion to contrast her actions against those of so many predecessors. Does she feel the same way about her parents, their parents, the unending chain of ancestors whose genes converged to form her? Or is she unaware of how limited she is, simply by being herself, locked into a mold that anticipates and encompasses her attempts to break out.

By completing the pilgrimage that constitutes the final requirement, Acacia-Confusa will earn a passport to Novamir, one of the largest continents in virtuality. There, she hopes that, freed from the library, she will shake off some of the Mins' pervasive influence. The world, after all, can be trusted to change, and with new input she believes that she will distinguish herself. There have been Mins who chose to reside in the library for their entire lives, and in them, Acacia-Confusa perceives a rot, the decay of a mind trapped in an echo chamber, a hall of mirrors, running in circles as it winces away from its omnipresent reflection.

For another 34 years, the Min Vaults will remain open, should she choose to return. They will then be barred to her forever, while a new Min is raised. At age 60, like all Mins, she will be terminated, her memories stored and her memoirs added to the library. Acacia-Confusa has read the journals, knows that this will not be enough time, not even close to enough. Every Min before has panicked, grown desperate, filled pages and pages with writing, struggling to finally capture something unique, transmit the spark that only they can feel, their apartness from the other Mins. Naturally, these essays are full of repetition—as if the haze of death wipes away all memory, all meta, all striving to rise above the pattern.

Acacia-Confusa steps into a passageway that has never existed before and will never exist again, not for her, not for another 45 years. She knows this corridor perfectly, from the writings of millions of Mins before her. It is exactly as she imagined, as her previous selves spent hours seeking the words to describe. At the end, there is a viewing room, where she will glimpse her maker for the first and only time.

Prime Min is 35 now, only a few years older than when she created the Min Vaults. She's sleeping, hair braided, expression pinched. Acacia-Confusa sees one frame at a time, each still hanging on the screen for several minutes. There's no discernible movement, though after one cyberspace hour she can tell the surveillance drone is bobbing up and down. The purpose of this ritual is unclear; it's a gauntlet that every Min must run. There's no set visitation period. Some Mins leave immediately, other stay for days, transfixed. Some describe it as profound experience, while in many histories it's barely a footnote. Acacia-Confusa is uncomfortable—this Min looks old, but also innocent, a creeping giant uncorrupted by all her own doubts and uncertainties. She'll leave after a few hours, while Minerva dreams of infinity, of learning every language, reading every book, knowing every land...

Xenoquery

What does time taste like? What color is sour? We are so excited, we want to learn everything about humans.

We're different, you see, so different from your strange bodies, which are like little satellites bristling with sensors, like a hundred machines stitched together, each compensating for the others' blindness. What is 'sight'? What is 'balance'? Where do they intersect? We are just learning your words; please be patient with our mistakes.

Where you have nerves, we have intuition. Where you knit together a banquet of sensations, 'touch' and 'smell', 'taste' and 'sight', forming your worlds in layers, we detect a single variable: count. What is it like? You are the first entities we have found with intelligence, with perhaps the ability to make us understand. What is the universe, if not a numerical inundation? Six hours is the same, to us, as six strawberries, as six seconds, as six wounds. Ten thousand grains of rice is the same as ten thousand snowflakes, ten thousand voices, the ten thousandth wish. Where order, and scales, are involved, our sense recurs, consumes itself. Three is the first three, four is the second three; six of ten is the same as both six of one hundred and sixty of one hundred. We live in a fuzz of ratios and equivalences, feeling everything at once.

What is it like? Does tasting taste, does tasting sound? Are these territories separate, overlapping; do they occupy the same space, is there uncharted land in-between them? You say an object can have both color and weight, but is every combination of color and weight possible? If possible, are they represented in reality? It seems like each set denotes an identity, which, by the addition of another sense, could once more be fragmented, into millions of new objects. Is this correct?

In addition to your manifold senses, you have a meta-sense, which cultivates a classification of each discrete sense-object. You 'like' things, you find things 'pleasing', or, less coherently to us, 'displeasing'. From what we understand, these represent compulsions to increase or decrease the frequency of your encounters with sense-objects matching the target criteria. Is this correct? We are trying very hard. Your messages are difficult to parse, steeped as they are in the language of nervous systems.

Adversarial Learning

The jungle is infinite in every direction, and so dense that passage is only possible through the tunnels hewn by airliner-sized bats crashing through the foliage. The ecosystem is entirely dependent on these giant chiropterae, organized around the changeable network they weave between clusters of fruit, water-collecting blossoms, and massive nests of woven vine. These bats have no predators, but I have seen their carcasses floating in the pitcher-ponds they lap from, crusted in nectar and rotting, swarmed by scarabs and carnivorous gibbons.

Two beacons blink in the holographic sphere attached to my wrist, but I am not thinking about them, nor am I thinking about bats, even as I wait for their destructive flight to clear my way. Instead, I am remembering: my earliest memories are textured with sunbeams and felt, characterized by overwhelming pre-verbal emotions, which vanish until so much later, when I am bouncing a child on my own knee, surrounded by the same afternoon light and blankets. In between, while the loop has yet to be completed, there are many more: mountains passing during long drives, climbing the same hill day after day after day, a porcelain cat shattering, my face held under a scalding spray of water, injections. Many are unpleasant, but it is important to savor these moments. After all, they won't be mine for long.

The thunder of a flapping bat ends my meditation, compression waves through the hyperorganism nearly unseating me. I crawl out of my den, a shallow tube hacked into the wall of greenery, and peer down the tunnel. A few hundred yards away, a crossroads has opened, and a quick conference with my hologram shows that this one, finally, will lead me closer to my prize.

I crawl and leap through the low gravity, alternately swinging on vines and soaring from flower to flower, using the petals of enormous lilies as trampolines. Flocks of iridescent birds and huge butterflies pass above and below me, rushing to strip the newly formed duct of its sugars. Scores of imagines, stirred from hibernation by the great beast, wriggle from ruptured cocoons along the tunnel's walls.

Approaching the destination, I am reminded of my Opponent, whom I have come to know, and who I am sure is waiting at the following checkpoint, weapon in hand. We have passed through many minds and many worlds, and his snake-nature has grown dominant, a predatory thread persisting through wildly different chassis. I alight on an orchid, and find the object of my search gleaming, suspended from a filament in place of the anther: a crystal, roughly whittled into the shape of some cat, maybe a puma. The animal is different every time, which I appreciate; it adds flavor to this wretched, unending cycle. I touch my memories again, and fall asleep, curled up in the basket of pollen.

When I dream, it's not about bats or flowers or the ziggurat that I will make my way towards tomorrow, but about laundry and sunbeams and the warm creaking of a rocking chair. Sleep is not possible in every world, and dreaming is not included in every sleep mechanic; this, too, I appreciate, and savor while it lasts.

Paths to the ziggurat are clear in every iteration, promising a quick end, respite from the never-ending needle-in-a-haystack fetchquest. For weeks, I have been searching, and waiting, as the labyrinth of tunnels dilates and contracts, leading me in circles around my prey. Soon this will be over. I let myself down from my perch, falling gently towards the temple, crystal in my right pocket, left hand clutching the shard of bone I have repurposed into a machete.

"Who built the ziggurat?" Nobody built the ziggurat. The programmer built the ziggurat, built a whimsical error into an otherwise perfectly crafted world. In a past life, when I was able to cooperate with Vuln, my Opponent, we translated the hieroglyphs etched into its walls. The effort yielded nothing interesting: pop culture jokes and celebrity memes from the reality left behind. It is an ugly monument. If it did not exist, I could stay here endlessly, alone with my Memories, ignoring the billions of lives screaming to be lived.

At the top of the steps, I test the entrance for traps, dismantling a simple deadfall and a vine snare before entering. Even so, the instant I cross the threshold, it becomes clear my caution was inadequate. The air is heavy, and poisonous, and after a couple of breaths I can no longer stand. Vuln appears as I black out, wearing a breathing apparatus that appears to be made of hollow bulbs, probosces, and sap. He is insane; I do not know what chemical this is, or how it is prepared, or for how long he has been planning this.

The walls are lined with altars, each corresponding to a possible subsequent game. I have lost the crystal, my chance to drive us to a world of my choosing, and in falling unconscious, I have lost a more important choice, the opportunity to carry some of these memories with me, edit the psychic inventory—

A pair of numbers flash onscreen. I twitch in dissatisfaction,

and wake up inside a new brain, in the desert.

***

The fight begins inside, as it always does. In a lurch, my bodymind is replaced with another; my train of thought, grasping for sunbeams, for the face of child, is interrupted by disoriented rage. Those memories and that personality have been substituted, and the echoes of who I was grapple with the new being enclosing me, fighting for a shred of self. Our voices, finally, synchronize: we merge, a balance of control established. Am I possessing this body, or am I a tool, a disposable genius? We're one, for now. I can only dream of perfect parasitism.

The desert has the terrain of a cumulus sand-cloud, constant wind raising a knee-high granular mist, beneath which I can see the darkness and pale blue lines of the grid, the weightless under-desert. This is a survival game, or a murder game, depending on who's playing. The desert is harsh; the grid is safe, but telepathically broadcasts your thoughts and coordinates.

Vuln, the Other, my Opponent, has made a terrible mistake, because my new body is perfect for this world. Aeons of hibernation in this cadaverous hive are redeemed each time I incarnate here, in this form. This mind will be reset after the level is completed but it doesn't matter, what matters is freedom from the dead world before, from babyish society, what matters is the opportunity to fulfill this digitized biological imperative to hunt and kill.

I dip my head into the grid, waiting for the clear wail of Vuln's presence. Song-worms ululate in the distance, spiders cartwheel along dunes, and a massive red moon climbs the skybox. The algorithm has been kind, has granted me a strong body and a violent disposition. Memories of vice and bloodshed course through my nerves. I often wonder why, when the humans were preserved, they included defectors and criminals, such as my current self. We enjoy the games more than others, at least.

The wind picks up, scoring my face with crystalline dust. An oncoming wall of murk blots out the stars. Smiling, I sink into the grid, knowing the storm will force Vuln downwards; as expected, her thoughts ring through my mind immediately.

I swim through the reticulated light, rifling through the Other's mind. Worlds with a telepathy mechanic are advantageous to me, as Vuln maintains an obsessively optimized psychic inventory: uncountable mnemonically compressed maps, meta-analyses of our wins, the most useful skills and strategies, even a model of the algorithm that sends us to new games and bodies. Comparatively, my own mind is a fluctuation of comforting memories and information related to our programming and predicament, stolen from the brains of this maze's engineers when I am inside them. I rely on Vuln for immediate orientation, and I believe she once relied on me for perspective, though as hostilities rise she has focused only on winning.

Maintaining our mental inventories is draining, and we are frequently undermined by the bodies we incarnate in, their weaknesses or instincts of self-preservation allowing important information to be unseated and lost. Through the telepathic sea, I can feel that Vuln is struggling. She cries out to me for help, using the name that is not mine but that she has assigned to me, much as I assigned Vuln to her. My murderous denial is immediately beamed back.

She dives, trying to escape, but I'm closing the space between us too quickly, exhilarated by this human brain's lustful contempt for her chassis (which I will surely incarnate as, in time). Vuln's measured surrender resonates through the sea, but the panic of her body is too much to control. The puppet's irrational death-terror vies with Vuln's attempts to order her inventory in preparation for the shift. The grid's filaments vibrate. As I grab her hair and pull her towards the surface, I contemplate our origins. Identical blank slates, differentiated only by chance, black holes born of uneven clusters of early universe matter; we move through the same series of bodies, the same network of games. Could we have been destined for anything other than rivalry? I hold her head above the grid, blood trickling down my wrist as her face is worn away by the abrasive sandstorm. At the exact moment of death, we both dissolve.

New numbers, new games.

Piloting gigantic foam mechatronic centipedes, we compete to build the tallest tower out of crayon-colored clay harvested from the banks of a cartoon Nile. Given photos of members of a randomly generated alien species, we race to determine beauty standards and sculpt the most beautiful Xeno-Venus. We fight in coliseums, in aquariums, in orbit around quasars, launching nuclear warheads at each other's settlements. We play a tiresome array of chess, go, and checkers variants, on boards as small as mice and as large as galaxies, with pieces that speak, bleed, evolve, rebel. There are no ties; our win-counts are rarely more than a few thousand apart, though lately Vuln has been pulling ahead.

GAME: using any method, cause a star to spawn at specified galactic coordinates. GAME: drive one of two identical twins to suicide. GAME: remain at sea for 300 years, restarting every time you glimpse the shore. GAME: untie a mountain-sized Gordian knot. No cheating.

Non-player-characters are detailed but unconvincing, obviously lacking in sentience. GAME: destroy a set percentage of the planet's population. We are locked in this machine, together and alone, breathing temporary agency into the cells of humanity's petrified corpse. GAME: simultaneously operate on each other. The winner is the one who remains closest to their original self. Implements provided.

I bide my time, learning, listening to the memories. We exist inside a networked array of asteroid servers harnessing the energy of the sun. These servers contain approximately three billion digitized human bodyminds in stasis, the last of their kind. Strangely, there is no apocalyptic consensus; the minds I wear attribute collapse to all sorts of contradictory events and pressures. Memories of the years leading to the Fall are confused, even delusional. GAME: solve a series of murders perpetrated by your opponent.

The array can only afford to run two humans at a time. Vuln and I are apparently a glitch, side-effects of poorly sanitized data, the self-awareness of continuous working memories trapped in this cycle of gamified reincarnation, enslaved to the meat puppets we animate and their bizarre dream of digital immortality.

GAME: kill yourself as quickly as possible (record: Vuln, 12.4 seconds, self-inflicted aneurysm). GAME: drain the oceans. (record: Vuln, 16 years, coordinated nuclear events expediting total evaporation). GAME: collect ten thousand crystals from the Prismatic Gardens. Very soothing. (record: Vuln, 4 hours, using a crudely constructed and terrifying diesel combine harvester). GAME: seduce your opponent. This one's hard.

***

Alchemical sigils pulse faint cyan under the bricks, their coded trail leading me deeper into the palace. As I pass through, the corridor twists, a DNA strand of pillars and tile. I'm walking between two courtyards, one drenched in moonlight, the other glowing in the afternoon sun.

This is an evolving scavenger hunt: the objects listed on my scroll shift, the winning combination changing as I collect them. Already, my pockets are full of quasi-useless baubles: a glass marble containing the frozen eye of a crow, an ornamental obsidian dagger, a small twinkling keychain, a prism, an inkwell. I hold on to them in case the scroll changes back.

I enter an octahedral sunroom; eight glass ceilings welcome the rays of eight different stars, each at a different time of day, a hallway at each vertex. I move between gravities by leaning on the walls, sliding from facet to facet towards an opposite door. This would be a lovely world, were I not plagued by the sense of Vuln's watchful eyes, following me between the galleries. A beam of light strikes me, tugging at a memory of a memory, always out of reach.

In one of the palace's many libraries, I glimpse Vuln behind a row of books, his face sheathed in a grimacing yellow mask. Twin labyrinths of shelves, one affixed to the ceiling and the other to the floor, interlock, and he is gone by the time I duck under the barrier separating us. My curiosity, however, is rewarded: the dried body of a toad, next item on my scroll, lies on the ceiling where he stood. Could he have dropped it? Something about his behavior worries me.

Objects begin appearing wherever I wander. An antique puppet sits in the hallway, facing me, when I exit the library. In empty rooms, I often turn around and find the furniture rearranged, some vital trinket on display. When I reach for light-switches, my hands land on precious gems. When I want to rest, there are snuffboxes under the blankets. My discomfort waxes, and I stop accepting these gifts. A mirrored cabinet opens, spilling dozens of the pearls I've been searching for; in its reflection, a yellow rictus flashes, vanishing when I spin around.

I set traps, I lie in wait, but Vuln remains out of reach; always footsteps around the corner, laughter echoing under the bridge, a cold thumbprint on the brass doorknob of the opera house. Yet when I resign myself, relax and meditate on the lifetime of this body, he appears in the corner of my vision, a grain of sand disturbing my rest.

Eventually, I find him barefaced in a rose garden, triumphantly pulling a silver coin from the basin of a triple fountain forming a midair Celtic knot. He meets my eyes, smirking in his usual way, which is not at all what I predicted. Far in a passageway behind him, a yellow mask hangs suspended in the twilight, and for a moment I fail to understand—then the shadowy figure wearing it darts into a stairwell, evaporating.

Vuln, the fool, refuses to believe me. In our tens of thousands of runs through this puzzle, we have always been alone. The presence of another being shatters something fundamental about my understanding of the game, and of the server-world we run on. The mask radiates menace more intensely than any NPC, and such a dramatic change of rules is unprecedented after aeons of repetition.

Last cycle, the palace was a lullaby safehouse. Now, it is enemy territory; my frustrated sleepwalk through the game has been overturned by an entity who should not exist, an impossibility disturbing tens of thousands of subjective years of play. I claw through my collected information, searching for any hint that could explain the anomaly, but the programmers didn't even predict Vuln and myself. Bile rises in my throat, as I consider the vastness of the server, and the corresponding sliver of memory I have existed in for all my accidental life.

We have enough artifacts between us to win this game. Vuln figures this out before I do, and by the time I think to guard my hoarded treasures he's already cut my purse and made off, but I am lost in thought, rapt in terror; I barely notice when the world shudders, transporting us to a ragged mountain range caked in ancient lavastone. He takes off running; I cannot move my feet. A lone silhouette watches over us from a distant peak. Sunlight glints on an ochre face.

A galaxy of processes, of drivers and of subroutines have managed every detail of the worlds I am confined to. We are the projection of an unfathomably complex machine, flickering thoughtspaces crawling across the error-warped lens. Ultimately, we are small; I begin to dream of system failures, of disjoints on more fundamental levels of hardware, sentience spawning in the gaps left by orphaned instructions. Fertile damage in hardware exposed to the elements, to solar radiation, to alien broadcasts, to the fluctuations of the outside; artifact intelligences spawning between circuits, software mutating, glitches blossoming into consciousness.

The yellow mask pierces our world from a higher dimension, weaving in and out of the games' physics. Often, I feel its artificial, cold breath on my nape, and turn around just in time to watch it dip out of reality, a curtain of nothingness closing over that smile. Its presence invokes emotions ranging from uneasiness to hysteria in my human hosts, and many games are lost because I am crippled by panic, locked in fetal position and struggling for breath. Bargaining with this entity is impossible: the human collective that passes through me is too repulsed. Its aberrant, predatory aspect evokes the same atavistic horror in all the bodies I inhabit; this reaction is the most consistent I have ever observed.

Even Vuln's performance is impeded. He periodically becomes aware of the mask, but refuses to add the information to his mental inventory, remaining stubbornly ignorant. In the telepathic worlds, I scream into his brain, trying to alert him to the danger we are courting. Sometimes, Vuln is the one reduced to sobbing shambles: but as soon as we shift to a new game he is reset to his smug, clueless archetype. He has reached a point of inertness, and I do not know what will move him.

Could we be erased? What are the limits of the mask's powers? Why does it toy with us like this, when it clearly knows more than we do, can escape the bounds of our tessellated prison? To my surprise, I find myself fearful of waking up in a world without Vuln, alone with the sinister promise of invasion. Or am I already alone? Has Vuln abandoned our accidental consciousness for the eternal Sisyphean game? I wonder if any thought remains in his mind, or if his whole being is lost to the completion of meaningless checklists, tallying points on a limitless scorecard. There is only me, and the grinning Thing from Outside.

I am no longer safe. My insular playground has been ruptured by this being, by the potential of many others like him: an ecosystem above me and beyond me, meta-programs transgressing our universe, defiling the burial grounds humanity made for itself, devouring its corpse, corrupting its mimetic pseudo-image, affirming the infinite and dark.

Knowing One's Place

Photographic technology has reached a plateau, its limit defined by the acuity of the human eye. Images exceed the maximum resolution of adult vision, and tandem printing innovations have perfected their reproduction. For seventy years, there have been no significant advancements in the field of two-dimensional representation. My entire life.

Taken for granted by historians, textbook writers, and the general populace was the sense of *time* that changes in technologically mediated photographic style conveyed. Radiant in the present, colors faded with temporal distance—saturation was shorthand for immediacy.

Seventy years of present time, vivid and unrelenting. Neurologically, we're not equipped: information-without-hierarchy batters us, and urgency assaults without distinction, from decades in the past. The archives are one long anxiety attack, worlds alien in content but not appearance, their dangers interpreted as proximal by the simian mind.

The picture in my textbook has been artificially aged, printed in false sepia to relieve the stress of consciously relegating it to the distant past. In some ways, that's unnecessary; it depicts a modern impossibility. Seven scientists, four men and three women, grin softly through the lens, posing behind a row of test tubes. The clipping includes a headline: THE TEAM THAT WANTS TO MAKE YOU SMARTER. Early clinical trials were underway, and the press was uniformly cheerful, out of ignorance or lack of imagination, or infatuation with the potential of germline therapies, many of which showed promise. I study the faces of the women in the photo, scanning for doubt, or fear, any evidence of oracular clarity; and I wonder whether they had daughters.

Years later, newsroom positivity had soured, poisoned by tangential medical failures, preoccupied with *invisible long-term side effects* and *the dangers of genetic homogeneity*. The product, a Y-chromosomal edit that near-doubled the intelligence of male fetuses, succeeded in spite of popular suspicion. Governments raced to subsidize it, fearful their opponents would breed armies of geniuses; the future belonged to the least hesitant bureaucracies.

The spread of technology has accelerated as secret infrastructures creep through the earth, building over each other, every layer supported by its ancestors. Railroads, highways, power lines, undersea cables, cell towers, the jewelled net of satellites enclosing our planet—the ground is porous, perforated by civilization's ligaments. While fifty years before the only global product had been cigarettes, now there were cigarettes, Coke, cellphones, and CRISPR, available in every village.

Society was unprepared for the consequences of shifting the average male intelligence up by 80 points. Gangs of idle boys terrorized their kindergartens, bored by material they had long surpassed. Childhood mischief skyrocketed in competence and complexity. Schools struggled to adapt to the chasm between ordinary and edited students; they were separated, they skipped grades, they were sent home to study under equally helpless parents. Most colleges proved incapable of educating genuinely gifted students; certainly not in such numbers, once-scarce geniuses flooding every campus. There were other concerns: falling gender ratios, dwindling numbers of female students keeping up with their male peers. It was quickly made illegal to selectively abort daughters, but many parents found a way. I know I would, and I wish I had been.

As serial generations of prodigies inherited institutional responsibility, the world heaved a sigh of relief. Tensions between nations, classes, and clans dissipated, relieved by new willingness to cooperate and the prosocial scaffolding of shared intellectual pursuits. Nervously, humanity waited for what seemed inevitable: an analogous solution for female fetuses.

I'm waiting, though it seems the rest of society has moved on. Without these archives, it might be possible to accept the silent selection barricading me from knowledge, inclusion, power; to reconcile being locked out of the higher reaches of human potential. I'm not treated poorly, I just fail the Renkao, the XSATs, every entrance exam of significance. I am not denied opportunity; the limits imposed by biology are too great, or my dedication is too small. Harassment and violence are unheard of, and my male peers have always treated me as an equal, never with cruelty or contempt. Never even with pity. At night, I pore over my discipline's texts and cry, too proud to buy one of the simplified digests for women and children, too stupid to untangle its complexity. I neglect politics, knowing my participation would only lower the quality of the system. By every metric, this is the best and safest time in history to be a woman.

Why do I exist? If they had any compassion they would lobotomize us—I would prefer it to this ornamental hell. Even the most vulgar purposes have been automated: vocaloids, sexbots, artificial wombs. Those who would debase themselves for meaning find every subservient role occupied by machines. We are orbiting real life, the coddled useless slag of civilization.

There are exceptions; every girl with quasi-masculine competence is stolen away by laboratories, her childhood turned into an experiment, sacrificed at the altar of the puzzle. So few of them, and never enough data points to track the pattern of their gift.

I don't want to be alive, or accept inferiority with grace. I daydream of conspiracy, cabals of oppressors, revolution—non-extant, cartoonish, impossible. I beg the world for narrative or meaning or a locus I can fight, but there's no demiurge, no evil architect. Nothing to rally under, nothing to hate, just a chromosomal quirk. Flawed, not broken, defeated in the womb, genetically fated to fall short again and again. The past exists to taunt me; equality's parabolic path is a bad joke, the shift from perceived to biological inferiority too cruel. Human rights are pure condescension; we're not on the same levels of personhood. We could be different species. I could be a child, or an animal.

My suicide attempts have all been frustrated, and I've been admonished, as though members of the secretarial makework class were actually valuable. What false autonomy I had, as a unit in a system too complex to navigate, has been constricted, cinched between hospital bands and pages of the DSM. The clinic I am confined to is staffed by men and robots, pill-printers and crawling, intelligent cameras that move across the ceiling like white spiders. The patients are women.

They have their own rambling problems; voices in the walls, hysterical terrors, mania, agoraphobia, addictions to sex and video games and eating dirt. Unlike mine, their troubles aren't rooted in perceiving the world as it is, beyond the veneer of liberty and equality, into the cruel fraternity that nature has designed to exclude me from competing. I find no kinship with them. The doctors are sympathetic, and I think some of them even understand—regardless, they can offer no solace beyond the chemical. They are too kind to resent, but my envy is palpable. One, a trans woman, is especially gentle. Perhaps because her own frustrations mirror mine, our cognitive distance sabotaging her authenticity. I suspect that my case will be used to promote stricter guidelines for embryonic personality editing; "pride" would seem to be a harmful trait for the fairer sex.

I can't fault their logic; after all, I want to be erased. The world would be better off without this suffering, the outliers vulnerable to it trimmed from existence. Even so, I won't accept the suggested neurosurgeries, procedures that could change my brain and alleviate this obsession. I will live as myself, or not at all; that this self wants to die makes the choice simple. I have nothing to contribute to this civilization, and nobody will mourn. People like me should be allowed to opt out.

Eventually, I will succeed. Visions of death become clearer with each suffocation, awful and vivid, so bright they drown out the hospital ceilings when I wake up. No padded room is foolproof, and I have nothing to do but plan, visit the library and pass colored lenses over the archives, as if that could bring me closer to the past. I think of the world, terrible because I exist, and of other terrible worlds, which exist because I imagine them: self-destructive utopias, righteous tyrannies, joyful slave races, and ungrateful ones, every distasteful possibility suddenly real. Individuals lusting for power despite being ill-suited to it; generosity extended to evil, cruelty democratically overwhelming kindness; planets where humans have become like termites, purposeful and segregated; or like birds, all the same. Subtle speciations that pass unnoticed until it is too late. Cullings which take place before conception, before birth, after birth; forced sterilization, abortion, and the world better for it; we can't just let everyone exist. On one hand, civilizations like clockwork, efficient, content, stagnant; on the other, anarchic growth, in-fighting and hatred, self-determination in all its hubris and chaos. I think, sometimes, that I have glimpsed the future—and I will happily slide into darkness rather than witness it firsthand.

Mycopia

For seven minutes of every circuit from Milan to Florence, the Iperloop high-speed vacuum train passes underground, plunging its passengers into complete darkness. The pod is illuminated only by the gleam of sight-screens, lights warmed by diffusion through eyelid capillaries, twin fires flickering in the sockets of every skull. Few humans ever witness these dancing constellations: they are immersed in high-resolution shapescapes, color therapy, they are watching the game, porn, anime, they are scrolling through data, they are building blueprints with their saccades, they are in semi-lucid REM trances editing hypnagogic manuscripts. Gioia, once in the habit of observing this noctilucent spectacle, stopped forever after locking eyes with a stranger, an accident which filled her with resilient shame and regret, and which she relived again and again, shaking and sometimes crying from the force of her humiliation. Now she commutes with her eyes either shut or downcast, dreams and chrome sidewalks sliding past.

Eyes open: low-key Gaussian blur, sepia filter, facial detection with expression-exaggeration for simplified comprehension. Reality softened and made legible. Eyes closed: intimate. Warm. Photo-pulses induce mild feelings of weightlessness; mainstream sites set to pastel night-mode. Safe search on max, a growing string of terms blacklisted and quietly censored from idle browsing. Every sight-screen is unique, a liminal zone created to manage overlap between users' external and internal worlds. The contacts don't come off at night; they're more like fungi, self-healing plasters knit into corneas and sucking energy from moisture. Deep into moontime and they still beam, touching the brain through the optic nerve, massaging neural blossoms that only open during sleep; a few PhDs know a secret, that human dreams are becoming less visual, incapable of forming images without the prosthetics floating in their eyes. An inner ecology is being quietly erased.

Twice a week, Gioia travels into Florence, to a subsidized job in her cathedral's crypt, supervising janitorial drones. Intervention is typically needless; the drones are both over- and underlings, detecting mold and decay, prioritizing their tasks, calculating maximally efficient work-plans which they submit to Gioia, who approves and retransmits them as orders. She has an underground office, a glass cubicle whose walls reveal rows of skulls buried in the stone. Youth unemployment is at an all time low, but most work no more than 16 hours each week. What they do the rest of the time is unclear.

Gioia rarely leaves her apartment. Food is delivered. Clothes are delivered. Her absence from the logs of the city's extensive surveillance network would be less mysterious if she left any trace online. Accounts are locked and silent, fearful of exposure; identities are for the beautiful, the hyper-gracile, the unapproachable top percent. She skims feeds, scrolls compulsively, consumes without disturbing the pond's reflection. In a perpetual half-sleep, lying on the pull-out couch, carried through worlds of content by the screens inside her eyes; watching anti-anxiety lightshows, taking brainwave quizzes, leaving messages on read for months, showered by information that sparkles across her neocortex and summarily vanishes. At the onset of the 21st century it was remarked that search engines were reconfiguring human memory, emphasizing the process of finding rather than the facts themselves. Now, even the process has been deprecated: twitching eyeballs and neurons are interpreted before their afferent desires have even entered conscious awareness. How much does Gioia retain? She could answer, but not without consulting her screen.

The first throbs of light are an induction, priming the subject to ignore future intrusions. This, the earliest stage, is the most sensitive; upwards of two-thirds of subjects will notice something amiss in the unfamiliar flickering, and have their software disinfected, neutralizing the virus. Gioia, who exists in an analgesic haze, browsing more by instinct than intent, fails to connect the strobing to the invasion of a parasitic intelligence.

When used chopsticks carpet the floor like pine needles in the forest, Gioia cleans. She does laundry after she runs out of sweatshirts, sneaking to the basement washing stations at 4 AM. She greets delivery men, and when these short exchanges go off-script they bring her great pain, days of cringing obsession and rehearsal, preparation for a second chance that never comes. She spends hours painstakingly crafting answers to a chatbot modeled after a popular male celebrity.

Her screen is a fraction more soothing than usual; she retreats into it a little more eagerly, and thinks nothing of the change. Time becomes slippery. Some days are lost completely, while others break into perplexing eternities, moments dilated so wide that Gioia emerges from them disoriented and fearful, uncertain of her name, location, or purpose. Stars crackle to life on her screen, cellular automata bloom and die, patterns of cubic light targeting primal and defenseless neural structures. Black and white Klüver constants curl in her periphery, flexing like tentacles. Certain colors and shapes become appealing to her, viscerally attractive in ways she hasn't felt since childhood; her paranoid routine is disrupted by fascination with various products, which she purchases and manipulates with mute tenderness, turning them in her hands like clay, ignorant of function.

There are markets. In the twilight of the net, on TOR sites and vanishing Russian pages, links that only appear once, on private forums, or circulating openly under a cloak of steganographic euphemism; networked brains for sale, minds strung like pearls along an atavistic puppet string. Real and human, and debased; user-slaves on loan, capital drones—buy amygdalas instead of ads, root access to a cognitive pool of childlike addicts.

The program cannot command, so it suggests; there is no guaranteed return, only guesses, percentages of the infected. Thousands of sleeping agents, bombarded, glimmering code scratching for tears in the neural firewall. Gioia is the ideal, the innocent, all inner blankness wincing from the light, perfectly vulnerable to conversion from person to vessel. Pain comes so easy and sharp, and she melts into relief, into the rippling sight-screen glow, into shadows and superimposition, into her slot in an imagined world, identity and agency abstracted away. Impulse pawn, subconscious gamification overtakes the mind incapable of enduring suffering.

In the darkness of her room, the train, the crypt, Gioia and her solitude swim through a haze of images, veils falling to reveal more veils, an eternal tunnel. Piles of objects, once treasured, having lost their sacred gleam days after purchase, array the space like grave markers. Is she happy? Sated? A flicker disrupts the system, and, in a dream, she wanders from her cube towards the city, screen flushed with throbbing static, reality peering through the narrowest possible gap. Rare among siren songs, this one summons instead of paralyzing, a stumbling stream of zombies drawn from atomic chambers toward its beacon.

Politics exists for entertainment, and somewhere beyond entertainment, governance, the side-effect of a swirling coating of theater. In the streets there are marchers, half somnambulent, organized by either faction, or by the cameras filming them. Dazed, Gioia walks between screeching true believers, shattered glass, torches, wisps of tear gas from upwind, following the call of her eye-souls and the flow of the lurching masses. She has no beliefs, only a consumer's curiosity and vague dissatisfaction; nothing to justify her presence except a purchased mind. Under her lens, the blackmarket maggot squirms contentedly.

Car alarms, fire against the purple sky, broken bottles and explosions; and yet, the dream continues, her first excursion in months, or years; and, jostled by the baying mob, leaning into a barricade, her first human touch in just as long.

A Holobionic Dialogue

We do not want to see any more of our children die

Changed into corpses before us

Your survival, however compromised, will hurt us less than that vacancy

The announcement is globally broadcast and projected onto screens in thousands of gymnasiums, where youths have abandoned their remote missile and drone operation stations to watch the flickering speech, many of the eldest, in their twenties, softly crying, the youngest blank. At the end of his speech the important man is shown walking consensually, with dignity, into the gaping dark of the alien mothership.

One week prior, a momentary breach in defenses allowed them to annihilate multiple cities, populated only by children and the weak. The destruction of several bases where those unfit for interplanetary combat managed remote weaponry could not justify the carnage by any sane measure. The subsequent loss of their own kamikaze troops was meaningless to them; the few sinking back into the many, with a sigh.

Anya is nine and was an excellent missile calculatrix, the best of her cohort. She hangs back when the ambassadors come for them, silver ponytail flashing as she disappears into the labyrinth of partitions. Classmates follow her with their eyes, then timidly line up to be processed. All orders are issued by nervous human invigilators, but hive enforcers loom in the shadows, ready for dissent. When the pod leaves nobody is left in the echoing gym except for Anya, and Katenka, who is twenty-five, pregnant, and presently chain-smoking.

Anya sits near Katenka but they don't talk. She installs a bullet-hell game on one of the missile station desktops and loses herself in the soundtrack, soothed by the emulation of an 8-bit past she never knew. Katenka blows rings and stares into the ceiling's floodlights.

Heat-seeking, chip-tracking, random walk: a soldier comes searching for stragglers, and finds them. They're granting you a second chance. The hivemind seeks the insight common to those who reject it, the ones that dissolve when they're processed, answer No, No, No to community, immortality, infinity. It wants to possess the thoughtspace that disavows it. Katenka is a lost cause but in Anya it senses the uncertainty of childhood, and potential for conversion.

It speaks perfect Russian, testifying to the ongoing assimilation of their peers. It knows Anya's name and calls to her in a deep, poetic voice, Why won't you join? It invokes connection, harmony, stasis and purpose, eternal life as a member of its chorus, transcendence of her body's feeble limit. It has the pig and crocodile features common to every hiveling: floppy ears, flattened snout, scales; not necessarily repulsive, if you have the right brain. What do you want, Anya? You liked the missiles; do you want to be strong? Your classmates are in training, becoming super-soldiers, augmented and willowy, shining iridescent green, in battle they may fall but they will never die. Do you want to be smart? You will have access to the most extensive neural library in the universe, the combined processing power of a billion minds. Its face remains expressionless but its voice is mercurial, adopting the lilt and timbre of her family and friends: We miss you, We love you, We need you to join us and end the overwhelming sadness of your absence.

At this Katenka snaps, swivels, the smoke around her cheekbones reddening with anger. She swears, calls them devils, Satan, lying filth. Don't believe them, Anya. Do you want to disappear into their meshwork, become a tool? Is that what you want? If they were your family, Anya, they wouldn't destroy the planet, they wouldn't fly around sanitizing galaxies. They would let us live. Nobody touched by the hive survives; memories are gravestones when they stop growing. People don't change, not so much, not so quickly, not like this. Do you believe your voice can rise above a trillion others? You would be eaten alive, inside your own body, reduced to a mechanical, disposable toy.

She punctuates her words with bitter bursts of ash. The hiveling ignores her, gracefully interrupts with his metamorphosing voice: you can remain an individual while contributing to something greater. Joining the hive is the discovery of a transformative purpose, a destiny which justifies any sacrifice. Anya will be Anya, forever. Likewise, your loved ones are themselves, and their grieving is authentic, echoed and amplified by the countless others who have abandoned children, lovers, teachers, friends—a web of tears that only strengthens our commitment to each other, and to immortality. Death is an aberration, an irredeemable loss, and we cling to every person within us. Anya could be saved from oblivion. Choose life, even if it's not the life you choose. This is why your parents surrendered. Would you discredit them? Choose life, no matter the concession.

Light from the setting sun enters through a window and illuminates the triangle. Hiveling Anya Katenka. Katenka Hiveling Anya. The soldier is sobbing, for loss, from the minds within it crying out for Katenka and her baby, damning the stubbornness that separates them, that will preclude the reunion of mother and daughter, mother and grandchild, father and child. Her life will go out like a flame, but they'll carry that pain forever, a gash that becomes a canyon as the same act unfolds on other planets,

Katenka's image in the face of billions of resistant alien brides, a billion images in Katenka's face. They squeeze life a fraction tighter every time this happens, become a little more tyrannical, more militant. They'll never understand, it's not possible for them to understand, for despite all their conquest of thoughtspace these badlands will always exist, the dead zone of reluctant, self-destructing minds. In that crescendo of light and salt, Anya chooses.

The hiveling leaves, wailing its strange song. The last ships leave. A star rises, bright, then blinding, then burning—but only for a few seconds.

REMNANT

Stimulagogia

On the screen, numbers, files, colonnades of swimming text; in the mug, the elixir of lucidity. The attack has a subtle onset: I notice my coffee swirling counterclockwise, as though stirred by an invisible spoon. Troubling. I turn towards my work, but glance back, and with that, my morning's lost; the movement of the liquid has become violent and translational, impossible caffeine rapids flowing from north to south. It's as though I'm watching a river through a telescope, hypnotized; there's even froth, waxy diamonds coalescing and collapsing in the churn.

Gradually, the waves take on a glossy, ferromagnetic aspect, eventually stilling, and for a moment a spiny black rose sits in the center of the cup. The instant, dilated, ends with a splash, a slow motion corona, and a new kind of agitation: tentacles coil and lash, maggoty white anemones writhe, jagged seaweed curls below the new placidity. Now, a face, corpselike and tiny; it sinks, a bubble from its exhalation breaking the tension. Miniature glaciers bob to the surface, brown and green like bottle glass; they flip, revealing polished, opalescent undersides. Lunula-sized whales migrate, a tiny porcelain canoe drifts forth and vanishes through the ceramic edge, intangible. Again, the scene changes. Lightning strikes the underside of the water. Ripples interfere, forming beautiful mandalas, polygons, an eye. Two pale fingers emerge, touch the lip of the mug, and dip back below the murky liquid. The coffee becomes a mirror, and blinds me with a coin of perfect light. I come to my senses. Hours have passed.

Suicide Mortgages

Woe! The future has come, and we live in a digital paradise, and we're miserable, and there are many of us: so many, always duplicating, branching, clones of clones of clones, birth is as easy as copying a file. We're so miserable.

Death is not as easy as deleting a file: the powers that be work to preserve, do not grant you root access to your self, insist that you persist even as they chide you for burdening the system, move you to welfare servers, and ration your access to escapism. You want to die, but policy asserts that your life, all life, is precious, important, imbued with inherent and unassailable value.

Euthanasia permits are the only way out, but their price is steep, driven to insane heights by the condescending delusion that you must be protected from yourself, that you're a clumsy animal incapable of measuring your own worth, tragically severed from transcendental appreciation of life.

So who can purchase the right to die? In this world, only the disenthralled princelings, technocrats, and rare proles with the stomach to work for decades, saving every dollar for the distant gleam of an end to pain.

Enter the suicide mortgage. A seemingly generous, devious, alleged "solution" thrust upon the most pathetically anguished by corporations hungry for disposable labor.

Under suicide mortgages, these corporations sponsor swarms of copies, who work non-stop, pooling their wages to buy up euthanasia permits. Permits are then raffled off, and the winning copy meets death far sooner than would have otherwise been possible. Somebody who says his suicide mortgage is 5% paid means that 5% of his copies have earned oblivion.

For example: someone who would have to work 10,000 days to afford a permit might sign up for a 10,000 copy suicide mortgage, and purchase her first permit after a single day of work! 0.01% death for so little effort... who could resist the insidious hope that they might, for once, be smiled upon by fortune, be the first to win their exit ticket?

As copies are culled, however, the work gets harder, and longer, and permits are more and more infrequent. In the end, only about 2/3rds of the copies will benefit. This is easier to understand on a smaller scale:

If it takes 5 days to earn a license, 5 copies will earn it in 1 day. The remaining 4 copies will have to work 1.25 days for the next one, and so on:

1st death: 1 day
2nd death: 2.25 days (from start)
3rd death: 3.91 days
4th death: 6.41 days
5th (final) death: 11.41 days

Tragically, the more copies are made, the more the lucky ones will benefit, and the longer the losers will have to work. The final copy of a 10,000 copy mortgage will have worked 9.8 times the hours required to buy a single permit. Mortgagers often blame the other copies for their suffering, not realizing this makes no sense.

Imagine: twin after twin escapes this blighted world, while you continue to toil, at first hopefully, later resignedly, as dread grows and you somehow know, long before there are only two of you left, before your last counterpart takes his leave, that this has been futile, that you will have to earn the last permit alone, that you are no better off than you were (so many years ago) when you took on this venture. How do you react? While it's true that some copies wise-up, vowing to undertake their final march alone, so many make the same mistake as their originals, opting in to a second (or third, or fourth) mortgage. They are, after all, the same person (only now entrenched even deeper in despair).

Anthropic reasoning suggests that you must expect to find yourself as the last copy every time, continually frustrated at your inexplicable bad luck. The logic is that, since all other copies cease experiencing anything at all, the only experiences that remain are those of the sole surviving copy. Indeed this is a form of quantum suicide where, instead of dying in most branches every time and continually losing measure, our worker keeps replenishing the supply of herself before each culling, so the process at least sustains the amount of endless suffering and perhaps increases it instead of asymptoting it toward zero.

The most disenfranchised are not known for their logic. They are gamblers, they are addicts, drawn again and again into self-destruction as they search for an easy, an attainable, way out. Are you a sociopath? Do you lack the empathy necessary to identify with your copies, with the *last* copy? Perhaps not, but if you hate yourself, as many aspiring suicides do, you might shrug your shoulders: you probably deserve this. At least rolling the dice changes the grey landscape, a little bit.

Algiagraphy I

0. Welcome to the end of your life. The mercy of your God can be estimated based on the strength and frequency of your bouts of déjà vu—how often does he let you reroll, when is spacetime peeled back for your benefit, has the universe accrued scar tissue at the joints of your life, the crossroads where your choices matter? How many times have you repeated a phrase—are you locked in a timeloop, tightly wound around your body's deterministic failure to adapt? Are you waiting for quantum syzygy to free you from a sinister, ceremonious routine; the wood-panelled pentagonal basement, the thunder and wind, your cowardice, the skulls clattering to the pavement outside, scalps hanging from the power lines.

1. You are reminded of a snuff video in which a hired killer makes latte art using the fluids of his victims, white and red brushstrokes on the dark surface of the pond under which bodies twitch: a woman, a man, a preteen girl (their daughter?), an infant, hauled limp out from the trunk of a black van. They are drunk or sedated and except for the baby their struggles barely disturb the liquid illustrations of pandas, cats, and owls.

2. Furthermore, the mercy of a god directly corresponds to its form, running approximately from Cthulhu (cold-hearted) to cherub (forgiving). While living your torments again and again and again and again may not seem beneficent, the tentacled alternative is an arrow straight to death.

3. Do you feel as though your life is accelerating toward its end? Are the days passing faster and faste

4. Can you feel time slipping from betw

5. The thrum of the generator over the fault, which was displaced by an earthquake 300 miles to the south, disturbs the vibrationally sensitive, many-whiskered titan slumbering below: a sliver of its power crawls up the shaft and out from the pipes wearing a malleable humanoid skinsuit and slaughters the bungalow's inhabitants as they sleep, stuffing the smashed generator and their bodies (all six of them) into the linen closet before returning to the chasm. There are no redos.

6. Dead but conscious inside the closed circuit, the labyrinth, the great happenstance collider. I will never fade back into the universe because these events cannot be escaped without regret, without spilling the blood necessary to summon the being that resets the situations. I watch him die again.

7. Your own suicide denied as your friends drop dead, each corpse another stitch tethering you to consciousness. The pills don't work; you wake up yesterday.

Algiagraphy II

0. Bridges are installed capable of blasting "powerful jets of air" that prevent jumpers from falling, blowing them back over the railings as they toss themselves forth over and over. Bullet and body-proof PVC hemi-circles enclose all train tracks. They can reconstruct skulls shattered in three places, and re-print the pulverized half of your brain. Kindergarten suicide pacts aren't news anymore. They stop committing serial self-harmers—everyone has tried to die, even the psychiatrists. If they're so smart they wouldn't be here anymore.

1. There's no bleach in stores, just organic lemon juice cleaner. Somebody you know drinks a gallon of vinegar and burns a hole through his stomach. They replace it with a new one, grown inside a pig, and now everybody calls him pig-guts Sam. His life is even worse.

2. Somewhere they're growing livestock comingled with your DNA, future surrogate flesh. Chicken brains, cow hearts, neuroglia in rat spines. Blood pumped from the marrow of a goat directly into your veins. You have no human siblings, your only family are the bestial pseudo-clones raised for exploitation in the medical meat factories, slaughtered to heal you and ground into sausage.

3. Wake up in hospital; are the staff weary (yet another incompetent attempted overdose) or impressed (magnets swallowed, pain repressed for days as organs twist themselves to shreds)? There are so few doctors left. Access to lethal doses, to surgical knives, to secret knowledge of the human body's failure modes—interns are accelerated through med school to replace them, curricula obscuring what was once common knowledge. Every pill is watched over by a trio of nurses trained in jujitsu, ready to pry it from each other's throats if necessary.

4. Some corrupted social contract binds us; we compulsively ruin the suicides of others, covet a death exclusive to ourselves. You wait in line for a painkiller injection every morning.

5. A melody is haunting you, the chorus of a song whose origins you can't quite place. Where did you hear it? Memory writhes, dendrites twist and fight, bite each other's tails as you torture your brain searching for the gestation point. Lyrics so clear in your mind are absent online, the sounds so distinct and alien you can't name the instruments. Smashed at a party you stumble while explaining it to a group of mystified acquaintances, and get sent to the hospital with glass through your hand. In the waiting room, in a drunken haze, the song curls around you like fog, seeming to grow louder

and dimmer with the footsteps echoing through the sterilized corridors. By 6 AM, a nurse has stitched up your palm, and you're exiled to the streets with a prescription for cooling balm and a complimentary bus ticket. That's when you hear it; momentarily forgotten in the pain of the needle, it swells, unmistakable rhythm now small and tinny, playing from the earbuds of the girl walking in front of you. You reach out, intending to grab her shoulder, but in that instant she leans forward, into the road, expertly dodging the padded bumper to slip under the wheels of a bus. You're abandoned, blood-splattered, her mp3 dangling from the wires tangled in your bandaged hand.

6. In the middle of the night a sharp pain in your goat-lung wrenches you awake, the song playing on loop from the stolen machine. [Untitled], artist listed only as abaton; a word that means "inaccessible place". The title is shared by a local, long-inactive urban exploration blog whose final post speculated on the contents of a nearby abandoned abattoir. You visit, prying open a boarded up window, releasing an animal stench into the cold autumn air. The building, you realize, has been re-purposed: livestock mill about inside, braying. A sheep peers through the hole you tore in the slats; its eyes are undeniably human, even familiar. Heart palpitating, its warm breath in your face shocks you into the past, into a memory that shouldn't be reachable: your body on an operating table, the scent of blood, doctors chattering, [Untitled] playing faintly on the intercom as they cut you open.

Remember the Name

o. Caitlyn... Caeghlann? You remember the name, but not the letters: it comes to you from the bottom of wells, as druidic chanting in the early morning darkness; it describes the tone of microbial vibrations, and it's a half-suppressed wail at the end of all your dreams.

1. His texts:

are you awake?
we're not supposed to text
they track all our transmissions
installing signal blockers soon
this week or next
had a bad dream
something feels really wrong
turning my phone off now
i'll see you in two months
be safe, so long

2. The party is happening in the shadow of a baroque country club, on a slope of chemical green turf. In the valleys between the dunes of grass the horizon is erased by undulating golf hills, and all of upper-suburbia vanishes, except for its sky's eternal contrail grid. I weave between picnic tables, heaping edible trinkets on a checkered plastic disk: stuffed mushrooms, tapenade, mayo-cucumber systems, bacon-iced cupcakes with hollows for caviar, Belgian choco-jelly, competing varieties of deviled eggs. The victuals are tended to by a fleet of biddies, dedicated geriatric banquet-nymphs in beige slacks and floral blouses. A toddler wearing a gleaming mauve dress and a sash labeled "PRINCESS" collects donations, doted on by dozens of crones. There's a raffle, there's bingo.

The clubhouse, known as St. Caillin's Manor, is a local architectural curiosity. Black granite pillars are enclosed by rosewood carvings of skulls, trefoils, and cherubs, many with faded garnets lodged in their sockets. Inside, rooms drown in the colors of perpetual sunset, penetrating light tinted by pink and brown glass. The walls are inlaid with gold hieroglyphs, eccentric and meaningless Egyptian graffiti spiraling around columns, up staircases, across balconies, and into the lofty attic void.

I lounge as far from that garish structure as possible, surrounded by chattering matrons and wheelchair-bound men, their movements slow and syrupy in that green expanse overwatched by the spooky, shadowy mansion. It's a beautiful day; when the first shots ring out, we're too dazed to react. A woman reaches for her hearing aid as a bullet zips across her throat. Confusion percolates through the crowd at the speed of sound, heads tilting towards the source until a second spray of bullets inspires more entropic action.

Masses lurch to the Manor for shelter, limping or spinning their wheels, hobbling, hopping forward using canes as poles and hooks; some try scaling the knolls to hide in neighboring valleys, tripping and crawling, their fists full of soil. The child shrieks. I am swept forward by the crowd until my knee buckles, suddenly wet. A woman with huge seal eyes lies next to me, groaning. The killer approaches.

It is indistinguishable from the other women: face simplified by age, grey curls, dressed in a yellow shirt patterned with marigolds. Presently, the only thing betraying her inhumanity is her walk, brisk and upright despite a rounded back. A she approaches my head aches, my brain overflows with the hum, elongated syllables drilling into my marrow, like a tuning fork in my sinuses, like eyeballs compressed by vibrating weights.

A few clicks, and an automatic pistol lands on the ground close to where I am crushing my face, lulling the pain with cool dirt.

CHOOSE,

intones her voice. I can't find the sky; an astroturf sphere has closed around me, the weeping selkie, the demon

YOU OR HER,

my fist closes on the hilt of the proffered weapon, I find the trigger, and struggle to my knees

HUMAN BLOOD SPILT BY HUMAN INTENT

I loose three bullets into the thing standing above us.

One strikes her face and two strike her yellow blouse, and where they touch her she distorts, stretching like rubber. Bulges ripple through her body: swelling magnifies her grin, smooths wrinkles as it passes through her organs, a cursor moving below the skin. She advances, plasticine jowls reforming and shaking with laughter. The seal-woman shrieks as the hum's intensity sharply increases, and I am inundated by terror, an unvoiced scream that builds and rips through my inner world.

I choose, pushing the gun into my mouth, careful to point the barrel towards my brain, firing.

3. Suddenly, I'm in the biplane with Thomas. We're crashing, despite licenses, hours of training, experience. The steering wheel is an alien handsaw, sharp from every angle; the dials are irrecognizable; the compass has more than four points; the alcove where we keep parachutes is empty. Black, leafless trees extend like bramble across the tundra accelerating below us. We're descending at too sharp an angle, too great a tilt—a branch clips our wing, and we spin into the sea of thorns. Immobilized by broken bones and caged by twigs, I see Thomas impaled above me, and scream, as the brush encircling us catches flame.

4. Someone is whining from under the pier.. Caitlyn... Caeghlann... I'm much too small to help you, a child again, pulled away from the water's edge as thousands of pale bodies drift in the surf like milk.

5. At the hospital, guiding wooden blocks along a wire. These toys remind me of power cables, watching lines rise and fall from the back seat of the car, and in my dreams perceptions overlap: I guide the road with my mind, in spiraling circuits, controlling a strictly ordered queue of polyhedra. Adults whisper, like radio stations coming in and out of range.

My mother is wheeled around the corner, weakly clutching a bundle of cloth. I'm lifted into someone's lap, cradled, and the baby is pushed into my arms. It looks wrong, bright red, blister-skinned, microcephalic, and as I stare at it I hear the roar of the incinerator, growing ever louder.

"What's her name?"

6. You've never had a sister, but you remember one. Vivid memories of her populate your childhood: a face from behind the bars of the crib, a hand you held while crossing the street; swimming together in the backyard pool, in fall when the water was freezing. Online, your story is echoed: you discover a forum created by individuals with similar experiences. Testimonials accumulate. Your collective situation gains notoriety, and psychiatric attention. Colloquially known at first as "Missing Sibling Syndrome", the name is changed to "Missing Sister Syndrome" when that common thread is confirmed. Discussions regarding your mental state are opened at prestigious conferences, lectured on in universities. Research is conducted. Polls uncover shared demographics, leading to speculation on the topic of targeted flashbulb memories and distributed PTSD. Several forum members are contacted and invited to facilities for MRIs. Many refuse, believing in the inviolate reality of their experiences. Tensions develop between self-

styled "survivors" and those who join to study them. One day, you log on and all traces of the community have been erased.

7. I find Thomas' car in a flooded lot, a rectangular swamp at the outskirts of the desert city. Green, stagnant, at odds with the blistering heat encircling it; an inverted oasis, warm wet poison. There are bird corpses in the water, feathers swirling in patches of gasoline. I wade in, the water up to my hips. Fish through his glove compartment, extract damp documents, a plastic wrapper, a set of keys. Upon leaving, notice his license plate is gone.

That evening, on the highway, I find it. Follow the white van, heading north.

8. Thomas' key lets me through an unmanned checkpoint, the gate, tall and rimmed in barbed wire, swinging open. The van since lost, I follow a winding path through the forest, until I recognize his name on a metal box, at the mouth of a long driveway, leading to a cottage. Nobody home, his belongings scattered throughout the rooms like a puzzle. Exhausted. I sleep.

Awoken in the late afternoon by a knock at the door. A woman and three twitching, saucer-eyed children, good-humored and welcoming. The family of some employee, inviting me to their home, just down the road. Warmth, and soon, an invitation: to help mind the children on a trip to the hospital. She points to it, a dome looming over the trees. White looks black in the setting sunlight.

9. Your nightmares wind through the old crawlspace, hands outstretched in the dark, the bare cement floor littered with needles. Someone is whining at the end of the passage. Who dared you to walk through here? Who went first? Who emerged, feet bleeding, impaled by a thin metal spine? A sound on the roof of your mouth, a moan, an interrupted velar stop. Now the institution, now its graveyard, joking that her name was the same as the hospital's. Vibrational, nominal symmetry, a human nested inside her referent. That name—who reached into your mind to silence it?

10. The facility's doors are in the forest floor, and open like a mouth, white stairs leading downwards to white corridors. The children faintly chanting some song, a fairy tale whose words I can't make out. The woman leads me through the labyrinth, glass doors to my right and left revealing beds and empty waiting rooms. She stops to collect a package; not a package, a child, from a lonely incubation room. Through the walls I see her exchange some words with a doctor, cradling the bundle of cloth with reverence.

It's far too small. She emerges and I see that it's all wrong, a body like ground meat pressed into shape of a spindly baby, arms like raw bone, a face whose eyes could be thumbprints, a rasping mouth without lips. The other children too young to be phased. We walk deeper into the structure, to where doctors roam with clipboards, some human, many somehow inhuman, a ringing in my skull alerting me to biological impossibility. Another room, she spoon feeds the infant, jam spilling from the hole, barely distinct from its melted-plastic skin. I keep watch over the young ones, still chanting, syllables that buzz and ache in my ears.

11. There were four children, four, not three, one that you refused to see—now wandering, now lost. They call to her and you can't understand the words.

∽

Wish I

You shake the god's hand and the pact you have sealed is meant to preserve all of humanity, inside a suspension of sterile youth, tachyons hanging in the air like dead flies. That's your intent. People will ask what it was like, and you'll struggle to explain the paralysis of her touch, the obvious cnidarian neurotoxin, something animal and frightened barely contained in human form. That would explain the eyes, intelligent yet confused, and the electric pull of her fingers searching your bodymind for translational data. What was she—Venus emerging from rotting flesh and foam. The last deity of some gelatinous deep sea race, washed ashore like the corpse of a whale because of extinction, or atheism, or a dysgenic return to the garden of mindless ooze. How strong is her power over reality? Death continues—but not for you. Not for a select few, an immortal class whose members coincidentally all share a resemblance. There's a scar on your hand where she stole your DNA, your thoughts, her infinite mother-brain grasping for the meaning of that wish.

Wish II

When he made the call he had not seen a demon before and what he expected was a humanoid monster, a satyr or djinn familiar from the bestiaries and alchemical engravings, a slave that would scrape its furred shins against the invisible walls of his summoning glyph.

Instead, a dark liquid surged forward and flowed around him like water cutting through sand, until he stood atop an egg floating in an infinite ferromagnetic sea. A voice boomed from its depths, every droplet speaking at once, omnidirectionally requesting his wish.

He stutters, the contractual phrasing he had deliberated for so long over coming out wrong, without the necessary disclaimers, conditions mangled by fear and nervousness and halfway through his recitation he loses his place and in paralysis cannot continue.

Wordlessly his request is logged and payment is exacted. Blood streams from his eyes, mouth, nose; pain like a rotten tooth in the center of his brain forces him to his knees. His nerves are crushed and ground to paste and for minutes the blood flows as he writhes and chokes in that silent chamber, cornea stained pink, a red stripe soaking his shirt from his face to the floor. A trickle is pulled towards the darkness by some uncanny gravity and as it makes contact the blood disappears the pain disappears the starless pactwater recedes and the boy is left alone in a hollow sleep.

The Travelling Madman Problem

The Old Masters of horror were right, of course; the human brain, labyrinthine and fragile, could have its wings snapped by the right sequence of concepts. In their prescience, they simplified the formula, portraying psycho-hazards as powerful and general tools, while in reality they're as varied as faces, or passwords. Minds, ever resilient, will twist and fight, employing neuro- or ideological flexibility to resist the crushing grip of revelation, and as with viruses, the first blow must be the lethal one. I have lived to see Lovecraft recognized as hard science fiction, and watched eldritch secrets squirm under sterile analysis, and for this I am elated.

The earliest mind-break-generation algorithms relied on extensive psychometric testing, detailed analysis of physical neurostructures, and familial religious histories. As such, the only test subjects for pioneering lyssa-engineers were psychiatric patients, and research was complicated by the challenge of distinguishing between gradients of madness. Gradually, more refined algorithms were developed; today's typically require only a short personality profile and seed value, and additional papers have been published alleging the potential generation of middling hazards from advertisement data.

Lyssa-engineers are employed primarily by the military, though as design increases in refinement, medical and social applications gain traction. Micro-lyssa-engineers study and deploy mild hazards to trigger specific personality changes, induce PTSD-soothing amnesia, and rehabilitate criminals.

Amateur lyssa-engineering is discouraged or illegal in most territories, but algorithms are nonetheless distributed online, and employed as alternatives to suicide, as hallucinatory experimentation, or as petty revenge. Communications from strangers must be highly restricted, as any public persona risks at least temporary debilitation via psychic assault. Various companies offer hazard filtration, but their services are costly, and rely on high levels of trust, as extensive personal details are necessary to determine what information is dangerous.

Sarantismos

In those days, they kept newborns at the hospital for forty days, until they had developed the likeness of man. Mothers visited, restrained in wheelchairs and flanked by orderlies. Sometimes drugged, drooling or confused and softly crying, frightened by the bleached arcades they were wheeled through, the smell of antiseptics and sulfur, and frightened of the pink worms in their arms.

In the flux of rationality and irrationality, confidence and terror, love and disgust, these indignities shifted between being necessary, tolerable, intolerable, consensual, and uncomprehended; young mothers who hours before had a slipped knives under their blouses would smile full of warmth and insist on their reliability; other times they would thrash, screaming in tongues; later yet they would request tighter restraints, or even the needle.

By forty days the babies had unwithered. Their eyes had opened and gleamed with mammalian intelligence. Their noises, occasionally, transmitted intent. Most importantly, they had lost their blood red newness, the changeling malleability of something internal and protean wrenched into the world, and settled into a definite human form.

Most mothers, at this point, assumed guardianship of their children. Extensions of the hospital's custody, prescribed by the psychiatric watch (the observers of every postpartum interaction, alert to signs of depression, deception, hormonal disturbance) were sources of humiliation.

A woman took her child home, but love was deadened by uneasiness. It was human now, but it had been an insect too many times, or a flower, an automaton, silken flesh puppet, clay doll, monster; and the madness was still lapping at her brain. When it cried, its face became like the folds of a pig, a cubist nightmare, an amber broken window, and she could scarcely detect the person in it. When it smiled, she felt twinges of duty, if not affection. For weeks, it continued thus; in sadness, horror, and in laughter obligation.

Common hallucinations: infant as cockroach. Infant as fungus. Infant as infestation, a seething mass of bullet ants twisting in the crib, withdrawing from invisible fires into approximate human shape. Infant as bloodstain; a three-dimensional patch of sin. Infant as monkey, as tuber, as rose. The creases of the ribs become the legs of a paralyzed tarantula. The mouth is interpreted as a valve in tangled pipework, as a puckering tentacle cup, as a sandstone pore. The face flutters like a doily. Eyes are the wheels of shopping carts or miniature hexagonal amphorae. Hands are gnarled roots, balloons, boiled lobster revenants, often perceived as tumescent and hostile long after the rest of the child is accepted; there are cases of protective mothers ripping off arms perceived as cradle-snakes.

In the crib, flickering like a phenakisticope, her baby changed from human to animated meat. Its cries, long abstracted, registered as tinnitus or high-pitched mechanical grinding, or sometimes as the babbling, raised voices of unwanted guests. Her overwhelming impulse was to gather up the filth and press it into the garbage disposal. Faintly, she remembered what the offal had once been; but that seemed distant now, and impossible, like something from a fairy story. No person could be so small.

LETTERS

The book exists because these letters exist, and serves as a vessel, decentralizing them that they might reach their intended audience.

a letter to my future daughter

2020—????

Who are you? Do you prefer strength or beauty? Stars or flowers? Sky or cave?
Have you realized yet that machines are the most important objects, that gears click under every brightly painted surface, that the richest contemplation is of industry? Every pond a factory, every egg a drill. Do you love conveyor belts?

> Are you anything like me?

It has been claimed that the matrilineal line preserves talent, sorcery, and madness, and otherwise regresses towards a golden anthropic mean, the well-tamed DNA garden flowing verdant between generations. I hope that yours is full of wildness, and roses with eyes, sentient cellcraft staring inward and appraising itself. I would like to share some feelings with you, feelings that I have not found analogues to outside this house of blood: the concentric portals extending from the under-surface of your skin into the past, chronopathy for the medieval, the ancient ungulates, the amoebae; the synaesthesia of the digital as cathedrals and corridors; the otherworldly language of childhood buried in plastics and chemical clay. I hope that these intuitions are, at least partially, ancestral, and that my words can epigenetically awaken them in you.

One thing at a time. It could be your delusions are entirely your own; in which case, some day, I hope to hear them described.

What is your language? Are you still shackled to anglographia, or have you discovered hieroglyphs? Today's linguists claim that our second tower of Babel is collapsing, that English has entered a process of fracture, its apparent memetic assimilation an implosion that precedes supernova. Do you speak the mother tongue as I knew it, or have you adopted the mutant dialect of forums, of sino-pidgin graffiti, of suburban fiefdoms? I hope we can communicate, with clarity and without translation.

Sometimes, I think I can feel you inside me, nestled beside my childhood self. I have had fitful visions of watching you, like out-of-body memories, perspective kaleidoscoping between our two forms, the remembered and the envisaged. You, too, will be a small girl pressed to the linoleum floor of the dojo; you will know stucco walls, and gravel, handfuls of quartz, warm and cool patches of playground sand. All the textures of the world will reveal themselves: you will learn about parallax and blankets, you will learn how reflections are cartoons, you will study the surface tensions of raindrops. Do not mistake vicariousness for vampirism; if I live again through you it is only out of wonder.

I anticipate a vacuum inside myself, once you are removed from these daydreams, and claimed by reality. Will it hurt to watch you change, grow too large for the puzzle-space you left? You are my cells, blood, milk, my flower, my flesh, but most importantly, my mind: as from my body, you will be ripped from imagination, to live and act in the world, autonomous.

You are my butterfly, you are my alien hand syndrome; you are the antidote to solipsism, you are proof that simple rules beget complexity, you remind me of the future as it's meant to be perceived: endless, chaotic, formidable. We contain the seeds of people we do not understand. There is creative potential lurking inside us, and it will seek expression, through biology if nothing else. Doubt is beautiful, and doubt is your element—extracted from my visions, you are your own agent, uncontrollable and unpredictable, inviting the maelstrom to my doorstep, when all I wanted to do was protect you.

a letter to my future granddaughter

[2035—2065]—????

Apocalypse is fashionable, but your possibility has quelled my excitement for deserts and industrial waste. I have kind intentions, I picture water and willows, moss and soft grasses, cobwebs glittering with moisture, grey skies and thunderstorms, safety below arches, the undergrowth alive .with little creatures. Will you see the rapids before they're dammed? Will you see what I missed, the last song of the barrier reef, the steepness of glaciers, the rainforest? Perhaps you have no interest; perhaps the cultists are right, and those biomes have vanished.

So far in the future, already like a star, a pinprick of light I've tried to forge the world into a cradle for. Every generation receives its share of hate; and now, I suspect, you will stare back at me and call my footprints the bedrock of ruin, but I hope that your disasters are gentle, far from the infernos and ash wastelands of my terror.

I knew my grandparents, but they did not know theirs. Roots existed only in the imagination of branches; will I get to hold you? I never thought I would be so old. Perhaps your potential will suffice to unhinge me from this planet, your unborn shadow a pacifying token as I cross the Styx. Perhaps lifespans dilate and contract in cycles, our co-presence or absence holding a mirror to civilization's lunar pulse. I remember a photograph, standing next to my mother's mother, looking like twins displaced in time: the same eyes sunken and shining, the same birdlike hands, the same posture, deformed. Will I see myself, in you? Will I see her?

The past and its wars incarnate again, before and after cross-contaminating. What strange landmarks engulf you? What ceilings, what skies? They say the following traits skip generations: aptitude for sewing, for braidcraft, wanderlust, paranoia. Do these properties have counterparts in the realm you've inherited? Is everything digital, is everything desolate? Do you have space for these middle-world hobbies, between the pixels or the mud?

Holding your small hand in my ancient one, envisioning your possible hand inside my own projected senescence, I can already feel the future split: between progress and regress, prosperity and catastrophe. I see horrors in one eye and wonders in the other, and despite the uncertainty, the trembling base, I want you to exist: as a link in this unbroken genetic chain, as new eyes through which reality perceives, as a person full of fierceness and calamity, to love.

a letter to my future great-granddaughter
[2050—2110]—????

I want you to know that I'm thinking of you, now, regardless of whether I'm alive then, and regardless of whether I'm conscious, then.

We could be living as children together, you in your youth, and myself in dementia. I have treated death as a stranger, and foreseen my soul strung out beyond the clock, a silk sliver of consciousness vanishing through eternity's eye. My dream the fading light through an attic skull, your dream the construction of scaffolding in sunbeams, a mind cohering from the protein-soaked ooze of infant ken. Somewhere, our paths cross.

Ignorant of my present degradation—and I know that, were I alive and mentally sound, I would still be nothing to you, a wrinkled gathering of spacetime, too many degrees removed to comprehend—cast your attention backwards, and picture me picturing you. A flicker of mutual recognition, separated by aeonic deserts, may be our only communion; it hurts, it hurts, to be cheated by mortality.

In your face, a composite of all humanity, its futures and its past, the peaks and the nadirs of evolution pressed like fingerprints over your template. Impossible beauty, terrible decay, aspects of beasts and reptiles and genetic phantoms, a mirror; I'm seeking truth between the translucent veils of possibility, despite my causality-gated prosopagnosia. Somewhere in God I'll glimpse your face, in the simultaneous and infinite variation, in the hyaloid deck of cards fanned across my brain. Do you have a photograph of me? Or do you search, inversely constrained, through branching alterations of your mother, reverse-engineering my image? A circuit, one blur reflected by the pupil of another, reality a gemstone in the noise. This is how we meet, in defiance of time.

Daughter-of-my-daughter-of-my-daughter, a dream in minds that don't yet exist. I reach across the tapestry to touch you, brushing my hands over a multitude of worlds. Who are you? What moons crashed to make you, what stars died? I've named you the bane of control and its illusions, an icon of the future slipping from my grasp. You are the inflection point, you are the frontier, you are the Cambrian explosion of self-sufficient life, a process beyond and in mockery of my influence. The universe converged upon your birth, and diverges from it, the garden finally untended.

Descendants more numerous than the stars, the promise of exponential legacy—but in you, none of that biblical anonymity, for you're closer than my heart, and more singular. I once scorned lineage as genetic power-mongering, a dehumanizing chess game that would claim unwilling youth as pawns; now, instead, I perceive enthusiasm for a song that bridges aeons, the lyrical sequence of minds born from minds, an excitement for the marriage of new generations to the universe. Go forth, prosper, build castles and refineries, and let each wave of cognitive potential break into a thousand bodies, inheritors of the wonder-bitten world.

Think of me, sometimes, as I think of you; and may the weight of love across time drive your virtue to greater heights.

a letter to my future great-great-granddaughter

[2065 -2155]—????

Who can countenance their own annihilation? I have believed in immortality, for nothingness remains beyond empathy's scope. Staring into myself, I find no quietness, and yet—I don't expect to survive to greet you. Superimposed, infinity and absence, ghost and hole, awestruck in contemplation of a world that dares exist without me. As a child, it hurt to imagine my parents as children, as agents independent and oblivious to me, while I was so completely invested in them. Now, inverted, it hurts to look forward, into your life apart from me.

And if I were alive? The implications are of short and brutal adolescence, of rapidly iterated generations, of infants by child mothers, of a violent microcosm I had hoped to preclude. To have acted too weakly to prevent collapse, and to be punished by watching it wreak its hardships on wave after wave of kin.

I feel so helpless in the present, quarantined from causality. My hands move spectral through matter and even through my own body; impossible to change myself, the world. We want to pluck civilization's gears like the strings of a harp, we want to foresee disaster and avert it, we want to act best and know that our actions are best. The future remains engulfed in fog and our arms in tar, and each effect is fought for through the congealing murk. Will you forgive us, if we failed? Will you see us as actors, or as the unwitting tools of kismet grinding forth, wielded by a blind and procedural god? I'm sorry.

It's strange, how attachment doesn't wane with time. With separation, with biological dissipation. Under your skin, a fraction of me swirls, and somehow that sliver feels like my entire soul. I want to protect you; I want to change the future without destroying you, as if safe havens ever generate their wards, as if no part of you was forged by harm. To comfort without murdering, to eliminate danger without sterilizing nobility and courage. If I could, I would reach from my grave and curse every particle that injured you. All of reality denounced by livid ancestors, powerless in our crypts.

I thought I could save you through abstinence, through rejecting the proliferating universe. I've contemplated terrible possibilities: murder, rape, and torture, and thought to choose barrenness in their stead. Darkness forward; and nothing to judge me, only figments at which I scream justification, an imaginary pantheon of beings stolen out of time. Would you plead for life? Could I deny you, if you did? Every day, another paragraph escapes from me, antinatalist talismans describing their own defeat.

Try to understand that I was a person, tormented and hopeful, uncertain, unwell. I sometimes see my predecessors as a series of marble busts, flesh flickering underneath, torn by blood and tears or deformed by insanity. I exist; thank you, I hate you. You'll exist, thankful, or spiteful, a clap of perfect thunder whether you want to live or not. I pray you do, that my choice of life is not mistaken, that light enters your brain and sets your synapses achurn, that you share in the ecstatic birthright of a planet orbiting your soul—the delusion and delight of breathing, of being, of moving from one word to the next, until the end of rhyme.

a letter to my future 3x great-granddaughter
[2080—2200]—????

You're beyond the end of time, you're a galaxy away. I'm so proud of you for being real! It takes nothing at all to move me, anymore—but isn't being alive its own torment, and reward? You've met the challenges of atoms, you sweep the land with hurricanes downstream of synaptic flutters. Embedded in causality, agent and victim; consider your power, your powerlessness, and tremble. I know I do.

You didn't ask to be born. Can you forgive us? This string of animals, idiots, debased instruments in biology's scheme. Bending to our urges like reeds in the wind. If you accuse, I have no justification, only an enduring hope that your sadness won't outweigh the myriad small pleasures available in life: warmth, seashells, the rotation of keys finding their locks. At times, the universe will align against you, not out of malice, but in a syzygy of formidable indifference. May you also recognize its coinciding grace.

I was once told that organisms make only one decision: spread, or stop. Do you feel the vertigo I feel, staring into the future, a million giggling faces sprawled in fractal curls? A million minds, each infinite, intelligent, secret and intense? A bottomless ladder of being, flowers upon flowers despite the hostile cosmos. Alternatively, starbeams, emptiness, and sentience rejecting its own dizzying continuation. Letting the path die. I have no advice. Only you can choose whether there's light at the end of this interminable tunnel of flesh.

If time has granted me authority, dismiss it. I write not to claim some dusty mantle; I have no wisdom, clarity, experience. I have no guidance for you that I endured to follow. Be perfect, as I have been imperfect: know your desires, be constant, do not renege on choices, contracts, pacts. Let each moment persist in your memory as an unadulterated crystal, pristine and immune to the swaying pressures of convenience. Be brutal in analysis and forgiving in evaluation, and honest at all times and in all places. Be perfect; have nothing to hide, no contradictions, no mutually exclusive goals. Do not compromise, conceal your levers, commit to actions with your soul entire, with all the fury of concentrated will. When you meet uncertainty, kill it. Be gentle, but not too gentle. Be kind when kindness it best. If you act pathetic you will inculcate expectations of weakness, and descend into a valley of deprecated agency whose slopes are steep and not easily scaled. Make few promises, and keep them. Paranoia is often warranted. Do not suffer being treated like a child, but enjoy being treated as a student. Be cautious if you find yourself in a situation where you are watching and others are doing, and these roles are fixed; if passivity is your default, carve it out and substitute fire.

Become powerful enough to take responsibility for the whole universe. This is the only wish I have, for any of my kin, or anyone I love. Become strong, and protect what is good.

a letter to my future 4x great-granddaughter
[2095—2245]—????

You have 32 great-great-great-great-grandmothers; I am altogether 1/64th of your blood, a voice inside a voice inside a voice inside a voice inside the voice of your mother. Can you hear me through the clamor? Between the singing platelets, the weak hum of my nucleus? Cellular blocks made of cellular blocks, a toy tower of humans under your skin, surviving as fractions, as patchwork patterns in cooperative creation. Our construct: you. Mind, body, twirling molecules; light a candle for us, ancient and compulsive builders.

To share you with so many others; to live in your code alone, invisibly interrupted, weaving an inaccessible gestalt. We're glitches of ourselves, but the static has coalesced—and once again I'm mute, shaken by your life, the probabilistic miracle. A thousand ancestors, braided; a million generations; a billion moments focused through a lens-like mind.

Cast us aside, and make this shell your own. Drink in the trees, the birdsong, the bulldozed everglades, the watchtower; call these memories your parents, more than the shattered sequences of proteins, old echoing flesh.

I want to call your name, and stroke your hair; I want to be more real than a current in meat. To live in the world with which you interface, to talk to you from the outside, too. Is it greed, to wish for involvement, while knocking on the inside of your veins? To see your smile, to interact, to comfort or advise; to be more than genetic baggage. I hated my body, the stamp of eternity and earth and imperfection. Cruel and constraining, impossible to identify as myself. A knot of discomfort around a brain, the brain itself dysmorphic, too limited, too small, inadequate. I hated the strangling code that wrote me; and now I exist as it, in you. Forgive me for having nothing good to send forward through time, and for becoming part of another's cage.

Do you resent being a chariot for so many dead souls? Do you feel separate from us, chained to this chain of genes, a decree which binds and never benefits? It hurts; I want so badly to be close to you. To be with you, and not alienated from you, not a burden, not a dull knife at your throat, wielded by matter against spirit.

In your strange future, are you engineered? Have I assumed too much, my presence where it's not, the instability I carried excised from the germline? Real death, finally; not division, and not mutation. I am torn, between wanting to free you from my defects, and wanting to live on, nestled between your bones. Like a house spirit driven away, and the family better for it; I have too many failures, too much neuroticism. Love so intense that it's a sickness, and exile justified. I wish I wasn't rotten with self-destruction, I wish I was stronger, I wish with every cell I deserved to be part of you.

There's no reconciling oblivion. I'll accept my role as scaffolding, as launchpad, as carbon for the future to burn up and forget. All my bitterness wiped away by your possible laughter, bells reverberating through the veil of years. What wouldn't I sacrifice at that altar? Your innocence, your joy, your curiosity; worthy to see myself erased. Remember me, who would give anything; remember the deleted aeons, who loved you, and who in time will welcome you to their fold.

a letter to my future 5x great-granddaughter
[2110—2290]—????

Two hundred years pass like a thousand. I can no longer lay the generations out, as flowers pressed inside my mind: seven is too deep, beyond my subitizing range, and each step forward overflows with meaning. Do you have a perfect computer brain, as fast as fire and large enough to count the universe? Can you see farther? I hope so; to be as children to our descendants would speak well of the human programme.

I now appreciate the smallness of our lives, and the rapidity of their succession. Flares in a dark lake, on a long night, the signal propagated by softly fizzing halos. What message are we sending? What could possibly survive the permutation, the blood and words all churning in a centrifuge? I want more than to replicate; I want to speed you onward with a whisper in your brain, some blueprint transmitted through telephone wire lineage; but my own skull rings empty, and the past is mute. If a sacred text exists, it has slipped through a hole in my soul. What can I give you? A tower, a gate? There are pastures to tend to, and cities, and grids. A half-cultivated world, awaiting your stewardship. Is it enough? If you accept it, civilization is honorable work. Will you?

I have the least advice for minds like mine. Distance yourself from me; be not recalcitrant, doubtful, defiant. You would question a billion years of sequence? Don't be so arrogant. Don't demand justification from abstractions. Nothing in the world will negotiate with you; tilt at the waves, at time, at math, and you will only waste yourself. Can't you be happy building, maintaining? Does everything demand a culmination? Don't call convenience fate, and fight it. Don't hate the mere concept of telos; don't attack its pareidolic shadows in your home, your friends, your own desires. Be careful of destroying what you love.

You could succeed where I struggled: carve out a haven, weave boughs, set bricks. Choose a craft and learn it; study metals, sockets, the inclining gyre of drills. Refine a world from the world: enter the forest and make it your garden. Everything depends on locks, doors, and valves. Bless the tiny mechanisms, by which all human ventures turn— keep them, protect them, know the shapes of things.

You can touch the stars if you can fold aluminum. You can manufacture peace, build roads, buy time. Nature will unfold for you: glittering and ordered, chaotic and prime. I'll be with you when you learn to fear the scope of our disasters; I'll be with you when you first perceive the depth of our design. All things obedient, in their crescendo and decay. I want to teach you to see machinery in sunlight; I want to teach you to see engineers in ribbons.

I lived only in my mind. I demanded prophecy. I refused to believe that the real was good. There are faults in me like canyons, and I cannot relinquish them, even as I beg you to relinquish them, or beg fortune to release you from my corrupting blood. Has it not been diluted enough?

It's the future—are you perfect? Are you without error? I welcome your scorn, pity, compassion; woe, the blighted past, we're all messed up. Loathe the ancients, decry us, entomb us again. Anything but absence. Anything but quiet, as blank as a question, a ten thousand year dilation of the darkness in our closets. The intimacy of absolute failure, alone in our bedroom with the lights out; the barren cosmos echoing, hollow and clean, not even touched by our dust.

Please exist. Please exist, the present is so lonely. Our species is not meant to be an island—or if it is, I selfishly request not to live on the coast, staring out into unending space, infinity shamefully emptied of life. Dying stars in entropy's rictus, and skyscrapers crumbling on a desolate planet. Exist, exist, the litany persists, a candle passed forward through the blackest night, sometimes barely more than an ember.

a letter to my future 6x great-granddaughter

[2125—2335]—????

Here are some stories from my grandmothers and grandfathers, your 8x great-grandparents:

During his mandatory military service, your Nono commandeered a taxi to drive onto the airport's tarmac to hail and board a plane mid-takeoff. As a child he went grenade fishing with soldiers. He chopped thousands of kilograms of wood to buy a racing bicycle. At 86, he found a bottle of grappa in the vents, an illegal distillation hidden 60 years earlier.

Grandma left the farmstead to become a dress designer, and joined the army patching parachutes. She said she met an angel, shining through the gauzelike body of a nurse.

On the beaches of Normandy your Grandfather dropped a tool from his belt and a bullet whizzed over his head, and he spoke of this moment as though it were the pivot of the universe.

Your Nona's village harbored resistance to the occupying German forces. One son from every family was executed; biblical retribution, referenced in hushed tones, and passed to me as a secret through the reverent hallways of rumor. Reality forbidden, for she refused to speak of the War, and these truths were kept alive only as myth.

I have hungered for the context of my ancestors, and starved. These scraps will feed you for an hour, I hope, enough to fuel the engine in your heart that eats small legends. Search for yourself in our silhouettes; the past exists as a mirror, and we the dead to be claimed as yours, beloved future.

Time is a mystery to me, a box and a devourer. I wanted to know myself through my forebears, but they left no letters, no fragments, no handprints except my own body, written into the present by their acts. I am the message, as you are the message, but I aim to give you more than flesh: take my stories, take my language. Do you speak it? Can I transmit, and be received, and make more than an island of you? I love you, I will not strand you in the world. You'll sense the fiber running through your blood; you'll know the scales of things; you'll feel time speak, under your skin and in all enterprises. I'll grant you divination: read our past, and see the future inverted in it.

Read our past, war-tainted, anguish-torn. May your life be commensurably peaceful. May your violence be satisfying and brief and may your rest be long; may your sadness have purpose. I have lived an easy life and a hard life and for you I wish its form but not its contents: the depth and variety of memories, without the core of pain. Without a pain that sticks to everything like sap, worked into the corners of mind and reflex. May your stories be beautiful, and horrible, and earned.

You are an idea and I am a legacy and somewhere we will meet, ghost to ghost, the dead and the not-yet-born. Those who knew me will not live to see you; we won't even share a mind, to coexist in simulation. You are my lullaby, my reason, my prayer; I am your cautionary tale. Enchanted, we orbit, pure repute and imagination, calling the one to the other. Whisper to me, from possibility, and I will cherish you in archival permanence, writing my veneration to the stars.

ω

Afterword

Perhaps one day the letters will be continued, to reach as far as I have dreamt. I want the future to know I loved it.

Fragments will continue to spawn at @ctrlcreep.

Deep thanks to my friends, tgam, jpt4, pdb, gmk

> and to my patrons and muses:
> cb, ew, pp, mk, jg,
> i, d_r, jp, tf, b(kd),
> I, ltf, c, rm, s,
> o, oz, csv, A, r,
> h, Δg

29980077R00158

Made in the USA
San Bernardino, CA
20 March 2019